Wanted:
A Forever Home

Janet Goodwin

authorHOUSE®

AuthorHouse™ UK
1663 Liberty Drive
Bloomington, IN 47403 USA
www.authorhouse.co.uk
Phone: 0800.197.4150

This book is a work of fiction. Human characters, places,
and incidents are either products of the author's imagination
or are used fictitiously. Any resemblance to actual locales,
events, or persons, living or dead, is entirely coincidental.

Published by AuthorHouse 11/16/2016

ISBN: 978-1-5246-3302-8 (sc)
ISBN: 978-1-5246-3301-1 (e)

Library of Congress Control Number: 2016911858

Print information available on the last page.

Any people depicted in stock imagery provided by Thinkstock are
models, and such images are being used for illustrative purposes only.
Certain stock imagery © Thinkstock.

This book is printed on acid-free paper.

Because of the dynamic nature of the Internet, any web addresses or
links contained in this book may have changed since publication and
may no longer be valid. The views expressed in this work are solely
those of the author and do not necessarily reflect the views of the
publisher, and the publisher hereby disclaims any responsibility for them.

Contents

Chapter 1

A Night of Terror

George stood up hurriedly, his rug slipping on the stone slabs beside the iron-framed bed. He shook his head, causing his metal dog tag, engraved with the name Gentleman George, to rattle against his well-worn collar. There it was again! The eerie howls penetrating the thick, stone-clad walls of the hundred-year-old cottage, which stood amongst the lush pastures on a hillside in north-eastern Spain. The howls were distant, but there were many.

He stealthily padded towards the entrance, glancing across the small, sparsely furnished, oak-beamed room. He did not want to wake his master, who was dozing peacefully in his rocking chair in front of a blazing fire. Sniffing along the bottom of the ill-fitting wooden door, George caught strange animal scents drifting in on the wind. With a well-practised motion, he lifted the latch with his nose, at the same time pushing the door open with his paw. The rain was heavy, with thunderous clouds filling the darkening sky, threatening a storm. Howls, sounding even more ghostly now he was outside, came from the direction of the forest high up on the ridge overlooking the valley. Something bad was happening up there.

His master, awakened by the sudden draft, joined him in listening, and his face changed from tranquillity to alarm. He recognised the howls. He had only heard them once before, when his father was a shepherd – and that time they had led to disaster.

'The sheep, George! Come! We must make sure they are safe!' As he spoke, he pulled a thick coat from the peg on the wall and buttoned it tightly across his chest. He hastily poured water over the burning logs, causing a small cloud of steam to escape into the room. He then hurried to a wooden cabinet holding three shotguns; on a shelf, there were small bags containing shells. He stuffed two bags in his pocket and took down one of the shotguns.

George shivered. He was always nervous when his master took out the long rod. The omens did not look good.

Once outside, his master covered his head with a deep hood and strode purposefully up the pathway leading towards the sheep pen halfway up the hillside. George dutifully followed at his heels, feeling an icy chill penetrating his thick, brown fur.

The day had been long. From dawn to dusk, George and his master had been out on the hillside, feeling the brunt of the winter weather whilst guarding the flock. George loved this work and had been doing it expertly for the past six years.

The flock was small, made up of three rams and twenty-five ewes, some of which were about to give birth. Of all the year, lambing was the time George enjoyed the most. As soon as the lambs were born, he loved the extra responsibility of caring for both mothers and their babies. He delighted in hearing the woolly babies make soft, bleating sounds as they were suckling. Sometimes a lamb would stray too far away from its mother, and she, trying to care for two or three lambs at the same time would make frantic noises while looking for her infant. George, with the command of 'Go find' from his master, would search for the scent on the hillside and undergrowth. He and his master worked as a team. When he found the baby, he always gave a warning bark, telling his master where he was. In turn, his master would whistle for George to carry the lamb gently back to its mother. It always gave George a sense of pride watching their reunion.

Early in the year, the wool on the backs of the sheep was long, thick, and ideal for shearing. His master would open the first of a series of gates leading to a narrow track to the shearing shed. At these times, his master whistled different commands, telling George to shepherd one sheep at a time to where he was waiting. His master then deftly took hold of the sheep by the rear legs, and with the use of a hand tool, he swiftly sheared the wool down the back and sides before letting the animal go into the pen by way of a turnstile.

George had his own method of counting and was never satisfied until he knew he had pushed all the animals into the shearing pen. By the time his master had finished, great piles of wool lay ready to be put into sacks and taken to the market.

The pathway up to the sheep pen was slippery from the rain beating down hindering their progress. All the while, George could hear the eerie howls above the noise of the wind. Then, just when they had left the pathway and were making their way towards the pen farther up the hillside, his master stopped suddenly. 'Lie,' he whispered sharply. George instinctively lay flat. 'Stay,' came the next command.

George watched his master disappear into the darkness. Why had he been commanded to stay? What if his master was in danger? How would be able to protect him? Indecision flew through his brain, but George knew better than to disobey a command. He pricked his ears, listening, all the time sniffing the air, and endeavouring to follow the fading scent. George became alarmed. Should he follow him? No, his master had told him to lie and stay. Obedience had been instilled into him since he was a tiny puppy, and although his instinct was now telling him this was something different, he didn't dare disobey. There was nothing he could do but wait for his master's return.

Strident reports filled the air, followed by screeching. The long rod had obviously hit its target. George sat up, barking loudly. Surely his master would return now. He waited and waited. With the rain soaking everything around him, he was soon lying in a pool of mud. He looked up at the sky and could see forked lightning in the distance; somewhere, the storm was raging. The temperature dropped sharply, and he began shivering.

Eventually the rain diminished, and the wind dropped, giving way to a deadly silence. Why hadn't his master whistled, telling George to go to him? That is what he always did after using the long rod. Something must have happened, but what, and where was he? Had he gone to look at the sheep? So far George had not heard a single bleat. He comforted himself that they must be all right and safely in their pen. Maybe he should use his instinct and go in search of his master. He knew it was his duty to obey the command to stay, but if his master had been hurt, George had to find him.

Without hesitating any longer, he stood up and cautiously crept up the hillside towards the sheep pen. He sniffed the air. A strange scent dominated, one he had never smelt before, although he knew it was a scent from an animal. Very soon there was another scent: blood. He kept very low to the ground, all the time creeping towards the pen. His eyes looked from side to side, and his ears were pricked, listening for his master's voice.

When he reached the pen, he took one look, threw his head back, and howled as loud as he could. The pen gate had been torn down, the surrounding fences were broken, and before him was a horrendous sight. The mauled bodies of dead sheep lay all over the ground. Some sheep were still alive, bleating in agony. There were no lambs left. George now knew why the howls had stopped: the sheep had been butchered. He slowly walked around the outside of the pen, trying to pick up the scent of his master, sensing the direction of the loud bangs coming from the long rod. He must find his master.

Alert and no longer caring for his own safety, George decided to go in search, knowing his master would never leave the pen without a good reason. He barked and barked. If he could hear him, his master would recognize his bark and give a return whistle. But there was nothing.

All night George searched in vain. He returned to the cottage and found the door still open, the embers from the log fire burned out. There was no sign of his master. Even Nobby, the ageing horse, stared blankly when George looked in his stable. Eventually he climbed back up the hillside, and for many hours he sat by the remains of the sheep pen, continually lifting his head and letting out loud howls of anguish. The wind was picking up and bringing with it the familiar scent. He stared towards the brow of the hill.

George had been up there only once, and he remembered backing off when he had reached the edge, seeing the deep crevices of rock jutting out below him. His master had immediately whistled, urging him to return. George had never forgotten the scolding he had received that day, and since then he had always been careful to never let the sheep wander to that part of the hillside.

But on this night, things were different. The scent of his master told him he was up there, and George had to find out if it was true. He left the sheep pen and very carefully made his way up the steep hillside, following the scent as he did so. As he moved closer, the scent was becoming much stronger, and it was as he reached the summit that he saw the bodies of two large, grey animals lying on the edge of the clifftop. He cautiously closed in, fearing they could still be alive, but when he saw the large wounds similar to those made by the long rod when he and his master hunted for hares, he realized they were dead. They were animals he had never seen before. Four young sheep were lying on the ground a short distance away. George crept up and nuzzled them; there was no movement. They had been slaughtered by the savage beasts.

Knowing his master must be nearby, George barked loudly. But there was silence, no answering call or whistle. He tentatively looked over the edge of the cliff. The clouds cleared and gave way to shafts of moonlight illuminating deep crevices, making them look very dangerous. Below him, he caught sight of a body lying very still at the bottom of a crevice. Farther below lay the bodies of large animals. He didn't know what to do except howl into the night.

The ground was muddy. George's paws kept slipping as he made his way down the deep ridge, whining his greeting as he did so, but his master did not respond. He was lying quite still with his rod beside him. His master's coat and hood were soaked with blood. The night air felt very cold. George licked his face, snuggled up to him, and made soft whimpering noises. Every now and then, he growled softly, telling his master to wake up. Not giving up, George sat up barking loudly, nudging him with his paw. Still nothing; his master made no movement. Hour after hour, George waited, hoping something would wake the master he loved more than anything else in the world. He made a vow that he would guard him forever.

On that same treacherous night, far away from the ridge where George kept his lonely vigil, another drama was about to unfold …

Chapter 2

Wynken, Blynken, and Nod

Claps of thunder sounded in the distance. Bright flashes from lightning cast eerie shadows across the night sky and scared Bella. Running as fast as she could, she desperately tried to find somewhere to hide. She felt the gale-force winds knocking her sideways, and the rain soaked her body. She knew if she didn't find shelter soon, her kittens would be born in an open countryside and under the most horrendous conditions.

The storm was moving in. With every moment that passed, she felt the pains inside her becoming stronger; her heavy body inevitably slowed her down, making her feel exhausted. Along the pathway in front of her, something was moving in the wind. Could it be shelter? She breathlessly quickened her pace, only to find it was a large bush blocking her route. But however temporary it was, she was relieved when she managed to crawl under some of its small branches. She badly needed to rest.

By now the storm was directly overhead, with lightning striking every few minutes followed by great crashes of thunder. Bella had never been so terrified in her life. There was a blinding flash followed by a searing noise as one of the tall trees broke in half, its long branches spreading out just a few feet from where she was hiding. Panicking in case more branches fell, she ran, slipping and sliding in the mud and looking a pitiful sight. Her white fur was soaking wet, and her black tail was heavy with sludge, drooping sadly behind her.

She didn't see the deep furrow in the ground until it was too late. There was a sharp pain as one of her forelegs caught the edge of a rock just below the surface. For a long while, she lay unable to move. Eventually, by using her tongue, she managed to massage some life into the wounded leg, enabling her to stand. She was frantic to be on her way, knowing the longer she remained unprotected, the greater the danger to not only herself but her unborn kittens.

Bella struggled on as best she could, limping heavily and feeling the birth pains becoming sharper every moment. Stumbling on the rough ground, she felt a surge of movement inside her. She knew she could go no further; her kittens were about to be born. There was no alternative but to stay where she was until it was all over.

Wynken, Blynken, and Nod, three beautiful ginger kittens with patches of white fur on their tiny bodies, arrived into the world on that treacherous winter night.

By the following morning, the storm had passed. Just before daylight, Bella carefully tongue-washed her three newborn kittens, at last content when she felt

10

their tiny paws press deep into her stomach suckling her milk. All three appeared to be strong and healthy. Her next task was to find a safe hiding place. On the other side of the meadow, she saw a farmhouse with a barn alongside it. It was dangerous, but she had no alternative, knowing she must hide the kittens from predators as soon as possible. With luck, the barn would be empty.

Her leg was painful, and her progress was slow. She carried one kitten for a few yards, hid it under some leaves, and returned for the second, and then the third. It took all her strength. All the while, her senses were on full alert, aware of the danger from foxes lurking nearby and awaiting easy prey.

It took a long time before she cautiously approached the barn. All was quiet; so far, so good. Breathing a sigh of relief, she looked around for a safe hiding place for the kittens before investigating inside. It didn't take her long; the strong winds of the previous night had done her a favour, with plenty of leaves left lying on the ground in a nearby orchard of orange trees. It was a good hiding place. When she had finished making a nest, she gently tucked her kittens inside.

She crept along the side of the barn and looked for a gap in the woodwork. She was in luck. At the far end, she found some broken planks of wood. Pushing with her paws, she poked her head through the opening, stopping abruptly. One of the planks above her was moving. She waited some moments before trying again. This time nothing happened, so she continued crawling slowly, making every effort to keep her body from touching the sides.

The interior was large, and she could hear mice scurrying everywhere. It seemed they too were on the alert for predators. Her eyes soon adjusted to the half-light, and she was able to look around. Large bales of hay stacked everywhere indicated the barn was used for storage – a good sign. Up in the rafters were several birds' nests, now empty; the eggs had hatched, and so the birds had flown. She set about making a bed by dragging old papers and straw that were scattered all over the floor into one of the corners. When she had finished, she stood back, pleased with her efforts. Nervous that she had left the kittens for too long, she carefully crawled through the gap in the woodwork and ran along the side of the barn to the orchard.

The kittens didn't stir as she gently carried them one by one, until all three were safely inside the barn in their new bed. Relaxing, Bella lay down beside them, purring contentedly while manoeuvring all three to her nipples. It was their feeding time. Outside, the sun shone brightly.

As the day progressed, Bella became more uneasy while listening to the noises coming from the farmyard: chickens clucking, the firm tread of someone walking past the closed door of the barn and scattering corn, the heavy breathing of a dog. She was both frightened and depressed. What if she was discovered and her babies were stolen? The nightmarish thought kept ringing in her head. The sooner she could get away, the better. Her only option would be to search for a safe home each night whilst out hunting for food.

No one seemed aware of her existence, although Bella had been living in the barn for two weeks. Not even the dog had picked up her scent. Most of the time the mice kept themselves hidden, but on the occasions when they carelessly exposed themselves, she used the opportunity to pounce. For most of the daylight hours, she occupied her time by feeding and cuddling her kittens, and sleeping as much as possible. Every night, as soon as it became dark, she carefully hid Wynken, Blynken, and Nod in an old box filled with straw before venturing outside to hunt. She always headed away from the farmyard for fear of waking the dog or attracting the attention of the humans living in the farmhouse. Fortunately, the weather had now changed for the better, and with temperatures rising with each day, there were always a plentiful supply of small rodents, enabling her to produce enough milk to satisfy three greedy mouths.

Her leg had now recovered, so she was able to hunt a little farther each night, all the time searching for a safe home. It was a difficult task, and wherever she looked, she found dangers. After walking all night, she would return to the barn just before dawn, exhausted and depressed.

Bella had always been an agile and active cat, but now it seemed feeding three kittens added greatly to her fatigue. She was no longer young and knew by instinct that unless she was able to find a safe haven soon and search for food both day and night, her milk could dry, with the result that her kittens would become weaker with each passing day.

One night whilst she was out hunting, she came across a hillside on the edge of a woodland thick with pine trees. The moon was bright enough and enabled her to see a blanket of wild flowers below, indicating the hillside was untouched by humans. Tired from her long walk, she sat down, putting a dead mouse in front of her. For some unknown reason, Bella felt safe.

Sprucing her whiskers, the scene below reminded her of the happy times she had spent on a similar hillside with the large, handsome male cat called Ginger, named after the colour of his fur. She had met Ginger while she was walking around some rubbish bins in a small village. They were immediately attracted to one another and seemed ideally suited for mating. They became good friends, spending most of their time in each other's company while looking for food under the covers of the stalls in the daily market, picking up scraps of meat or (if they were lucky) the head of a fish. On other occasions, they went to the nearby forest, where they hunted for small rodents, taking them back to the village for their supper. But for Bella, the nights were always the happiest, when they lay relaxed in each other's arms with their paws encircling their warm bodies. She'd never known such contentment in her life, and it seemed her happiness would last forever, especially when she found she was expecting Ginger's babies.

They were in the forest trying to catch a large rabbit when loud bangs shattered the peace. Ginger looked up sharply; it seemed the whole forest was alerted by the noise. Insects buzzed loudly, and a flock of birds rose to the sky. Their prey rapidly disappeared into the undergrowth.

'Hurry, Bella. We're in danger. Run as fast as you can. Hide! Don't wait; I'll follow.' His meows were long and piercing. As instructed, she ran deep into the forest and climbed a tall tree with long overhanging branches nestling herself amongst its leaves.

There were several more bangs, and then silence followed by laughter disappearing into the distance. Bella waited, not daring to come out from her hiding place until she was certain the laughter had stopped. Eventually she peeked through the leaves, wondering if Ginger was hiding somewhere in the same tree, too scared to move like she was. 'Are you there, Ginger?' There was no reply. Surely he had followed her as he'd promised. No longer caring for her own safety, she climbed down to the ground, deciding to make her own search.

Hours later, she found his limp body covered in blood. Weeping silently, she tried washing his wounds, willing him to wake up. He didn't stir, and Bella knew she had lost him forever. Purring softly whilst gently covering his body with leaves, she vowed to give his kittens all the love they deserved until, like all young adults, they went their separate ways and found their own mates.

Chapter 3

A Hostile World

Daylight came and went. Throughout another night of bitter cold, George waited. He was hungry but refused to move, knowing he must protect his master at all costs. Many nights later, during a full moon, George at last began to accept his master would never call him again. His friend and lifelong companion had gone from him forever.

Hunger eventually drove him back to the cottage, but even though he searched, he could find nothing to eat, so he sat in the doorway day after day, barking and howling. He didn't care anymore; he too wanted to die.

It was early one morning when an old cart drawn by two large horses came trundling up the hill. George got up slowly and painfully, and as he did so, he recognised that the man riding in the cart was a friend of his master. He wagged his tail, and even though he was exhausted from lack of food, he ran towards the cart, barking furiously.

'What's up, old chap?' The man got down from his seat, tethering his horses to a tree, wondering why the door was open with no sign of his friend. He called out, but when there was no response, he decided to take a look inside the cottage to see if his friend had been taken ill. When he found the cottage empty, he returned to the lane where George was still barking furiously and running a little way up the hillside.

'What's the matter, old chap? Where's your master?' George's frantic barking continued. There was obviously something wrong. It was plain George wanted him to follow. It took them half an hour to reach the pen. He gasped when he saw all the dead carcasses. 'My God,' he breathed. 'Grey wolves.' He turned to George, 'All right, all right, George. Let's go and find your master.'

He carried his friend's body back to the cottage, with George running around him in wide circles, making sure no more danger could hurt his beloved companion. 'Maybe master will be all right again now that he is back home.' But in his heart, he knew it was hopeless.

The ground was rock hard, but his master's friend axed out a large hole, gently wrapped his body in a blanket, and lowered him into the ground. He spent a long time carving two pieces of wood, which he tied together making a small cross. As he placed it in the ground, he quietly said a few words. George lay down and whimpered softly. He knew he would never see his master again.

It took many hours before his master's friend could persuade George to move. 'You can't stay here any longer, old chap,' the man pleaded. 'I must go to the police station and report what has happened to your master. Come home with me. I'll look after you until we can find you another home, and we'll also find someone to take good care of Nobby.'

The cottage was far too small to accommodate the family of five. George tried to make friends with the dogs and cats living in the yard, but they would have nothing to do with him, adding to his loneliness. There seemed to be no future for George. He was a lost soul.

Each day after his master's friend left for his day's work, George sneaked back to the only home he had ever known. The cottage was empty, as was the stable and small paddock. Hour upon hour, he sat by the wooden cross, deeply saddened knowing his master was beneath the earth. On some days, he ventured up the hillside to the old sheep pen, but there was nothing left – just signs of new grass growing where the slaughter had taken place. As each evening approached, he returned to the family cottage for his evening meal before settling down to sleep on the rug given to him by his master so long ago.

Early one evening, while the family were sitting outside in the yard eating their supper, four travellers, each carrying heavy bags on their shoulders, walked along the lane towards them. When they saw George they stopped at the garden gate and called out pointing at him. He barked a warning. What were strangers doing here, and why were they pointing at him? He barked again but relaxed when his master's friend walked to the gate, smiling and shaking hands with the two youths and the two girls. Then, after talking earnestly for a few moments, he looked back across the yard, patting the side of his leg as he did so. 'Come here, old chap.' George obediently walked towards him, wagging his tail and wondering who these strangers were and why he was being summoned. He looked up questioningly.

'George,' his master's friend said while patting his head. 'You remember I told you that one day I would find you a forever home? Well, these kind people would like to look after you and give you that home. What do you say?'

His voice was gentle as always, and although George didn't understand the words, he had an uneasy feeling his master's friend was saying goodbye. He looked back at the smiling woman sitting at the table with the three children precariously perched on her knees, waving their small hands. Then he looked up at the man who had rescued him and who had taken care of the dead body of his master all those months before. Was it really true he was no longer welcome, and he was being asked to leave and go with strangers?

One of the youths patted his leg. 'Come!' It was a word George understood well, but this voice wasn't a command; it had a weak sound. George took a pace back and breathed in. He didn't like their scent; they had a bad smell. He knew the word 'Come' was a command, but he was hesitant, not wanting to obey. The strangers picked up their bags and put them on their backs. The youth bent down and tied a long rope to George's collar, giving it a quick tug repeating his command. George and his master's friend looked towards one another. It was quite clear: he was to leave the family and walk with the strangers.

From then on, George, led by the travellers, roamed the countryside, making camp each night either in woods or open fields, dependent upon the weather. As hard as he tried, he couldn't understand why they didn't take him to a new home, as his master's friend had promised.

They lived frugally, throwing George the odd chicken bone or bad-tasting rice. He became thin, and his coat was matted with neglect. All the time they were in camp, he was tied to a tree. Late into the night, they danced to their strange music, drinking liquid from brown bottles, giving him a sharp kick if his rope became tangled in their feet. Their routine never changed with the passing seasons. Each week he was led to the nearest village, where they stole the odd chicken, potato, or cabbage from an unobservant stallholder. George knew what they were doing, but he didn't dare give them away for fear of the thrashing he would receive.

George's once glossy coat became more and more matted. He was continually scratching from fleas, but nobody cared – or even noticed his plight.

Chapter 4

The Reunion

A dim crunching sound coming from farther down the hillside alerted Bella's attention. What now? She slowly crept behind some bushes, trying to see what was coming towards her. The crunching sound seemed too light for a human, or even a dog. Whatever it was, it was obviously small. Then in the moonlight, she saw a skinny-looking tortoiseshell cat walking jauntily up the hillside, pausing every now and then to sniff the flowers.

From her hiding place, Bella breathed in deeply, trying to catch the scent drifting towards her. Was she imagining it, or was there something familiar about that scent? Still unsure if the cat was a male in search of a mate, she stiffened, putting her body into a pounce position.

As the cat came closer, she heard loud purring, and a strong scent filled the air all around her. Shocked, she sat bolt upright. She had no doubt: this was the scent from her own daughter. She hadn't seen Tia for more than fifteen moons. Not since the tragic day when she had scratched and fought as hard as she could, trying to rescue her kittens. The day when those large gloved hands had been too strong, and she could only watch as they were taken away in the back of an old cart. Frightened for their future, her only hope was that one day they would be free to find their own mates, as she had done.

Staring with disbelief, Bella stood up and called out, 'Tia?' Not waiting for an answer but purring with contentment, she walked down the hillside towards her.

The scent from the large white cat with a black tail and ginger and black patches on her face and ear was strong. Tia hesitated, not sure what she should do. Should she run? Somewhere she had smelt this scent before, but where? A warm, loving scent when she was very young, perhaps? The only affection she had ever known was from her mother. Could this white cat be her mother? Was this one of those miracles she had heard so much about? She didn't know what to think. Could it really be true that here on this hillside, she was looking at the mother she hadn't seen for such a long time?

Bella could contain herself no longer. In her excitement, she nearly knocked Tia to one side, brushing against her affectionately and rubbing her head along Tia's body, attempting to give her a tongue wash. 'It's so wonderful to see you! I can hardly believe it! I've never been to this hillside before. I was hunting for food for my new babies.'

Tia purred. Was there a memory of this white cat's scent tucked away somewhere at the back of her mind? She wasn't sure. 'Are you my mother? I don't remember,' she said tentatively. Then, with her confidence growing, she continued. 'If you are, I would be so happy. I could show you my forever home. It's just down there.' Lifting her paw, she pointed to a large white house at the bottom of the hill. She stopped, suddenly feeling shy.

Bella sat down. 'Of course it's true. I shall never forget your wonderful scent. When you and Tio were taken from me, I was frantic. I tried looking for you, but it was impossible. How is Tio?'

With no more proof needed that her mother was really sitting beside her, Tia told the story of how they had been taken to a place where humans drank from brown bottles while in an alley beside a building then throwing their bottles at anything that moved. 'It was always the same,' she continued. 'Eventually we managed to escape and lived on the streets, stealing from the rubbish bins. Tio soon got fed up and went off somewhere. I think he wanted a mate. I haven't seen him since.'

'What happened then?' Bella wanted to know everything. Eventually after all the excitement of their reunion abated, they sat close together, and Tia told her mother the story of how she had managed to survive street living.

Throughout the harsh winter, Tia found shelter on the doorstep of an empty house in one of the many alleyways. Each night, along with the other street cats, she was able to find scraps of bread, vegetable peelings, or if she was very lucky, a few bits of meat. She told her mother how a large black cat kept watching her, wanting to mate, and how after the mating had left her.

Finding enough food for her kittens was very difficult. She always waited until darkness before creeping out into the open to search for food, but she was very nervous of the night, aware of the constant noises coming from local bars where humans continually drank from cans of liquid until they fell out into the street in screaming hordes.

One night as she was creeping back to her hiding place, she felt a sharp pain on her side and another on the back of her head. Then there was more and more pain all over her small body, where she was pelted with stones by a group of youths who were standing around and laughing. She ran as fast as she could, but the stones kept hitting her until the pain was so great she had to lie down. She was too close to her kittens for safety, and now, unable to move, she knew the youths would find them. Screaming and hissing, she watched one hold up a plastic bag, tying it tightly before throwing it into a large rubbish bin by the side of the alley. There was nothing Tia could do but listen to the tiny cries.

Some hours later, the street lamps were switched off, and with the darkness came silence. She pulled her wounded body to her feet, gingerly making her way along the village lane away from the houses. She had no idea where she was going or how she would live. She simply wanted to feel safe.

One sunny spring morning while she hunted for food, she came across a pathway winding down a hillside covered with flowers. At the bottom stood a white house, and it looked inviting. Trembling, she crept along the pathway. She was nervous of moving too close, so she hid herself under one of the many bushes of wild thyme and sat, endeavouring to see if there was any activity inside, but there was none.

As her confidence grew, she decided to take a closer look. She crept towards a narrow lane dividing the hillside from a small garden gate, behind which were steps leading up to a wide terrace surrounding the house. To one side was a large pool of crystal-clear water.

A wall, built from large rocks in places crumbling with age, separated the steps from an area of grassland covered with sweet-smelling herbs. In the middle stood the thick, gnarled trunk of an ancient olive tree, its wide-spreading branches giving deep shade throughout the hot summers.

Laughter coming from the direction of the terrace suddenly attracted her attention. She looked up sharply, not daring to move in case she was discovered. The laughter ceased as quickly as it had begun, and once more the only sounds were the loud chirping from crickets brushing their wings together.

By hunting mice and insects, and occasionally lizards, Tia kept herself alive and spent her days enjoying the happenings of the household. As far as she could see, an elegant white cat with two black spots on her head lived in the house with a tall, fair-haired man and a pretty lady with dark curls touching her shoulders.

Tia cautiously watched the man, shivering with fright and remembering when she had been used as a target by youths. But this man seemed quite different, often stroking the cat, who seemed to enjoy nothing better than to alternate between sitting on his lap and sleeping on a rather comfortable-looking cushion. Other times, the lady of the household would talk to her, every now and then picking her up and giving her a playful hug. Tia didn't think too much of this idea. If she decided to adopt this household, she would always keep her distance.

Each morning and again in the evening, the pretty lady, wearing a brightly coloured floral apron, brought a bowl filled with delicious-smelling food, which she put on the terrace. It took no time for the cat to leap off her cushion, brush herself against the lady's legs, and purr contentedly. Every time Tia watched, she was filled with envy. She couldn't get over the fact that this elegant white cat never went hunting. Often the aromas coming from the bowl were so enticing that they caused Tia, perched high up in the old olive tree, to wobble precariously.

Tia didn't dare approach. What if they threw stones at her, or worse still, water? She thought of the time she had climbed through an open window, and before realizing what was happening, she had been drenched by a jug full of water. She watched patiently for an opportunity to slip quietly towards that increasingly appetizing smell of food.

One evening her chance came. She had been watching the white cat for some time whilst she was eating her meal. For some reason, the cat seemed to have lost some of her composure and was hurriedly snatching at the food as though there wasn't a moment to waste. Then she abruptly twitched up her ears and darted away.

Keeping her eyes on the bowl, her ears well up so she could hear the slightest sound, Tia ventured forward and took a mouthful. Oh, what wonderful flavours! After all the months of near starvation, this food tasted like the most sumptuous meal in the world! A banquet, yes; that's what it was, a banquet! *Oh, what luck,* she thought, munching as quickly as she could.

She was so busy eating that she forgot to listen and didn't hear quiet footsteps a few yards away – until a sweet smell, unlike anything she had ever smelt before, drifted towards her. Only then did she realize she was not alone. Immediately she rushed towards the wall. If only she hadn't been so stupid and become so engrossed in eating. Now she was sure to be chased and have stones thrown at her. *Never again will I be tempted,* she vowed as she leapt into the undergrowth. But all she could hear was the sound of buzzing insects. She hadn't been chased.

'Puss, Puss!' a soft, warm voice called out. From her hiding place, Tia could hear footsteps walking towards her. 'Puss, Puss!' The voice called again. Tia shivered. Maybe the voice would go away. The voice called a third time. 'Puss, Puss.' Something seemed to be telling her not to be afraid. There was a clinking sound. She peeked out from her hiding place and saw the lady wearing the brightly coloured floral apron putting a bowl at the top of the steps on the other side of the wall. Then the lady quietly walked back along the terrace before disappearing through a doorway into the white house. Now, why would the lady do that? Enticing smells from the bowl were definitely reaching Tia's nostrils, causing her whiskers to twitch wildly.

She stayed quite still for a very long time – so long, in fact, that when she eventually sat up, she realized she had fallen asleep. It was dark, and no longer could she see the lights from the white house. Even the crickets had finally ceased their endless chattering.

Dawn was breaking over the glistening blue sea far below. Tia finally decided it was safe enough to creep up to the bowl, which was still on the ground where it had been left the previous evening. She put her nose down and then shook it violently as it encountered a sweet milky liquid. She tried again, but this time she managed to judge the distance and began drinking. She couldn't believe her luck, it tasted so good; sweet, but not too sweet. Tia thought it was the nicest thing she had ever tasted in her life. As she drank the last drop, she gingerly looked around her. No one was about. She still had time to lick the bowl quite clean before returning to her hiding place in order to take up her daily watch.

Every now and then throughout the morning, the lady walked towards Tia, calling softly and sometimes putting out a hand. As she did so, the white cat followed, brushing herself against the lady's legs and purring softly. Tia cautiously showed herself, and the three of them stood staring at each other.

By evening, the smell of food once more reached Tia's nostrils. It really was too much to resist. She sat up boldly and then, after a good deal of indecision, crept towards the white cat. 'May I share your supper?' she asked politely.

'Share my supper!' hissed the white cat, looking down her nose at the scraggy, multi-coloured specimen of a cat creeping alongside her. 'I should think not, indeed. In this household, we each have our own supper – we don't share, you know. Go and ask Dear Lady for your own.'

'Oh, no,' said Tia. She was very nervous and shocked at the thought. 'I wouldn't dare do that. Please, Mrs White Cat, I am very hungry. Please, may I have just a small morsel?'

Senora eyed Tia haughtily. 'If you must know, my name is not Mrs White Cat. My name is Senora.' She looked down at her bowl and then at Tia. 'Oh, well, I've finished anyway. It's too much for me, so you might as well try a bit.' She then tossed her head in the air, giving Tia a playful pat with her paw as she turned away. Tia, immediately terrified at the quick movement, darted back to the safety behind the old wall. 'Oh, don't be so stupid,' Senora said, climbing over the top. 'I won't hurt you. What a silly cat you are, all scrawny and moth-eaten. You really do look awful. I'm going to bring Dear Lady and Dear Man and introduce them. Wait there, stupid cat. Don't run away, or you'll regret it – I promise you.' With that, she turned quickly and ran the length of the terrace before taking a flying leap through an open window.

Not sure what the white cat meant, Tia didn't dare move, although she wanted to run as far away as possible. A few moments went by, and then through the open doorway came Senora followed by the man and the lady. They were each carrying a small bowl.

'What's your name?' asked Senora, not too unkindly.

'Tia.'

'That's a funny name, isn't it?'

'I don't know,' said Tia helplessly. 'I've never known any other.'

The lady and man put down the bowls of food close to where Tia was hiding, and they slowly walked back along the terrace before turning and taking a look, wondering what she would do.

30

With her confidence returning, Tia stood up. Taking a deep breath, she bravely climbed back over the wall and walked towards the bowls. As soon as she reached the first bowl, she began eating. She was no longer afraid. At last she had found her forever home.

Chapter 5

A Forever Home

Having finished her story, Tia turned to her mother. 'So you see, Mama, it really is a wonderful home. Of course, I have to be careful to keep out of Senora's way because she can be very spiteful. She keeps telling me that I should wash myself more often, and that I smell. It is very upsetting because I do try hard, but I think I have something wrong with my skin; horrid things keep jumping out of my fur, making me scratch. Senora calls them fleas and ticks. One day I saw her whisper into Dear Lady's ear, and the following day Dear Lady sprayed my nest with some horrid-smelling stuff. But I have to say, my nest did feel better afterwards, and I don't need to scratch so much now.'

Tia bent towards Bella, pushing her head into her mother's neck and at the same time giving the side of her face a tongue wash. 'Wouldn't it be wonderful if we could all live together? I want to meet Wynken, Blynken, and Nod to help with their lessons. They will have so much to learn about living in this scary world.'

Bella looked at her daughter quietly contemplating the thought. 'Well, I would have to find a safe nest. And you say there are no dogs? Just this white cat called Senora? I wonder where she's from.'

'Oh, royalty, I should think,' replied Tia, sitting down and gazing towards the white house in the distance. 'Nothing is too good for her. Dear Lady and Dear Man always treat her with enormous love. Yes, I really think she must be descended from some very rich, noble family.'

Bella purred contentedly at the thought of finding a safe home. Without a doubt, the more she thought about Tia's idea, the more it appealed. It seemed that her daughter was presenting her with a golden opportunity – and one that would be very difficult to resist. To have a real home and not have to go searching for food was beyond her wildest dreams. 'And there's plenty of food, enough to feed all of us?'

'Oh, yes, I'm quite sure there would be plenty for all of us.' Tia optimistically crossed her front paw, just in case she was mistaken. 'Dear Lady and Dear Man are always very kind, and I'm quite certain they will fall in love with the kittens. Also, I promise you there are no dogs.'

'But where would we sleep?'

'Well, the very old olive tree has a great big hollow inside. Wynken, Blynken, and Nod would be quite safe in there. It is not too high from the ground, so if they fall, they would not hurt themselves.'

And so it was decided. The next night, Bella would visit the white house and inspect the tree for herself.

When she arrived, Tia was already sitting below the old olive tree keeping watch. 'I've been here since the new day dawned,' she said, yawning. 'Not a soul has disturbed me. Such a lovely place. Look, Mama: you can see ever such a long way, so no one can possibly approach without your knowledge. Dear Lady, Dear Man, and Senora stay up at the house most of the time, so they won't bother any of us whilst we are resting.' Tia was so excited at the prospect of her family coming to live with her. She went on and on, singing the praises of her good fortune as she led the way on to the terrace. Bella nervously followed at a safe distance, not quite sure what to expect.

After sitting down outside the glass doors leading into the house, Tia meowed loudly. The door opened, and Dear Lady appeared. When she first saw the large, straggly white cat, with a black tail drooping behind and one ginger and black ear badly torn from some past escapade standing in the shadow of a pot plant, she couldn't believe her eyes.

'Who on earth have you brought me, Tia?'

Tia sat and quietly purred, wanting to show her mother how brave she was.

Dear Lady said nothing more. She quietly retreated into the house returning after a short while, carrying a bowl of food and accompanied by Dear Man.

'Well, well, well. What have we here?' Dear Man said as he looked down at Bella. 'I must say, you do look as though you've been in the wars. I suppose you want some breakfast, do you?'

Although the voice was soft and gentle, Bella hastily moved backwards when Dear Man bent towards her and put out a hand.

'Don't touch me,' Bella hissed.

'They're all right, I promise you,' whispered Tia. 'I was like that at first, but now I let them stroke me. Only very occasionally, mind you, but I must confess it gives me a nice feeling. Dear Lady has this wooden stick with soft bristles on it. Senora calls it a brush, and when Dear Lady puts it up and down her body, she says she is in cat heaven. I haven't dared try it, but I think I would love to find out if she is speaking the truth.'

When Dear Lady put down the bowl of food, Bella's fear left her, and she needed no further persuasion. Unable to resist any longer, she snatched large mouthfuls of the delicious-smelling meat. Licking the bowl quite clean and making sure there wasn't a morsel left, she sat back and washed her paws. Oh, yes, Tia had quite definitely spoken the truth. The food did taste good.

For the next two weeks, Bella regularly made her long journey over the fields and through the wood to visit the white house. She was fed regularly, and it wasn't long before she felt her body becoming healthy and strong. She thoroughly investigated the old olive tree and built a comfortable nest halfway up, inside the hollow. There was no doubt: the tree was a very safe home for her small charges.

Once or twice she came across Senora, but Senora always seemed much too preoccupied with her own thoughts to take any notice of Bella. One day, however, she did quietly inquire after Bella's health and hoped that Bella would find the tree to her liking.

'Just don't think you can come and live in the house, that's all! That is my prerogative.'

Bella had no idea what the very long word meant, but she understood Senora's meaning. 'No, I won't do that,' she replied.

From dusk to dawn for two nights, Bella and Tia carried the six-week-old kittens passing through villages, orange orchards, fields, and woodlands. At all times they were on the alert for predators, resting only during the daylight hours hiding under bushes or in the long reeds growing close to the banks of a stream.

Tia, thinking the whole escapade was tremendous fun, took great delight in rushing ahead, climbing trees, and carefully smelling the air until she was sure there were no predators slinking in the shadows. When she was convinced their path was safe, she called out to Bella, telling her to bring one of the kittens.

The kittens also sensed the excitement – so much so that Wynken and Blynken disobeyed Bella's order to remain hidden until she returned. Smelling all the delicious unknown smells was far too much of a temptation to remain hidden for long, and they were oblivious of the fact that they may become lost as they scampered off into the darkness. By the time Bella returned, having left Nod tucked under a bush, there was no sign of either kitten.

'Where are you hiding?' she called, but there was no answer. 'I'm losing patience,' she warned.

'Here we are,' came a little meow. 'We can see you, we can see you!'

Bella stared into the darkness, looking around and listening to their high-pitched cries. She breathed a sigh of relief when she saw both kittens happily dancing amongst a clump of fallen leaves.

'Tia,' Bella meowed loudly, 'come over and help. We haven't much further to go, so we'll carry them between us.' Before long, they left the wood. There, directly below them, they saw the white house bathed in moonlight. Bella nodded to Tia at the same time, brushing against her and purring with happiness.

Full of contentment, Bella stretched out beneath the large olive tree. The tree had long thick, knobbly branches spreading out like great tentacles, sometimes twining around each other. They gave a heavy blanket of shade from morning sunshine. For fear of waking the three fluffy ginger and white balls of fur pressed against her stomach, Bella had great difficulty in purring quietly. It had been a long, difficult journey. They were tired, but Bella was particularly exhausted, having carried the kittens for most of the way. All she wanted to do was sleep.

Although the sun had risen only an hour before, it was already high. With no breeze, the trees on the hillside were still. Far below, the sea shimmered and glistened, reflecting the rays from the sun and making beautiful soundless patterns as it moved slowly back and forth against the red rocks. All around were the constant chirping from crickets and buzzing insects constantly at work in their fight for survival.

She idly watched a lizard scaling up the old wall, the great slabs of rock piled loosely one above the other giving the appearance that the slightest breeze would cause the whole wall to collapse, but to Bella, it seemed safe. *Probably as old as time itself,* she thought, stretching lazily.

With one eye open, she watched the lizard make its way up the vertical stone, its head held alertly erect and its tail flicking back and forth as if in defiance. Bella silently shifted her position, making herself ready to spring, but then she relaxed. Too late – the lizard disappeared into a small crack. She thought, *Ah, there'll be another time.* She slowly rolled over, closing her eyes before falling into a deep sleep.

Chapter 6

Senora enjoyed the daily lessons. Today she was watching the progress of the stalk, certain the kittens must be weary at having been tracking Bella's tail since daylight.

As soon as the sun had risen, she took up her position on the stone steps above the wall, patiently waiting for Bella to climb down from the old tree followed by Tia and then the three kittens. Refreshed from their sleep, the kittens were always eager to play, chasing each other through the tall grasses and sweet herbs surrounding the olive tree. Inevitably this game was followed by playing hide and seek amongst the bushes of rosemary, curry, and thyme littering the hillside, collecting pungent smells on their ginger and white bodies, which were soon glistening from the dewy grasses.

But their favourite game was Catch Tails. The object was to run as fast as they could in and out of bushes and up and down the hillside, trying to catch the tail in front of them. Often the game ended by falling head over heels in a circle, nipping their own tails by mistake.

The family had been living in the old tree for four months, and the kittens were growing quickly. Senora still found difficulty in telling them apart, but she had never dared to take a closer look. She remembered that first day when she had climbed over the old wall and had been met by ten pairs of eyes plus a great deal of hissing and spitting, with Bella making it perfectly clear that the territory beyond the old wall was hers.

From her vantage point, Senora was content to watch their games from a safe distance and learn whatever she could from Bella in the hope that one day she would be able to teach her own babies in the same way. However, something deep down inside her told her she would never have a mate or babies. Every time she thought about it, she came to the conclusion that it had something to do with the old lady who had looked after her before she came to the white house.

That old lady had been very old, always bending heavily over a wooden stick as she stumbled along. Her sight was so bad that when she had opened her front door one rainy winter's day, she had barely seen the white kitten curled up asleep on the doorstep. She bent down as far as she was able, gently stroking the tiny head as she lifted the thin body. She pressed it closely to her chest as she wondered what she should do. It was obvious the kitten was defenceless and probably abandoned by some uncaring person. The old lady shuddered at the horrible thought. How could anybody be so heartless?

From then on, the old lady had nursed the kitten, whom she called Senora. She fed her every few hours with a mixture of warm milk and water from an old eyedropper, which she purified in boiling water. Eventually Senora was fully weaned and could eat the morsels of food from the old lady's dinner plate.

The old lady decided she would look after Senora until she was able to find her another home. Throughout the following weeks and months, she smothered Senora with all the love she could muster, especially the times they spent together after their midday meal, with the growing kitten asleep on her lap. During the nights, they'd cuddled in each other's arms under the blankets.

Inevitably, as Senora grew, she became more and more playful, often rushing around the room in pursuit of some imaginary quarry. As a consequence, the old lady fell, at times unable to get up until she was able to summon help by calling for her neighbour. On those occasions, the neighbour would give the old lady a severe reprimand, telling her she was far too old to have a kitten in the house. Senora had many painful memories of the times when one of her paws fell under the foot of the old lady, causing her to meow loudly as she scrambled to the nearest hiding place.

One day when Senora was about four months old, a visitor came to the house, gathered her in her arms, and put her into a cage. Scared, Senora hissed and screamed as loudly as she could, trying to explain that she hadn't had her breakfast, but nobody seemed to be listening. As she was being carried from the house, she was aware the old lady was crying and calling out her name. There was nothing she could do to escape.

The visitor put the cage into the back of a machine making a loud noise Senora had never heard before. Similar-looking machines had often moved back and forth along the street outside the old lady's house, but to Senora, behind closed windows, they were mostly soundless. Now she was very scared.

The ride was bumpy. From the inside of her cage, Senora could see nothing except the tops of trees as they quickly passed by. But thankfully the ride was short, and very soon the machine came to a halt outside a brick building. Then, as soon as Senora was carried into a large room and put on a table, she could smell strong disinfectant, similar to the one the old lady had used whenever she washed the kitchen floor. Senora remembered how she had always been forbidden to enter the kitchen until the floor was dry.

Waiting behind a table was a man dressed in a white coat. With gloved hands, he immediately opened her cage door and put her into a larger cage, which was standing on a long table. She spied two other cats in similar cages.

'So what's going on?' she asked nervously when they were finally left alone.

'Oh, they do funny things to you.' The answer came from a large ginger cat sitting alongside her. 'Stick pins in your leg. I had it done yesterday, but I don't remember what happened.'

'It was the same for me,' called the black cat from inside his cage at the end of the table. 'I have no idea what happened after I had that horrid pin stuck into me. Anyway, I feel better today, and I am waiting for my mistress to come and fetch me, so it's not so bad, really.'

Very soon both cats were removed, and Senora was left alone. After a while, a lady dressed in a white coat came into the room. *I bet she's the one with the pins,* thought Senora, shivering and giving a loud hiss.

The lady was efficient. She spoke soothingly, and before Senora realized what was happening, she felt a sharp pain in her neck where the pin pricked her. Very soon she felt relaxed and sleepy.

It was sometime later when she woke. She felt a little weak with a pain in her stomach, and as she tried to wash herself, she found it was difficult. She peeked through the wires of the cage. At first she thought she must still be dreaming, although knew she wasn't. No longer was there a smell from the horrid disinfectant, and she couldn't see the man in the white coat or the lady with the pin prick. But neither could she see the worn sofa in the old lady's cottage.

This was a room with a nice smell of flowers, comfortable armchairs, and two sofas covered with lots of soft cushions. Alongside one of them, she spied a small bowl. Senora sniffed the fresh aroma of fish and instantly felt very hungry; she meowed loudly. The visitor who had brought her here, and whom she later named Dear Lady, walked towards her and bent down to open the cage to let her out. Then whilst showing her the bowl of fish, she gently brushed her back with a soft brush. Sighing happily, Senora realized that this was to be her forever home.

Continuing the kittens' lesson, Bella moved deftly through the grasses. Every now and then, she crouched low on the ground and crawled along, her large body swaying with the motion. She stopped and remained quite still, her ears alert, her eyes fixed on her prey, this time a baby lizard. Quietly, Wynken, Blynken, and Nod followed in her wake, imitating her swaying movements. With a swift flick of her tail, she gave a signal, and simultaneously each kitten flew through the air as far as their small legs would take them, towards the lizard. But the lizard, wiser than they, had watched the proceedings with slight amusement, and it waited until Blynken's front paws touched the ground before it dashed off, knowing that his green body would merge with the grass.

And so the lesson proceeded. With each stalk, Bella took a different prey, always careful to choose something small enough for the kittens to handle if they were lucky enough to make a catch. Very seldom were they successful, but they tried and were good pupils; obedient and silent. On an occasion when Nod succeeded in leaping on top of a sleeping butterfly, there was great excitement. Wynken and Blynken rushed up and danced around Nod, mewing at him and giving their encouragement. Nod, excited by his achievement, forgot to keep his paw over the butterfly; as he lifted his paw, the butterfly gracefully flew away. He received a very sharp reprimand from his mother, and this time she flicked her tail in anger whilst giving him a sharp nip behind his ear with her paw. He wouldn't let it happen again.

'The cardinal rule,' she said sternly. 'Always keep your head, and never allow yourself to be distracted until you are quite sure that you have your prey under control.'

Teaching them to climb trees was difficult. The first thing they had to be taught was although it was always easy to go up, it was never easy to come down.

Bella would be the first to climb the tree. Calling to the kittens she instructed them to climb up the trunk slowly before passing from one branch to another, until they were alongside her. Tia would always wait at the bottom, ready to catch any kitten who had the misfortune to fall. Finally, each kitten would reach the highest branch where they balanced precariously, the weight of their bodies making the branch dip and sway. As soon as the last kitten got to the top, Bella would take a flying leap to another branch and race down to the ground, leaving the kittens hanging on for dear life.

It took a long time before the kittens had the courage to move from their perch. Finally, with Bella's persuasion, Wynken took a few steps. As he did so, he overbalanced and slid, holding on as best he could before tumbling to the branch below. Then Nod and Blynken copied his movements, wobbling from side to side, backwards, and then forwards before finally sliding down the trunk of the tree head first. By the time all three reached the safety of the ground, they were quite exhausted.

With lessons over for the day, they lay together in a pile at the foot of the tree and fell asleep until awakened by the smell of food. In anticipation, they sat silently watching from the safety of the old olive tree whilst Dear Lady, always accompanied by Senora, placed a bowl at the top of the steps. At first they had been too shy to approach the bowl, but with their mother no longer able to give them milk, they soon forgot their shyness, bravely creeping nearer until reaching the bowl with the tantalizing aromas, whereupon they ate hungrily.

Senora, becoming bored by the activities of the morning, returned to the terrace for her own meal. She always tried to ignore Tia, who was still nervous in her presence. Senora couldn't think why this cat was so nervous, because she tried to be polite whenever she met her.

Tia said, 'Oh, dear. There it goes again. I shall never be able to eat now.'

'Why on earth not?' Senora could not resist the question, although she suspected she knew the answer.

'I just get so frightened, that's why,' said Tia, twitching both ears towards the loud, crackling sound coming from inside the house. 'I just don't like strange sounds when I can't understand what they are. Do you have any idea what those sounds could be, Senora?'

'Of course I have. For heaven's sake, stop asking questions and get on with your meal. You're fussing over nothing.'

'No, I'm not,' retorted Tia, trying her best to hold her tears back. The crackling sound got louder. 'It's coming towards us! Quick, Senora – let's run,' she cried, taking a flying leap towards the old wall.

'Tia, really, it's nothing to be afraid of. It's only Dear Man fiddling with his box again.'

Tia, safe in her retreat on the other side of the wall, was weeping silently. 'What box?'

'Oh, the box he's always fiddling with. He does it all the time. Surely you realize that. Sometimes he makes quite pretty sounds come out of it. Dear Lady says that's called good music. Other times it speaks with a very deep voice which I know doesn't belong to Dear Man. Perhaps something has gone wrong. I've heard that sort of crackle noise before, and it makes Dear Man really mad. Why don't you come with me, and we'll find out?'

'Oh, no. I've never been inside the White House. I wouldn't dare! If it is Dear Man, I shan't be frightened anymore. I let him stroke me yesterday, but nothing more. It wouldn't do to let him to be too familiar, would it? You go and find out, Senora, just to make sure.'

After her brief inspection, Senora sauntered through the open door as though she hadn't a care in the world. Oh, how she loved her home. *This really is the way to live,* she thought. *Lots of loving from Dear Man and Dear Lady, lots of good food, and plenty of sunshine every day.* Yes, Senora really did count her blessings when it came to thinking of her good fortune.

Having filled herself with the delicious bowlful of chicken, she decided that it was time to persuade Dear Lady to give her coat a good grooming. Since discovering how clean she felt afterwards, she thought it was much nicer to let someone else do the work. Senora took great pride in her glistening white coat, and she hated even the tiniest smudge to be seen anywhere. When she had been living with the old lady, she had never been looked after properly and had never even seen a brush. She thought Dear Lady was wonderful. Senora knew that the old lady had loved her in her own way, but now she believed that Dear Lady loved her even more.

As the sun rose to its full height, quietness fell once more over the terraces surrounding the white house. Bella guided her charges into the shady hollow of the old tree, Tia dropped off to sleep in her retreat on the other side of the low wall, and Senora curled herself up on her favourite cushion in the shade of the grapevine. It was very hot, and it seemed that the only sensible thing to do was to sleep. Faint sounds from the white house penetrated the quiet as Dear Lady busied herself with her household duties whilst Dear Man surveyed the view from his armchair alongside the large pool filled to the brim with cool clear water. The peace was almost electrifying.

Chapter 7

Nod's Escapade

Nod opened an eye. Something was crawling over his tail. He yawned and sat up, twisting his head to get a better look, but he could see nothing. *Funny,* he thought. *I must have dreamt it.* Now fully awake, he looked across at his mother lying stretched out with her legs encircling Wynken and Blynken. All three were fast asleep. He breathed a sigh of relief, guiltily wondering if he would be able to creep away without waking them. Maybe, at last, this could be his opportunity to investigate all on his own. He hesitated a moment, trying to pluck up the courage to disobey his mother's orders. *Perhaps I shouldn't. If I get caught, I will be in terrible trouble.* While slowly tongue-washing his paw, he tried to make up his mind. Was the risk worth it? *Yes!*

He stood up very slowly, nonchalantly stretching his limbs and keeping his eyes firmly fixed on his mother, all the time praying she wouldn't wake. But fortunately, she gave no sign of stirring. *Ah,* he thought, *this is going to be easy. Just a few steps, and I'll be away.* He quietly crawled down and crept around to the other side of the old tree, his heart thumping far too loudly for his liking. He stopped, listening for any movement above. There was nothing; they were all still asleep. He took a little leap into the air with excitement at the prospect of adventure, and as his confidence grew, he quickly made for the old wall.

He remembered a large hole on the other side. Taking a peek inside could be a lot of fun. It didn't take him long to find it, and after a quick sniff, he reckoned it was a friendly hole and crept inside. Overhead, he could make out a rough roof forming the shape of a tunnel. After adjusting his eyes to the darkness, he was able to see trickles of sand falling onto the ground. He was immediately fearless. His tail went up but just as quickly went down again when it came in contact with the roof. More trickles of sand fell, this time behind him. Something scurried. Could it be a beetle, a fly, or maybe a spider? *No, this is much bigger than any of those!* He excitedly moved deeper into the tunnel, still hearing the scurrying sound in front of him.

He saw a pair of staring eyes. They were very small bright eyes, and he could just make out a slim head surrounding them. 'It's a lizard,' he meowed loudly. At the sound of his cry, the lizard scuttled away, disappearing into the darkness. Realizing his mistake, he began crawling on his stomach as quickly as he could, completely unaware that he was loosening the sand all around him.

Although it was becoming difficult to move, Nod continued pushing himself forward, pressing his front paws as hard as he could in an attempt to catch his prize before it escaped, all the time imagining how proud his brothers would be when he returned to the nest with a lizard in his mouth. *Yes, they will all be very proud of me,* he thought. *And Mama will be especially proud.*

'Too late, too late.' laughed the lizard out of the darkness. 'You won't get out now – you are trapped.'

Bella was awakened by the loud humming of a bee as it attached itself to the bark of the old olive tree just above her ear. *Bother,* she thought. She had been dreaming of a banquet of mice, ready for eating. She yawned and curled up tighter in an effort to recapture the luxury of the imaginary meal. Then she opened one eye to check on the sleeping kittens. There was something very wrong. Nod wasn't by her side! Immediately she began meowing, calling for him. There was no answer, and Wynken and Blynken woke up, stretching and yawning, quite sure it must be time for their next meal.

'Stay where you are,' Bella snapped. The two kittens shuddered at the sharpness of her voice and sat down again. 'Nod is missing. Don't you dare move until I return.' With that, she hurried off, calling as she went.

She searched the surrounds of the olive tree, around the wall, and under each rosemary, curry and thyme bush, but she could find no sign of Nod. Her calls of alarm awakened Tia and Senora from their siesta. Both ran along the terrace as quickly as they could, wondering what on earth could be wrong.

'Oh, for cat's sake,' said Senora crossly as they arrived at the top of the steps. 'What on earth is the matter with you this time?'

'Nod is missing,' Bella said worriedly. 'He must have crept away while I was asleep. I keep calling for him, but he doesn't answer.'

'Well, why on earth don't you pick up his scent?' Senora was irritable at having been disturbed. 'Surely if you pick up his scent, you will find him in no time, and then we can all have some peace.'

'Of course I've tried, silly cat!' Bella's reply was bold. She had never dared to confront Senora like this before. 'He's probably been rolling amongst the curry bushes or something, because I can't find his scent anywhere. Now, I don't know where else to look, but I am sure he can't be far away. After all, I was just having a short nap when he disappeared. Where on earth do you think he can be hiding?' Her voice became more anxious, with her tail flicking back and forth.

'If that's the case, let's go and get Dear Man,' said Senora practically. 'He will know what to do.'

'Oh, goodness me, no.' Bella was shocked at the thought. 'I can't go near him!' With that, she promptly rushed off in the opposite direction.

Senora vigorously washed her neck and looked across at Tia. 'She really is frightened of Dear Man, isn't she? Oh, well. I've done my best. If she doesn't want our help, it's too bad.' She sauntered back to her cushion.

Tia stood, worried at her mother's alarm. She wanted to help her find Nod, but she too was nervous of approaching Dear Man, despite the fact that he had always been very kind to her. *I expect he will turn up,* she thought, trying to put her worries behind her. *Mama's right: he's probably playing hide and seek somewhere.*

Nod was scared. He couldn't go forward because the tunnel was too narrow, and as hard as he tried to push himself backwards, he was blocked. There was no longer any sound from the lizard, just silence all around him. He tried meowing, but his little voice echoed back at him, and every time he opened his mouth, it was filled with sand, which he had to promptly spit out.

Bella spent a long time searching along the old wall. All the time, something told her it was connected with Nod's disappearance. Breathing in deeply, at the same time scratching at a small hole between the cracks in the rocks, she caught his scent.

'Horrors!' She gave out a terrified meow. 'Tia, get help as fast as you can. Nod is buried in the old wall. Hurry, or he will die!' She began scratching harder and harder, trying to make the small hole larger, but it was no use. She kept coming across hard rock.

Tia rushed along the terrace where Senora was fast asleep and stretched out on her cushion. 'Quick, quick, Senora! Wake up! Get Dear Man. Nod is buried in the old wall!'

Senora responded immediately, and both cats raced to the poolside where Dear Man was reading. Senora, using her mouth, tugged at his trouser leg, Tia jumped onto his lap, having forgotten that she was meant to be nervous, and together they meowed loudly.

Dear Man was quite perplexed; he didn't know what was going on and didn't particularly like his afternoon peace disturbed. 'Now, what's the matter?' he asked crossly. 'Go away, both of you. Tia, you are being very brave all of a sudden.' His voice took on a tone of surprise.

'Oh, quick, quick,' came the meows from both cats. 'Nod is buried in the old wall. Come quickly, or he will die!' Senora and Tia jumped off his lap, rushing back and forth along the terrace, their agitation very evident.

Dear Man stared at them in amazement, unable to fathom out what it was they wanted, although he realized it had to be something very urgent for them to behave this way.

He stood up and followed them towards the steps. Senora excitedly rushed back, giving his trousers a tug of encouragement until a tiny split appeared in the right leg. 'Senora, for goodness' sake, stop it.' Wynken and Blynken, discipline and fear forgotten, rushed to meet

Dear Man, meowing frantically and pleading with him to hurry.

He reached the steps and leant over the wall, surprised that Bella was scratching at the stonework and taking no notice of his arrival. Wondering why she hadn't backed off, he looked around and counted. 'Oh, good grief,' he exclaimed. 'One of the kittens must be trapped inside the wall.'

Bella continued scratching as hard as she could while Dear Man gently removed a large stone, then another, then another. But there was no sound coming from inside the wall. There seemed no doubt that Nod was buried very deeply.

'Wait here, Bella. I'll go get something to dig with.' He ran down to the garage below the house, returned quickly carrying a large spade in his hand, and began digging. It seemed a very long time before he made any real headway, but at last he found a tunnel, only to be blocked by a mound of stones preventing any form of exit.

Bella drew back, hearing coughing and choking coming from inside. She was frantic. 'Oh, hurry, hurry!' She pushed her paws into the stones dangerously close to Dear Man's spade. 'Come on, everyone. Help me save Nod. He must have been swallowing sand for ages. He will die, I know he will die!'

'Calm down,' Senora said, pulling her tail. 'Come away, Bella, and leave it to Dear Man. By getting in his way, you are making matters worse. You must have faith. You'll see he will dig Nod out.' As a way of consolation, her irritation at having her sleep disturbed had completely disappeared, she gently licked Bella's dirty head.

Eventually, Dear Man lifted Nod from his prison, brushing off the loose sand covering his head and body. 'He's had a nasty shock,' he said, 'but I don't think he has come to any real harm. Here, Bella. We'll put him back in the old tree, and then you can wash him clean.' With that, he made a soft bed from some dried leaves and laid down Nod.

'Thank you, Dear Man,' meowed Bella, not forgetting her manners.

'Thank you, Dear Man,' echoed Wynken and Blynken.

Soon everybody settled down for a good sleep, and peace reigned once more.

Chapter 8

As summer continued, the days grew hotter. Everyone and everything felt lifeless, wishing there would be a break in the heat. Unusually, there had been no rain for several months; the hillside was parched dry with deep cracks appearing all over the ground. Flowers were already dead from a lack of water, and the birds had long since left to seek cooler air.

Dear Lady and Dear Man, both in their sixties, spent most of their time lazing by the pool whilst the cats sought the deepest shade they could find. The olive trees on the hillsides were still, bent almost double by their burden of succulent, shiny fruit.

Since Nod's escapade buried under the old wall, a great change had come about. Bella, Tia, and Senora were now firm friends, and instead of Dear Lady bringing food to the steps by the wall, the three kittens bravely took their meals on the big terrace within the shade of the house where, they were now spending a lot of their time. Sunning themselves in the early mornings after their lessons were over, they spent the hot afternoons sleeping under the vine that covered a wooden trellis, dividing the terrace from the swimming pool.

'I think we have finally won them over,' sighed Dear Lady contentedly as she looked down at the sleeping bundle of fur on her best deckchair.

The evenings were the happiest time. Dear Lady and Dear Man would take a walk on one of the many paths winding up and down the hillside, enjoying the cooler air whilst watching the sunset. The red rocks in the bay were reflected in the setting sun, and the sky changed from yellow to pink to deep red streaked with turquoise. As the shadows lengthened, giant shapes hid the contours of the bay. It was always a magical experience.

Whenever she watched them set out, Senora always thought how much she would enjoy going to the top of the hillside with them. She hardly ever left the grounds around the white house, so she imagined it would be exciting new territory to explore. Then one evening, she decided to follow. At first she remained at distance in case they should see her and send her back home. But they never did, and it wasn't long before Dear Man called to her every time they set out. Always upon returning to the white house, she would breathlessly tell her friends all about her excursions stalking the rabbits burrowed high up on the hillside. It wasn't long before they all wanted to go.

And so each evening, any stranger who happened to be passing would be able to watch an enchanting sight of the silhouetted figures of Dear Lady and Dear Man, followed by six cats of varying shapes and sizes making their way along the winding pathways taking them to the top of the hillside. There they would pause whilst Dear Lady and Dear Man contentedly smoked their white sticks. Together, cats and humans sat quietly contemplating their idyllic world.

Early one morning in late August, Senora had already spent a pleasant hour watching Bella and her family on a stalk around the swimming pool. She returned to find the household awake. She looked in on Dear Lady, who was (as usual) in the kitchen cooking breakfast and preparing food. Then, becoming quickly bored with watching and not getting any attention, she decided to stroll down to the garage, where she found Dear Man carrying two large cases that were normally stored under some blankets.

'Good morning, Senora,' he said solemnly, puffing under the weight of the cases.

Senora replied with a little skip, her tail standing erect as she walked up to him. 'What are you doing?' she asked politely.

Dear Man, wishing he could understand cat language, continued, 'It's another lovely day, isn't it?' He continued walking up the steps towards the house with a case under each arm.

Senora immediately went to investigate the empty hole left by the removal of the cases, thinking it was very peculiar behaviour. What on earth was he doing? She sat down, staring at the empty hole twitching her whiskers. Why had he left the blankets in a crumbled mess? As far as Senora was concerned, those cases had been there forever. There was only one thing she could do, and that was to keep an eye on things. After all, he may need her help.

A scuffling sound came from one of the bedroom cupboards. That noise was something she should definitely explore. She crept into the bedroom and leapt onto the windowsill. Dear Lady was taking clothes out of the cupboard, folding them neatly and putting them into the same cases she had seen Dear Man carrying. Goodness knows what was happening; this was certainly all very odd. She jumped down from her perch in order to take a closer look, and then she ran across the room, took a flying leap, landed on top of the cupboard, and peered over. She had never seen such strange goings-on as she was seeing this morning.

Oh, they surely need my help, she thought. With that, she leapt down from the cupboard and into the middle of the nearest case, her paws destroying the folds of Dear Lady's best dress. *Of course, why didn't I think? This a new game! What fun,* she thought as she took a leap into the second case, burying herself amongst the clean underwear. She was quite oblivious that by this time, Dear Lady was irritated at having her neat packing ruined by a cat.

'Sorry, Senora, but this won't do. Out you go.' With that, Senora found herself sitting outside the closed bedroom door.

'Well!' Senora was quite indignant at being banished before she'd had a chance to join in. 'That really is too bad. I was only trying to have a bit of fun, as well as help.'

It was sometime later when Senora saw the offending cases standing on their own outside the front door. She stared at them intently, wondering why Dear Man hadn't put them back under the blankets in the garage where they belonged. She gave her paw a quick tongue lick while she thought about the problem. *I suppose he has forgotten. Anyway, they're in the shade, so they will probably make a comfortable bed.* With that, she took a leap onto the nearest case. 'Ouch!' she screeched, realizing something hard was sticking into her back leg. 'That was definitely a mistake.' She spied Dear Man coming up the steps from the garden gate, so she hurriedly crept behind the offending case, hoping he wouldn't see her.

'Come on, Senora. Get out of the way, for goodness' sake,' sighed Dear Man, picking up the cases. She watched him carrying them down the steps, through the garden gate, and out into the narrow lane where the car was parked. He opened a door, put the cases inside, and slammed the door. Senora simply couldn't understand what was happening, except that she seemed to sense all was not well. Some mysterious change was taking place. Both Dear Lady and Dear Man seemed to be in much too much of a hurry to bother about her, and although they had all been given their breakfast as usual, Dear Man did not linger as was his normal habit. She sat at the top of the steps, watching whilst Dear Lady hurried down the path and got into the front seat, calling up to her as she did so. 'Be a good girl, and look after everybody.'

'Now, Senora,' Dear Man said when he returned to where she was standing. He gently stroked her back. 'I am putting you in charge whilst we are away, so you be a good girl, and look after the others.'

He was obviously telling her she was rather beautiful, so she promptly showed her appreciation by brushing herself against his legs, purring loudly as she did so. Apart from the words 'good girl', she was not sure what he was saying, but she guessed he must be very pleased. She was certainly ready for more strokes and loving talk – so she was rather surprised when Dear Man turned his back on her, ran down the steps two at a time, and got into the driver's seat. 'Goodbye, Senora,' he called from the open window. 'Maria will come here and feed you'. Then they were gone, leaving Senora – who by now was sitting on top of the garden gate, completely bewildered – to watch the car disappear down the lane, causing a great amount of dust as it travelled quickly over the loose gravel.

'Phew,' she exclaimed out loud. 'They were in a hurry.' With that, she went over the wall to join Tia and Bella, who by this time were playing their favourite game of Catch My Tail.

Dear Lady looked back at the white house. She wasn't sure why she was feeling guilty. After all, they were only leaving the cats for a short vacation, their first since they had arrived in Spain. Of all the cats, she loved Senora the best, having adopted her as a kitten. She had always been comforted by the fact that Senora was a home-loving cat, entering into all their household activities, coming and going as she pleased; none of the others had ever even set a paw inside the double doors leading to their living room.

She remembered how it had taken her weeks to persuade Bella and her family to come onto the terrace for food, and that was only since Nod had been trapped inside the wall. Nevertheless, she had to admit she felt fondly towards them all – and even guilty about leaving them. Her husband put a comforting hand on her knee as they drove down the bumpy lane, assuring her that their friend from the village had promised to visit the house each day to feed them and that they would be quite safe. Nevertheless, Dear Lady couldn't help feeling apprehensive.

Senora was awakened by the sound of the latch being lifted on the garden gate. Peeking through a small tear in the back of her favourite chair in the shade by the swimming pool, she saw a large, jolly woman walking up the steps to the terrace. The straw basket she was carrying was bulging, and even from her vantage point, Senora could smell food. Flicking her tail back and forth, warning off a fly about to settle, she jumped down and ran towards the woman as she was unlocking the kitchen door and going inside. Senora stood back, watching the woman collect some empty bowls lying on the scrubbed table and fill them with food before carrying them back to the terrace and putting them on the tiled floor. Without so much as a glance in Senora's direction, she left as quietly as she had come. The cats gathered round to take their meal in silence.

'Where have they gone?' asked Tia, having digested sufficiently and cleansed her bowl.

'Maybe to get us more food,' offered Bella, hurriedly licking the remains in her bowl.

Senora looked wistfully towards the bedroom. 'Well, they've never taken cases before, and they have emptied all their cupboards.'

Tia was shocked. 'You mean they've left nothing at all?'

'Well, no, not exactly,' answered Senora. 'I think there are still things in some of the other cupboards. They never opened those.'

'Well, I hope they are back in time for our evening meal.' Bella was getting irritated at the thought of having to go without her supper.

'And, what about our evening walk?' Senora returned. 'I don't want to miss that.'

The following day, there was still no sign of Dear Man and Dear Lady. The jolly woman called at the house both in the morning and in the evening, each time carrying her basket filled with food. She was kind and even managed a smile of satisfaction at watching three adult cats and the three kittens tucking into their food.

Senora inspected each room several times in the hope that she would find Dear Lady somewhere in the house. *Maybe they returned during the night and forgot to wake me.* On the third night, she decided to sleep on the large bed – something she was normally not allowed to do. She liked the bedroom with its spacious windows overlooking the distant bay. She also liked to peek out from behind the blue curtains, watching the swifts swooping down over the swimming pool and skimming the water as they did so. One day, while she had been hiding behind the curtain, she had seen a swift catch a beautiful dragonfly whilst both were in flight. But today she contented herself watching a baby gecko as it skimmed up the wall in an effort to find shelter behind a window shutter. At first Senora was pleased with the comfort of the silken coverlet, but when she realized there was no one to scold her, she became bored and went back to her usual chair.

The days and nights passed. Senora taxed Bella frequently on the subject but soon realized that Bella wasn't worried. *As long as she's not hungry, what does she care? But then, she's not really their cat like I am.*

'Come to the woods with us. We are going hunting,' called Tia on the morning of the ninth day. 'Come on, Senora. It will be fun.' But Senora ignored her and quietly went back into the house. She was thoroughly depressed, certain her family would never return.

In the late afternoon, she was dozing in the middle of the large double bed when she was awakened by a loud knocking on the front door. Alarmed at the suddenness of the noise, Senora ran under the bed for cover. The knock came again and again. Then a short time later, she heard footsteps retreating and the latch gate click. The strangers were departing and talking loudly amongst themselves. As they did so, Senora was convinced she could pick up an unfamiliar scent that wasn't human. She breathed in deeply, wondering what else was outside beside the humans.

Curious, she crept from under the bed and took up a position behind the blue curtains, cautiously looking out. She could see the backsides of four strangers, each carrying a large sack on their back. Beside them stood a large brown, shaggy dog. So that was the unfamiliar scent. It was the scent of a dog! Remembering both Tia's and Bella's fear of dogs, she shuddered at the thought of a strange dog being so close.

Ah, well, she sighed thankfully. *I expect they will go now they know the house is empty.* But she was wrong. She watched the strangers cross over to the old wall, throwing their baggage carelessly onto the ground before leaning lazily in the shade of the old olive tree. There were two youths and two girls.

What a cheek – that's our tree. What gives them the right to be there without permission from Dear Man and Dear Lady? One of the girls handed out bottles of brown liquid whilst the others emptied their sacks and began eating large handfuls of bread and cheese. After they had eaten and drunk several bottles of the brown liquid, a youth called out sharply. From behind a bush appeared the large shaggy dog. Senora noticed it had a bad limp.

Senora was worried. *What about the others? How on earth am I going to warn them there's a dog on the other side of the wall?* Her meow was quiet but anxious. *It won't be long before they'll be back from the woods, so I've simply got to try. But how?* Although Senora was trying to be brave, she knew she would never dare to go out on the terrace. She paced up and down the bedroom, wondering what she could do. *Maybe the jolly-faced lady will tell them to go away when she brings us our food.* The thought consoled her for a little while.

At last, just before sunset, she saw the jolly lady coming through the gate, pausing for a moment when she caught sight of the strangers. Senora heard her calling to them. A young girl called back and waved. The dog stood up, giving a sharp bark of warning. Nobody else stirred, so the lady went into the house with her basket of food, filled all the bowls, and placed them on the terrace as usual before leaving.

Senora was astonished. The jolly lady had allowed those strange people to stay. Now how would all the cats be able to reach their food with that big, shaggy dog close by? She needn't have worried because as soon as the jolly lady disappeared down the lane, the shaggy dog leapt up from his sleeping place, jumped over the wall, ran up the steps, and began eating from a bowl, licking it clean before going on to the next. 'Well, of all the cheek!' exclaimed Senora. 'Now what am I supposed to do?'

More horrors – the strangers were putting up a tent. They pulled blankets from one of the sacks, and from another sack they produced a bag of food One of the youths stood a large iron frame alongside the tent, and it wasn't long before the other youth was cutting branches from the trees climbed by Wynken, Blynken, and Nod. Senora was beside herself with worry and anger. She hissed loudly but then stopped. What if they could hear her? She jumped down, hurriedly hiding herself under the bed.

By the time Senora had plucked up enough courage to take another look, all the wood had been chopped and stacked under the iron frame. One of the youths was opening a metal can and pouring a pungent-smelling liquid over the wood, spilling it on the ground as he did so. She thought the smell was horrid. This whole episode was becoming a nightmare.

Senora was inconsolable. *If only Dear Lady and Dear Man would come back. If they were here, nothing like this would be happening. They would certainly send these horrible strangers away and make everything better.* For a closer view, she stood up on the windowsill, pressing her front paws against the glass and making sure she was well hidden behind the curtain. A girl was mixing something in a large wooden bowl. The other put large slabs of meat on a wooden board, turning her back and not seeing the shaggy dog creeping up to take a sniff. He yelped loudly when a heavy boot kicked him out of the way. Senora watched him crawling off meekly, hiding himself as best he could amongst the herbs growing alongside the old wall. Senora felt sorry for him.

A youth pulled a box of sticks from his pocket and made a flame. Senora had seen Dear Man do the very same thing whenever he wanted to puff on his long, brown stick. But this youth threw his small stick onto the wood. Immediately tall flames shot up into the air, causing Senora to draw back from the window. *What on earth were they thinking?* In fear, she meowed loudly. She had often seen Dear Man and Dear Lady make a flame. Sometimes on cold nights during the winter months, they would make a flame in a large opening in the living room wall; other times, it was by the swimming pool. But there they never used wood. They always made their fire with small black shapes, which never sent up high flames.

Wonderful aromas from the cooking meat soon reached Senora. She could hardly contain herself, and the smells were so inviting. They must have had a similar effect on the dog, because he was again creeping closer, obviously wanting a taste. *I don't blame him,* thought Senora. *After all, he does look very thin.*

Another kick caused the dog to fall back against the wall. He squealed, scrambling away with his tail between his legs. But it wasn't long before he determinedly tried again. One of the youths shouted out, kicking him on his backside, whilst the other tied a rope around his neck and dragged him over the old wall and on to the terrace. The boy tied him to the railing before kicking him on the head. Shivering with fright in case the youth came into the house, Senora had no idea what to do. Should she run as fast as she could, or would it be more sensible to hide? She tried to think logically and intelligently.

By this time, the youth had returned to the fire. Maybe Senora would be able to creep past the dog, run up to the woods, and warn Bella and the others. No, that would be far too risky. Anyway, Dear Lady was always telling her she was beautiful, and she certainly didn't want to get her white fur dirty by running up to the woods in case Dear Lady returned. She would be dreadfully upset if she was grubby.

Eventually Senora made up her mind and retreated under the covers on the large bed in order to think about matters.

Chapter 9

Fire!

Bella, Tia, and the kittens had a very exciting day hunting for mice and insects in the woods at the top of the hillside above the white house. They were all tired, so before returning home Bella, decided they should rest a while, knowing secretly that she was probably sleepier than any of the others. 'After all,' she said, 'we've had a very energetic day.' She found herself some soft leaves, lay down, and called out to the kittens to find themselves a place to sleep close by her. Finally, when finally all was quiet, Bella closed her eyes and slept.

Something was unsettling Tia. While lying in the shade of a large tree, she became aware of strange scents permeating the air. They were scents she remembered from her past but, for the moment she couldn't make out what they were. She didn't like them. For a long while, she tried to catch the different smells drifting around her. There was one in particular that was quite different from the normal scent given off by rodents, birds, or even humans.

So as not to wake the others, she decided to investigate and walked slowly out of the woods and halfway down the hillside. As she did so, she heard a loud bark coming from the direction of the white house, and she knew immediately it was connected to the scent. It was the scent of a dog! She raced back up the hillside and into the woods, calling out to Bella. 'There's a dog at the white house,' she exclaimed.

'Oh, don't be silly, Tia. How could a dog be at the white house?'

'There is, I promise you, I heard it bark, and I think I heard people. Bella, we must decide what to do. Senora is there on her own. She might be eaten by the dog if we don't save her.'

'Oh, really, Tia. Don't exaggerate so much. I'll come with you, and we'll look together.' Bella spied a pine tree nearby with a hole halfway up its thick trunk, which was just large enough to house the kittens. 'Wynken, Blynken, and Nod, wake up,' she ordered sharply, pointing to the hole. 'Climb up to the branch of that tree and crawl inside the hole. Hide there. On no account are you to come down until I return. Do you understand?'

Each kitten reluctantly followed her command, not knowing why, after such an exciting morning, they had to hide in an uncomfortable tree until their mother returned. But without voicing their question, they obeyed.

Bella and Tia crept down the side of the hill until they were able to get a good view of the house. In horror, they watched the strangers tying ropes around the old olive tree. Tia was right. They could hear loud barks and howling coming from a dog. 'That dog sounds large and very angry.' Bella whispered in Tia's ear. 'We can't possibly return whilst that's there. It's much too dangerous.'

'What about Senora?'

'Well, we can't do anything about her. Let's hope she stays inside the house until the jolly lady who comes with our food sends away those strangers and that dog. Come on. Let's go back and wait.' Together, they slowly crept back up towards the woods, nervously looking behind them every few minutes and making sure that weren't being followed by the dog.

'I'm hungry,' called Wynken from his hiding place. 'Please, can we come down? It's too hot up here.'

'It won't be long now, but we must make sure everything is safe.' Bella was trying to keep calm, having no idea how long it would be before she could allow the kittens to return home.

'It really is annoying,' said Tia. 'If Dear Lady and Dear Man were here, they would never allow strangers to sit by our tree. How can we possibly go about our normal business with strange humans so close to us? And, what's more, they have that dog.'

They returned to the hillside as the sun set, and they sat quietly watching the strangers, who were moving around and swaying to some kind of loud noise. It was the same noise Tia had heard many times in the villages late at night, and she didn't like it. There were too many bad memories.

Bella sniffed the air, and strange scents reached her nostrils. In the twilight, she saw the strangers running around, lifting large bottles to their lips and throwing them to the ground. After a while the noise grew louder and louder. The strangers were running around the old tree, grabbing bottles from a makeshift table as they did so. Eventually, with squeals of laughter, they fell over each other helplessly, landing in a big pile on top of one another.

Bella said, 'Wait a minute, Tia. I am sure I can see a large, shaggy dog tied up on the terrace. What do you think?'

Tia peered through the growing darkness, not able to see very much. At last she answered. 'Well, if it is tied up, it can't be dangerous, so if we decide to go down, maybe the strangers will give us something to eat.' But as soon as she voiced her thoughts, she dismissed the idea. No, it would be too risky to take the kittens amongst humans they didn't know. Anyway, they would probably throw stones and hurt them. 'There is no sign of Senora. Maybe she has stayed inside the house.'

'Or maybe she has escaped. I do hope she is safe. She can be very snooty at times, but I think I love her dearly.' Bella gave the white house one last look. It was getting too dark to see any more. 'We might as well settle down here in the woods for the night. It's not very pleasant, but it will have to do. Go and see if you can catch a mouse or two; otherwise, we are going to have three very hungry kittens, especially if they have nothing to eat until morning. I just hope the mice haven't disappeared. We've been up here for so long that they must surely have caught our scent by now. Try not to worry. I am sure the strangers and that dog will be gone by morning, and things will be back to normal. Don't get downhearted, Tia. It always turns out right in the end.' Bella was not entirely convinced at her own words of comfort. Sighing, she walked up the hillside to give the kittens the bad news.

The family didn't get any sleep that night. Bella and Tia couldn't sleep for fear the shaggy dog would be let off its rope, take a walk up the hillside, and seek them out. The kittens couldn't sleep because they were hungry and cramped together in the hole of the pine tree.

Senora couldn't sleep because of the shouts and loud singing coming from the strangers. From the safety of the bedroom, she listened to the noises coming from outside. The loud music, shouting, and laughter mixed with cooking smells lasted late into the night. But it was in the early hours when she heard the sound of breaking glass. She leapt up to the windowsill and peeked from behind the curtain. In the darkness she couldn't see very much, but every now and then, she heard a squeal coming from the dog. She reckoned someone must be throwing things at it. She stretched her neck as much as she dared, but it was difficult to see what was happening below. The sound of breaking glass followed by loud howls of pain were becoming more frequent.

Senora knew something very bad was happening. She shivered, terrified and not knowing how she could escape. She couldn't understand why the strangers were deliberately throwing things at the dog, who couldn't run away because it was tied up. What if the strangers came into the house and did the same thing to her? She jumped down from the windowsill and ran to the other side of the bedroom, where she slid her paw under a crack in the door of the clothes cupboard. She was an expert at the art of opening cupboard doors, and this one was no exception. With her paw, she pulled the door until it was fully open and crawled inside, hiding at the back amongst a pile of Dear Man's shoes, wishing desperately that he was here.

Even from her hiding place, she could hear the loud shouting and laughter from around the tree. But now the mood had changed; instead of laughter, there were angry voices and screaming. Curiosity overcame her fear, and she once more leapt up to the window. The moonlight illuminated the depravity on the other side of the old wall. She watched in horror at the scene. Sprawled on the ground were the girls screaming, at the two youths having a brawl. A foot hit out, catching the side of the iron frame, whilst another foot pushed over the metal can.

It was too late to do anything. Black liquid spilt over the ground. A small flame shot out, multiplying as it did so until it was wide enough to consume everything in its path. The corner of the tent began burning. With the flames growing taller, great bellows of smoke sent black cinders across the terrace and into the swimming pool.

'Oh, no – the tent has caught fire!.' Senora meowed loudly, giving her neck a quick tongue wash in an effort to disguise the fear building up inside her. On the terrace, the dog was howling and pulling hard on his chain.

When Senora looked again, she could see the breeze was taking the flames away from the house – but towards the old olive tree. For the moment, she was safe. She called as loudly as she could, telling the strangers to put out the fire, but they took no notice. Within minutes she saw them gather up whatever belongings they could, quickly stuffing them into their sacks as they ran away down the lane. 'Oh, how wicked!' exclaimed Senora in horror. 'They are not going to do anything. They are just running away!.'

She crept down the stairs and onto the terrace, keeping well away from both the dog and the old wall; the latter acting as a barrier from the flames, which were swirling all around the olive tree and flying across the hillside. The acrid smell of burning, together with thick smoke, was strong. Senora, now very frightened, ran past the swimming pool, all the time glancing over her shoulder at the fire, not knowing what she should do. She was aware of heavy panting and whimpering coming from the dog. One look told her the poor creature was in great pain because he had been used as a target. He needed help, but what could she do? She turned around, walking timidly towards him. Instead of fear at being so close to a strange dog, she felt a deep sorrow for the animal. There was a great gash of blood coming from a long wound down a back leg, and another deep into the neck. The dog's head was covered with tiny cuts from broken glass.

'Poor dog. What's your name?'

George whimpered, trying to lift his head. He was unable to do anything else.

'Well, if you can't tell me your name, I'll just call you Dog. That will have to do for now, but I do think it is very important for everyone to have a name, animals as well as humans. I am called Senora, by the way. Dear Lady and Dear Man always call me Senora because I am a real lady.' To emphasize her words, she quickly turned her head and tongue-licked herself down the side of her body. Raising her head, she stared at the fire, which was now spreading widely across the hillside, the strong breeze taking the flames to the top towards the woods. How could she possibly warn Bella and the others?

Chapter 10

The smell of smoke coming towards them became stronger, so much so that Bella and Tia couldn't believe what they were witnessing. By the light of the moon, they watched as flames surrounded the old olive tree – the very tree which had been their home all summer. Tears rolled down their faces at seeing their forever home being destroyed before their eyes.

'The breeze is definitely blowing this way,' Bella said anxiously. 'If it continues, I am sure it will bring the fire up the hillside towards the woods. It is far too dangerous for us to stay. Once those flames reach these woods, it will be too late to save anything.'

'But, Mama, if the breeze has changed direction, the white house will be safe. Why don't we use another path and go back?'

'No.' Bella looked up at the bright, starlit night. There was no sign of rain, and no one to put out the flames. It was a desperate situation. 'We daren't risk it in case the breeze changes direction again.' She looked across at her daughter, surprised that her memory was so short. 'Tia, have you forgotten about the dog? And what if the strangers are hiding inside the house?' She didn't

80

wait for an answer and was adamant. She would take charge. 'We will take the path on the other side of the woods away from the direction of the flames, and we'll go down to the village. We'll find some food amongst the bins, and then tomorrow, when the flames have died away, we can go back and find Senora. What do you think of that idea?'

Tia sniffed the air. Bella was right: the fire was definitely coming closer.

'Come, everyone,' Bella meowed loudly. 'We must hurry as quickly as we can.' Within moments the three kittens, hearing the urgency in their mother's voice, jumped down from the tree and stood by her feet, waiting to follow. Tia stood behind, whispering authoritatively in their ears. 'You must understand, once a fire catches, it will spread very quickly. This one is definitely coming in our direction, so we must hurry.'

It was dawn by the time they reached the village. They took a narrow track down the other side of the hill and quickly left the woods behind them. At the bottom, they came across a road with a stream running alongside. It was the same stream where Bella had hidden the kittens amongst the reeds the day before they'd journeyed to the white house.

The road was busy with traffic, so Bella quietly ordered Tia and the kittens to keep themselves hidden every time a car passed. The last thing she wanted was for a kitten to be run over. Eventually they entered the small village, and Bella hesitated. 'We must be very quiet. There are a lot of dangers in a village, so we must try not to be seen, especially if there are dogs about.'

'Or youths,' added Tia, nervous at the very thought of walking down the village street. 'We'll look for some bins, and then we will be able to find something to eat.' She remembered the many times she had been able to find scraps of food inside bins in the middle of a village square.

'I can see some over there, on the other side of the square. Look, next to those market stalls,' whispered Bella. 'Come on, everyone. Follow me' She immediately perked up at the thought of being able to find some food.

With Bella leading the way, they crept around the side of the market square, all the while hearing dogs barking and howling from nearby yards. Then they heard another sound: the sound of caterwauling. Bella put up her paw, warning the others to stop where they were.

She crept carefully to the edge of one of the market stalls and peeked out through its canvas covering. There, to her horror, she saw eight or ten cats fighting over a small piece of meat. As she watched, one of the cats backed off howling and running around in circles before disappearing down an alleyway screaming in agony. Cats began running in all directions. Immediately Bella ran to the waiting group. She pushed Wynken, Blynken, and Nod into the shadow of a wall, fearful they would be seen. 'It's too dangerous here. We must leave.'

Once away from the village square, she felt safer. 'I was very suspicious of those bins from the start. We'll have to find somewhere else. Tia, you have been here before. Do you have any more suggestions where we can find food? This time I would like a sensible suggestion, please.'

'Well.' Tia's voice shook, upset at her mother's reprimand. After all, she had been doing her best. How was she to know there would be so many cats around the bins? She thought hard. 'I do remember when I was last here, there was a place where the men were making a lot of noise while drinking from brown bottles. I also think I remember some large bins down an alleyway by a tall building. We could try there.'

'You lead, and we'll follow. Let's hope you are right.' Bella was tired and irritable. 'Keep to the shadows, everyone.'

Tia was as good as her word, and it didn't take her long to find the tall building. It was quiet, and no lights were showing. Bella breathed a sigh of relief and took a quick look around, making sure it was safe. When she was absolutely certain, she beckoned to the others. 'We are in luck. There are two large bins in the corner. Nod, you climb up and look inside. When you move the lid, be careful not to make a noise.'

There was a tremendous clatter when Nod let the lid slide from his grasp, and it fell onto the concrete ground below. Immediately they heard several dogs barking loudly at the noise, and then all went quiet. 'For heaven's sake, Nod, be more careful!' chided Bella. 'What is in the bin?'

'Just brown things, Mama. Those same things we saw Dear Lady and Dear Man drinking from.'

'Can you smell any food?'

'No, Mama, no food.' Nod sighed sadly.

'Well, there is nothing for it but to look for some more bins. Maybe in the next village we will have some luck. Come on, everyone. Keep as quiet as you can.'

Tia knew her way around, and she quickly found a shortcut across some fields, taking them to the next village. When they arrived, they followed her along deserted streets until they came upon the market square. The layout was exactly the same as the previous village, with market stalls encircling a large open square. On market day, there would be a throng of traders and villagers buying their weekly merchandise.

'There is sure to be something to eat here,' Tia whispered, dearly wanting to regain her mother's favour. 'Look, over there by that stall. I can see some bins.' She held up her paw in the direction of three large dustbins. 'See them? And what's more, there are no cats in sight. I think we are lucky. Just to be on the safe side,' she warned softly, 'you must keep as quiet as you can while I take a look around the back.'

Bella herded her charges into the shadow of one of the stalls and waited for Tia to beckon them that all was clear. It was only a few moments before she heard a familiar meow coming from the direction of the bins. As they approached, Bella saw Tia standing alongside three large cages, the smell of food reaching her nostrils. She turned to Wynken, Blynken, and Nod. 'My goodness, I really do believe we are in luck. There is definitely the smell of delicious fish, and it's coming from inside the cages.' But Bella wasn't the only one smelling fish; they were licking their lips in anticipation.

'I think the jolly woman knows we are here and has brought us our breakfast,' said Bella proudly. 'Wynken and Blynken, you go into that cage. Tia and Nod, you go into the next one. I'll go in here. Then we shall all be able to have something to eat. Be quick, all of you, in case some other cats want to steal this food.'

Each cat obeyed her instructions and ran into the cages. Not waiting for any encouragement, they began eating hungrily. In fact, they were so hungry they were completely unaware that the openings by which they had all entered snapped, closing behind them. When Bella finished eating and turned to leave, she let out a huge yell of horror, realizing they were trapped inside the cages.

Chapter 11

A Life Saved

Unaware of what was to become of Bella, Tia, and the kittens, Senora sat on the terrace, watching the olive tree burn. She knew that she would be putting herself in grave danger if she tried to go searching. Luckily, the breeze was not very strong. She prayed it wouldn't change direction; if it did, all would be lost. She looked across at the dog, still whimpering in pain and seemingly unaware that every time he moved his head, the chain around his neck was becoming a little tighter. Senora wondered how she could set him free, but as hard as she thought about it, she imagined the task to be impossible. The jolly lady wouldn't be coming until the following morning, and Senora didn't know where she lived, so she couldn't contemplate trying to find her. But one thing was certain: Senora knew the dog needed help badly.

Maybe he will die, she thought, grimacing at the prospect. *Well, if he does, I'm not going to stay the stench would be quite undignified.* For a long while, she sat and wondered what she should do next. *Maybe it would help if I wash his wounds. Surely that would make him feel better. After all, when I don't feel well, a good tongue wash always helps.* She shivered with concern, listening to the dog's heavy gasps of pain and seeing his tongue hanging loosely from the side of his mouth, his eyes tightly closed. *He looks so sad and helpless. I mustn't let him die.*

'Will you bite me if I touch you?' she asked.

The dog opened one eye and lifted his tail a few inches as if to tell her that he was her friend and was quite harmless. Carefully avoiding pieces of glass from broken bottles which were littering the terrace, Senora walked over to him and sat down. She lifted her paw as gently as she could, put it on a clean part of the dog's body, and carefully stroked him. Once again the dog lifted his tail as if to say thanks. This time Senora was convinced she was safe; this dog wasn't going to bite her.

With so many thoughts running through her head, Senora forgot about being scared of either the dog or the fire. As she continued to stroke his body, an idea formed in her mind. She remembered seeing some rags in the garage under the house.

'I'll just be a moment,' she whispered, and she quickly scampered around the edge of the terrace and down the steps leading to the garage. The cleanest rag she could find was in the corner. It had a bad smell of rotting vegetables, but she thought it was better than nothing, so she picked it up with her mouth and carried it up to the terrace.

She ran across to the swimming pool and leaned over, holding the rag tightly between her teeth so as not to drop it while she soaked it in the water. When satisfied, she went back to the dog, who was still lying in the same position. She placed the rag on his wounded leg, gently patting it with her paw. His leg shuddered, and Senora quickly took a step back for fear she had misunderstood. Maybe he would jump up and attack her? But she needn't have worried; he immediately became quite still again, whimpering quietly.

Senora repeated this exercise several times, making sure that she didn't rub the wound but gently patting it as much as she could. She attempted to clean the wounds along his back, but it was impossible. There were so many bits of glass embedded amongst his thick long fur that she didn't dare touch for fear of scratching her own paw. It seemed there was nothing she could do to relieve his pain.

All the time, whilst washing his wounds, she was purring and telling him not to be afraid, adding that she would take care of him. Every now and again, he lifted his tail. Senora knew he couldn't understand, but she also knew he was grateful. After she had finished, she slowly and gently washed his face with her tongue. As she worked, she was watching the course of the fire, making sure it was still safe to stay on the terrace.

The fire was moving quickly over the hillside, already engulfing the edge of the woodland. Tall pine trees were well ablaze. Above her, she heard a loud chugging noise. Scared at the strange sound, she stared up to the sky and saw three large flying objects drop water over the flames, causing clouds of black smoke to rise from the ground. Gushes of water poured down to the earth, soaking everything in its path. By the time it had disappeared over the horizon, both Senora and dog were completely sodden. Senora blinked, clearing the moisture from her eyes, and she looked over to the old olive tree. The flames had died, leaving a pitiful sight; the magnificent tree was now no more than a stubble.

The machines flew back and forth over the hillside, dropping water from their large buckets until all that was left was blackened earth. When the flying objects finally left, there was an uncanny silence around them. Not an insect buzzed, and no longer were there the continual chirping of crickets. All that was left was a pungent smell of scorched wood. Not even the swimming pool had escaped a coating of ash.

After giving the dog's head a final tongue wash, Senora decided that now she had helped ease his pain as much as possible, she could leave him whilst she investigated inside the house. Once inside, she looked around, shocked at seeing the dirt covering everything. *Poor Dear Lady,* she thought. *She will be so distressed when she sees all this mess.* Nothing had been saved, from the smoke-blackened floor to every piece of furniture being covered with soot.

While she was looking at the dirty bedroom, a nasty thought came into her head. Was the fire the reason Dear Lady and Dear Man had gone away in such a rush? Had they known the fire would be coming? *If they did know, why didn't they tell me? I thought I was important to them.* She gave one last look at the room, doing her best to put such thoughts out of her mind. She returned to the terrace to investigate what had happened to the garden, walking slowly and inspecting each plant. It was a depressing sight: no plant had escaped the ash.

She decided it would be a good idea to clean her grubby fur with some water from the swimming pool, but it didn't help very much. She pushed some ash away with her paw and glanced at her reflection, hardly believing what she saw. The cat looking back at her had lost its beautiful white fur and had instead become a dirty grey. She quickly looked around, making sure she was still alone. *I can't possibly be seen looking like this,* she thought whilst hurriedly using her tongue trying to clean herself, but very soon it became so sore, she had to give up.

Oh, my goodness, she thought. *What if Dear Lady and Dear Man should return now? How will they possibly be able to cuddle me?* She gave another fleeting glance at her reflection in disgust before returning to see how the dog was getting along.

To her surprise, when she reached the railing where the dog was chained, she found that he was standing up. Unable to hide her pleasure, she immediately went up to him and nuzzled against his good leg. As her head moved up and down against him, she realized he was much larger than she had first thought; the tips of her ears did not even reach the top of his leg. She felt his wet tongue stroking her head as if he was trying to communicate with her.

He moved the direction of his head towards the railing and then back to Senora, limping a few paces forward; in doing so, he tugged at the chain. It was as though he thought Senora, having helped clean his wounds, would be able to free him. Sadly, Senora knew this was one thing she couldn't possibly do. They would have to wait until the jolly lady came with her basket.

They lay down on the terrace side by side and waited patiently for many hours. Senora watched as the sun sank on the other side of the hillside, knowing that it was long past their normal feeding time. She was hungry. What could have happened to the jolly lady with the basket?

It was getting dark, and Senora was losing her patience. She stood up and stalked around. She was thirsty as well as hungry, and she guessed that the dog felt the same. Eventually, she decided she would have to find some way of having a drink before it became too dark to see.

Once again she went down the steps to the garage, where she had found the rags. She didn't really know what she was looking for, but she felt that maybe in some way, the garage where Dear Man stored so many things would give her the answer. She was right. As soon as she walked in, she spied an old, chipped plastic bowl lying in the middle of the floor. Holding it between her teeth, she slowly dragged it up the stone steps and onto the terrace. Once there, she pushed it towards a tap, which was attached to the wall. She had often watched Dear Man tying a long rubber pipe to this tap and moving it with his hand until the water spurted out the other end. In an effort to copy him, she balanced on her hind legs, put her front paws onto the tap, and with the aid of her teeth held onto it firmly, managing to turn it until the water gushed out. Then she quickly pushed the bowl underneath the running water until it was filled to overflowing and dragged it across the terrace to the dog. When he had lapped up every drop, she repeated the exercise, this time for herself.

Having satisfied their thirst, Senora thought about a new problem. She had managed to turn on the tap, but however hard she tried, she could not turn it off again. She looked in horror as the water continued to flow over the terrace towards the dog. Unable to move out of its path, he lay down again, seemingly enjoying the freshness of the water soaking his body. Senora watched with amusement. Maybe the water was actually relieving his pain.

By now both animals were extremely hungry. *Maybe there are some mice hiding somewhere,* she thought. *At least a mouse or two would be better than nothing. I wonder if this dog likes mice?* Looking across at the burnt hillside, she slowly dismissed the idea as being stupid. All the wildlife, if they weren't already dead, would have disappeared when the fire started. She decided to look inside the house, but although she searched every room, there was not a morsel of food anywhere. Darkness fell. The jolly lady never arrived, and however hard she tried, Senora could not understand why they had been abandoned.

The following morning, neither of them had had any food for two days, and Senora was very fretful. No one had been near the white house since the strangers had left. Time and time again, she wondered what had happened to Dear Lady and Dear Man. Why hadn't they returned? Why hadn't the jolly lady come with some food?

Of course! thought Senora suddenly. *The jolly lady has probably been badly hurt in the fire. I expect she lives in the countryside, and her house has been burned down.* She purred with admiration at her intelligence about why the lady hadn't come. Having thought of this solution, Senora felt relieved. Now she was certain they hadn't been deserted on purpose. *Everyone will think we all left the white house as soon as the fire started,* she mused. *That's why no one has been to rescue us. After all, who would be stupid enough to stay here amongst all this dirt? Even those horrid strangers who caused the fire ran away as soon as they could.* Senora knew that if it hadn't been for the dog, she wouldn't still be sitting on the terrace either. She would have long since left, although she had to admit she would have been very afraid.

Senora looked towards the dog, lying asleep in a pool of water from the running tap. She had no idea where she could find help, or how long it would take her. She would probably have to travel to the nearest village, and she didn't know which direction she should take in order to do that. Anyway, how was she possibly going to explain to a human – who wouldn't understand a word she was saying – that there was a badly injured dog lying on the terrace of the white house?

Whilst sitting in the shade of the grapevine, keeping a safe distance from the running water, she tried her best to clean her fur, all the time pondering their bleak situation and wondering if there was some way she could free the dog from its chain, but no matter how much she tried, her mind was a complete blank. She thought, *Maybe the best idea would be to have a good sleep. Then when I wake up, I will be able to think of something.*

She looked at the deckchairs, trying to decide which would be the cleanest, but they were all far too dirty. She glanced over to the sleeping dog, and then quite unexpectedly, an idea crept into her mind.

Although one end of the chain was tied to the railing, she remembered that the other end was fastened to something around the dog's neck. She walked over and looked closely. She had seen these leather things on dogs before and knew they were called collars. She could see the dog's collar was very wet from all the water, which had been running for so long. She nuzzled up against him and felt that the collar was soft. She thought, *I wonder if it would be possible to chew all the way through his collar and break him free that way?* She thought about the idea for a long time, knowing it could be a very risky thing to do. What if she were trying her best to set him free, and he misunderstood and attacked her?

With these thoughts in her mind, she knew that although he was in great pain, he could become frightened. Still, she felt so concerned she was willing to take a chance. She gently caught his attention by licking his nose. As she did so, she pushed a paw under the collar at the back of the dog's neck. The dog moved slightly, and as though by instinct, he had an idea what Senora was trying to do and remained very still whilst she set to work.

Senora moved her mouth to where her paw had been and slowly began chewing. It was tough, it was smelly, and it tasted horrible; but she kept on and on gnawing. After what seemed forever, she felt her teeth grind into a very small portion of the leather. Her jaws were beginning to feel very sore, but she kept going until little by little, the chewing became easier, especially where the collar was thinner. Suddenly Senora felt a snap, and the collar tore apart. The dog was free!

Although probably still in a great deal of pain, he pushed up against Senora, almost knocking her over, and covered her with licks and nudges in his happiness and gratitude at what she had just achieved. Then he immediately hobbled over to a dry part of the terrace and sat down, his head held high. He howled his thanks at the top of his voice. Senora went over to join him and sat contentedly between his legs. Then without so much as a grunt, the dog lay down, entwining his front legs around Senora and pulling her towards him. They cuddled up to each other and fell into a contented sleep. What happened next and how they would survive didn't seem to matter.

When George woke, his leg was hurting badly, so much so he wondered if he would ever walk again. The cat was still sleeping soundly, so he lay with the warmth of her body soothing his pain. Although the sun was at its highest, his thick coat protected him. He stayed quite still on the hard concrete, smelling the strong, acrid smoke hanging over the hillside.

Chapter 12

Nightmare Journey

It was after dawn when a white van drove up to the bins. A man got down from the driver's seat and walked quietly across to the cages. He knew the cats trapped inside the cages would be very frightened. When he approached, he heard their frantic hissing, screams, and scratching from all five cats trying to escape. Quickly he tied a label to each cage before carefully lifting them into the van.

Bella was frantic. She could hear everyone crying loudly, trying to break through the sides of their cages. There was nothing she could do except to soothe and console them that nothing bad would happen. She cried out, trying to convince them that they were on their way back to Dear Lady and Dear Man, and as soon as they reached the white house, everything would be all right again. But she knew her words were empty. Their forever home had been destroyed by the fire, and there was nothing left to go back to. The doors of the van slammed shut, and they were trapped and terrified.

As soon as their journey began, Bella listened intently to the sound of the engine. Her ears and nose were able to tell her a lot about their journey. There was an open window just above her cage, so she was able to see the tops of trees alongside the road as the van sped by. By concentrating very hard, she followed the line of trees, counting breaks in between each one. While passing a farmyard, she heard cocks crowing and sheep bleating in a nearby field, followed by the sound of galloping horses. No longer could she hear sounds from the sea; familiar scents were becoming fainter and fainter.

Inside the van, the cages rattled, precariously sliding from side to side as the driver manoeuvred the bumpy roads. When the driver negotiated a steep hill, the cages began sliding backwards towards the rear. To Bella, it seemed they would burst through the doors and out on to the road. Inside their cages, each cat and kitten was terrified by the sudden movement, their fear evident while they hissed, scratched, and spat, doing their best to escape. Then finally the van levelled out as they reached a straight road. Bella, recovering from the initial shock, meowed as loudly as she could, doing her utmost to calm down everybody. But the noise from the engine drowned most of her cries and did nothing to stop the fear of Wynken, Blynken, and Nod, still screaming every time their cage moved.

The van came to a standstill. They had no idea where they were. All Bella could see was the driver's head passing the open window. Immediately after he left, their meows subsided, and Bella was able to comfort them with assurances that they had nothing to fear. It wasn't long before the man returned, munching a sandwich. After he had finished eating, he sat drinking from a bottle, listening to the hissing and scratching coming from the back of the van. He was well aware that the cats inside the cages must be terrified. He gave them a sympathetic look over his shoulder, knowing there was little he could do to make their journey more comfortable. He was simply doing his job for the community.

They were all hungry, and although they were scared, Nod couldn't help licking his lips in anticipation of being given a mouthful. But he was out of luck. When he had finished his meal, the man walked around to the back of the van, opened the rear doors, and climbed inside, nearly deafened by the cacophony of noise as he did so. With a rope he had found by a rubbish bin, he securely tied the cages to a side rail in the hope that it would prevent them from bouncing about. Bella stared at him. His face was kind, reminding her of Dear Man. As he pulled on the rope, he spoke to them softly, hoping they would try to relax but at the same time knowing his attempts were in vain.

Bella stretched out in her cage as best she could. The sun was high, making the interior of the van hot and humid. The driver set off once more and took a turn, taking them along a bumpy track. All the cats were suffering from the intermittent bumps, their cages rattling with the motion. After a short while, the van gathered speed. Bella could see buildings; they were driving through a large village. She was able to see the tops of strange-looking vehicles and heard a loud hooting sound, which seemed to be coming from some long, black monster. Then to Bella's horror, the van stopped, and she saw they were alongside the black monster. The driver opened the doors, took three cages from a wooden bench, and hurriedly put them into the van alongside Bella. Each contained cats.

Bella could hear Blynken and Wynken crying out. She tried to call to them and tell them not to worry, adding that they would be kept safe. Tia, nervous as ever, was shaking, hissing, and meowing loudly. Nod, seemingly the stronger, did his best to cuddle up to her, consoling her as best he could. Suddenly under all the stress, Bella became angry, telling Tia to control herself and lead a good example to the kittens, instead of thinking of herself all the time. In turn, Tia hissed at her mother and promptly turned her back on her. Nod purred, licking her head and ears until he felt her relax.

Fortunately the strange arrivals remained quiet, so Bella was able to call out to them, asking if they knew what was happening. No one seemed to give her a coherent answer. One said he had heard about cats being cut up whilst they were still alive, and another thought they would be going to cat heaven, and a third insisted that the other two were quite wrong in saying such things and that they were all going to a forever home.

Eventually they heard a chugging sound as the black monster disappeared into the distance. The driver turned on his engine, and they were once more on the move, this time turning away from the village and travelling along narrow country roads, which at times were so bumpy that the rope became loose, causing the cages to bounce against each other once more.

They travelled farther, their constant noisy meowing filled the van. They were all hungry, thirsty, tired, and cramped with no idea where or when their nightmare journey would end.

It was the middle of the afternoon when the driver drove slowly down a narrow road towards a group of low buildings, coming to a stop in front of tall double gates. The driver hooted his horn and waited. The gates opened, and they passed through. The motor was switched off, and the rear door opened. Large gloved hands swiftly picked up each cage, placing them on a long table.

Bella shivered. Although the sun was high in the sky, there was a definite coolness in the air – quite different from the air she was used to at the white house. In the distance, she could see mountains. She meowed fiercely. 'What's happening? Where are we?' But no one seemed to hear.

'Are you all right, everyone?'

'Yes, Mama.' Tia's voice was weak with fear.

Again Bella meowed loudly. 'Where are you taking us?' Her voice was becoming hoarse with anxiety. 'Wynken and Blynken, answer me. Are you all right?' Filled with fear herself, she could do little to soothe their scared replies. Loud barking and whining came from an area to the left of her. Large dogs were jumping up at the tall fence separating them, each doing their best to reach the cats, who were frantically scratching the inside of their cages, meowing loudly, and adding to the raucous cacophony.

Bella called out, trying her best to assure they were safely out of the dogs' reach. 'Look over there. See the fencing enclosing the place, where there are dogs? They can't come here. We are quite safe.' Not knowing what would happen next, there was nothing more she could do except pray to her cat heaven, asking that she would be able to remain close to Tia and the kittens.

A man, followed by a young woman, both dressed in white coats, checked all the cages. Whilst she was waiting for her turn, Bella looked to the right of the entrance gate. The tall fencing continued as far as she could see, this time surrounding an open area filled with grassy banks, bushes, and beds of colourful flowers.

At last it was Bella's turn. A pretty face smiled down at her. 'Well, hello! For the time being, this is to be your new home. You must try not to worry I am quite sure you will enjoy yourself here.'

Bella had no idea what was said, but like the man in the van, the woman's voice sounded kind. To Bella, she sounded a little bit like Dear Lady. That made her feel more hopeful.

All the labels had now been checked. Bella nervously watched the cages being moved around into some sort of order. Finally, the cage holding Nod and Tia was placed beside her. What a relief! She watched Nod gently washing Tia's head as though to say, 'Everything will be all right. Don't you worry.' Bella once again prayed to her cat heaven.

Then, with a final look at the labels, the cage carrying Wynken and Blynken was placed next to Nod and Tia. The only thing Bella could do now was wait and see what happened next. At least she felt close enough to her family to give them some comfort.

One by one, all the cages were removed and carried into the building, leaving only Bella and her family on the table. The tall gates reopened. Bella watched the van disappear down the bumpy road and out of sight. They had been completely abandoned.

The young woman carefully lifted Bella's cage and carried her inside the building, where she was taken down a narrow corridor. The scent of cats was very strong. Silently filled with apprehension, she looked out of her cage. At intervals along the corridor, glass doors revealed separate enclosures, each holding cats. Eventually the young woman opened the door of an empty enclosure and put down her cage on the cement floor.

As she opened the gate of her cage, the woman spoke softly to Bella, coaxing her to relax and telling her not to be afraid. But Bella understood nothing and realized she was free. She rushed, hissing, to the nearest corner, arching her large body, spitting and stretching out her claws, scared she would be attacked. But with a few more softly spoken words, the young woman left, and Bella was all alone. Where were Tia and the kittens?

While despairingly looking at her surroundings, she searched for a way to escape. On either side of the large square enclosure was wire fencing; above her was a wooden roof. She slowly crept from her hiding place, inspecting every corner. More wire fencing separated her from the same play area she had seen when she had been waiting on the table. Several cats were lying lazily in the shade, and the younger ones were playing games on broken logs of wood. To her dismay, the whole area was completely enclosed by more wire fencing. Her heart sank, knowing there was no possibility of climbing it and jumping down the other side.

She walked up and down the separating wall, wondering how the cats reached the play area. She ran her paw along the bottom, hoping the netting would give way, but nothing happened. Then as she began inspecting it closer, her paw felt something solid just above the floor. To her surprise, she saw it was a small, transparent door. *Wait a minute,* she thought. *This is just like the opening Senora used back at the at the white house.* She remembered how she had often seen Senora push a transparent door like this one whenever she wanted to go inside the house, when the large doors and windows were closed. That was something Bella had never dared to do herself, always afraid of what she might find on the other side. She gave it a gentle push. There was some movement, but not enough to make any difference; she was still inside.

She pressed a little harder and suddenly found her head out in the open air. It was a miracle!

The sound of the door to the enclosure opening caused her to draw her head back sharply. She swung around to see the man and young woman putting two cages on the ground. Inside were Tia and the kittens, still meowing and hissing as loud as they could.

Within minutes of their cage doors being opened, they scattered, trying to hide somewhere. Nod took a leap upwards and landed on a wooden shelf, quickly followed by Blynken. Both kittens lay flat against the wall, cuddling each other. Tia rushed in a different direction and knocked into a bowl of water, causing water to spray everywhere. For a moment she shook her wet fur, and then she ran for cover. Wynken seemed to be the only one who wanted the protection of his mother. He rushed up to her, doing his best to hide under her tail.

'Come here,' the young woman said kindly as she put out her hand towards Bella. 'You will be safe now.'

Of course Bella couldn't understand. As before the voice was soft, and gradually, as though to tell the others she was not afraid anymore, she slowly stretched and walked over to the woman, allowing her to stroke the back of her neck. At the same time, she kept a watchful eye on the man leaving the enclosure. Bella began to purr hesitantly. Moments later, the man in the white coat returned with bowls of food in his hands, and he placed them in a corner, indicating that they should go and eat. Of course they were very hungry and thirsty, not having eaten since they were trapped the previous night, but even so, they were very reluctant to trust him.

'Sleep well. See you in the morning.' the young woman called out as they departed, closing the door behind them. Her voice was very gentle.

Bella sat down in the middle of the floor, listening to the meowing and crying coming from other enclosures. Thoroughly depressed and terrified by their situation, she decided to show everyone the cat flap and tell them that they would soon be able to go out and play. 'It's not so bad, really,' she said encouragingly. 'Of course, it's not as nice as being with Dear Lady and Dear Man, but we have food, and that lady seemed very nice. I think we should look on the bright side and enjoy ourselves while we are here.'

'But how long will we be here?' they wanted to know. Bella couldn't give them an answer.

Tia looked at the food bowls. 'What should we do now? Do you think it's a trick, and the food is full of bad things that will make us sick?' She remembered the screams of agony coming from the cat in the village who had been pulling on the piece of meat.

'Don't be silly, Tia. Of course the food is all right.' Bella tried to think logically. 'If the food is bad, they wouldn't put it into pretty bowls; they would leave it on the ground. Now, all of you, come and eat. Otherwise you will feel the back of my paw.' Although her voice was full of confidence, it was the last thing she felt. She was quietly shivering with terror, not knowing what was in store for them.

One by one, the three kittens began to examine their surroundings, inquisitive as usual and relaxing now that they realized they were safe. They walked around, sniffing the strange smells. They sniffed at the three beds lying on wooden shelves, each having a comfortable cushion inside. Nod immediately noted that there were only three beds. 'Mama, something is very wrong,' he exclaimed. 'Where are you and Tia going to sleep?'

'Don't worry, Nod. Tia and I will share the bed over there.' Lifting her paw, she pointed to a corner of the enclosure where, underneath a rack, was a bed covered with warm blankets and straw. 'That will do nicely. You will see: we will be very cosy.'

It was Wynken who discovered the three trays in one of the corners of the enclosure. 'Why are those funny things filled with hard stuff, Mama? Are they the only things for us to play with?' Without waiting for an answer, he ran across and pushed his nose in amongst the gravel, taking a large sniff and endeavouring to find a scent. Immediately he lifted his head, shaking off some gravel that had stuck to the tip of his nose. 'It smells really funny. Mama, what are these things for? Why can't we play outside?' His questions came tumbling out.

At first Bella couldn't answer his question, but again her mind went back to the white house when, one day with nobody about, she had peeked through the open door of Dear Lady's kitchen and had seen a similar tray sitting on the floor in one of the corners of the room. At the time she had been curious, so had asked Senora what it was for.

'Oh,' Senora had said proudly. 'That is a tray for me. If the rain is pouring down outside and I have to go pee in the night, I am able to use the tray. Dear Lady is the most wonderful lady in the world; she thinks of everything.'

The memories of that conversation were vivid in Bella's mind. Oh, how she wished they could all be back at the white house again. They had been so happy.

'Now, listen carefully, Wynken, Blynken, Nod, and Tia. Whenever you want to go pee in the night, you must use that tray. Whatever we do, we must keep our new home as clean as possible. I am sure these kind humans will look after us. We are safe. Now, please eat, and then we will all have a good sleep.'

It was a cold night, and although there were cushions, blankets, and straw, everyone was shivering. But with their bellies full, after they cuddled up together, it wasn't long before they fell into a deep sleep.

Chapter 13

Welcome Home

Dawn was breaking when Senora woke to hear the familiar noise of a car engine coming down the lane. 'My goodness,' she exclaimed, jumping high into the air. 'Dog, I don't believe it. Dear Lady and Dear Man have come back to us.'

Excitedly pushing George to one side, she leapt over plants still covered with soot, and raced down the stone steps by the old wall. Finally, she landed with a loud bump just inside the garden gate as the car came to a stop. Her meows were ecstatic. She leapt upwards, balancing boldly on top of the iron gate before taking a flying leap onto the bonnet of the car as Dear Lady opened her door, laughing at the sight of her beloved cat slipping and sliding over the shiny surface.

'We are definitely pleased to see you, Senora, and we're very relieved you are all right.' Both stood beside the car, staring in horror at the devastation all around them, and spoke to each other quietly. All the while, Dear Lady stroked Senora, who rubbed her face against their clothes, purring as loudly as she could. After opening the gate, they walked up the stone steps towards the terrace. Senora followed closely, brushing her body around their legs as they tried to walk, rolling over and over asking to be tickled, and stretching out her claws trying to stroke them.

'Ouch, that hurt,' said Dear Man. 'Come on, Senora. We know you are pleased, but you must let us pass and have a look to see exactly how much damage has been done.'

In reply, Senora jumped neatly onto his shoulder and washed his ear as fast as she could. She wanted to ask them where they had been and why they had deserted her, but she was far too excited to see them to bother with questions now – and anyway, they wouldn't be able to understand her. Oh, how she wished she could talk human language.

'Where are all the other cats?' Dear Lady asked as she looked anxiously towards the burnt out olive tree. 'Just look at that.' Tears welled in her eyes. 'It's such a dreadful disaster. How they loved climbing that tree and playing amongst the herbs.' She looked down at Senora. 'Where are Bella, Tia, and the kittens?' Senora rushed to the gate and back again. She knew what Dear Lady was asking because she recognized the names, but she could not explain in cat language exactly what had happened. Besides, she had no idea where the cats had gone.

'Let's at least take the cases in.' Dear Man went back to the car and pulled out a suitcase.

He heard his wife's cry coming from the top of the steps: 'Hurry, come and look. There's water everywhere!' When he reached the top, he realized what his wife had meant. There was water all over the terrace pouring from the garden tap.

'For heaven's sake,' he shouted. 'Some fool has left the tap running. What a stupid thing to do. Now we probably won't have enough water to last us through the weekend. It's far too late to call the water man to come fill the tanks; he'll be having his siesta.' With his shoes squelching, he crossed the terrace, quickly turning off the tap. Then, noticing the large, shaggy brown dog lying fast asleep by the grapevine, his frustration quickly subsided. 'My goodness, who on earth is that?' He called to Dear Lady, who was still stroking Senora at the top of the steps. 'Quick, come over here and take a look. We seem to have inherited a dog from somewhere. Whoever he is, the poor thing is in a very bad way.'

Dear Lady joined him and bent down, taking a closer look at the matted fur covered with blood and bits of glass.

'Just look at those gashes. He's in a terrible state; goodness knows what's been happening.' She picked up the bottom of a beer bottle. 'I guess it must have been those dreadful travellers we heard about.' She began picking up pieces of glass scattered all over the terrace. 'They were obviously using this poor dog as a target. What a horrendous thing to do!'

George opened his eyes, shuddering as he whimpered. He wasn't sure what he should do. Her voice sounded soft, but he had learned over the past few months to be very wary of strangers. He felt Senora brushing firmly against his body as she leant across to give his face a wash with her tongue.

'It's all right dog,' she said gently. 'These humans are my beloved family. They won't hurt you.' She looked up at Dear Lady and meowed loudly.

Dear Lady picked up Senora in her arms, cuddling her as she did so. 'Oh, sweetheart, you have no idea how pleased we are to be home. If only you could tell us what has been happening. Those people were criminals to cause this terrible damage and to be so cruel to this animal. I hope they get caught and are sent to prison.'

Dear Man bent over, putting his hand down for George to sniff. The scent was friendly, so George gave the outstretched hand a lick in return. Dear Man stood up and turned to his wife. 'I think I had better take him to the vet before I do anything else. These wounds might be infected. Just look at his gentle face; he must be suffering so much. It beats me how anybody could be so cruel. It is inhuman. Will you help carry him down to the car? Sorry to leave you, love, but I think he is more important than helping with the unpacking.'

'Don't worry,' Dear Lady said with a smile, hoping that he wasn't too tired after their long journey. 'I'll start cleaning up while you are gone.'

112

Senora was mortified at watching them carry the dog to the car and lay him on the back seat. Fearful that Dear Man would take her new friend away from her forever, she rushed after them and flung herself on top of the dog. He grunted with pain but put out his large tongue and licked her head.

'Look at that,' exclaimed Dear Lady. 'They must be very good friends for Senora to allow a dog to do that. I can't believe it!'

Knowing the urgency of getting the injured dog to the vet as quickly as possible, Dear Man spoke sharply. 'Well, let's hope Senora hasn't got bits of glass in her. I don't want to have to take two of them. Go on, Senora. You can't come with us. I promise I will be back soon. I'm going to try to make this poor animal better.' He too was surprised that the two had become so close to each other.

It was three hours before Dear Man returned with George. All the while, Senora had waited anxiously by the terrace steps, which by this time had been washed and scrubbed.

'Well,' announced Dear Man to Dear Lady with George walking alongside him. 'It appears we have a champion sheep dog boarded with us.' Senora sat beside them, trying her best to understand. Dear Man continued. 'The vet immediately recognized him. He told me that he has been treating this dog, whose name is Gentleman George, since he was a puppy.' He sat in his favourite deckchair. 'Apparently, he's a

Portuguese mountain dog, and that's the reason he looks so different from our sheep dogs back home. He's at least twice their size. And what's more, he is a pretty special dog because he and his master won first prize at the local sheep dog trials last year, which is remarkable because this particular breed is very difficult to train.

'The vet had even saved a newspaper cutting, which he had pasted on the wall, showing Gentleman George sitting alongside his master holding the winner's trophy. It was amazing. When George was lying on the table in the vet's surgery, he must have recognized his own photograph, because as we were looking at it, he suddenly whimpered and wagged his tail.

'But, the news isn't good, I'm afraid. Thankfully, George's wounds are superficial, so the vet gave him an injection of antibiotics, and he should be okay in a few days. But his owner, who was a sheep farmer, was found shot dead in a deep ravine up in the hills. About thirty sheep had been savaged. They also found the bodies of grey wolves, who are apparently very rare in these parts. The vet has no idea when it happened, or how George escaped, but when the sheep farmer's body was found, he had been dead for many days. The vet didn't know much else except that a friend buried the body and looked after George until some travellers came along and took him away.' Dear Man looked across to the burnt hillside. 'It certainly seems to fit doesn't it? Those travellers cleared off after starting the fire, leaving George behind. Poor creature.'

Senora washed her whiskers as she was listening to Dear Man. She kept hearing him repeat the word George and look towards the dog. *Of course,* she thought, once again proud at her intelligence. *George is the dog's name. Thank goodness for that. I hate it when an animal doesn't have a name.*

'I hope you told the vet he can stay with us for as long as he likes,' Dear Lady said while stroking George's head. 'He looks a lovely dog, and Senora is obviously very attached to him. After a good bath and grooming, he will be as good as new. But I must say, I am really worried about the cats. I can't help wondering what has happened to them. I just hope they got scared and ran away when the fire came. It's very worrying. They are such lovely animals, and I should hate to lose them.'

'Well, George, is obviously used to finding sheep who are lost on the hillside,' said Dear Man. 'Maybe if we ask him to look for Bella and the others, he will be able to do so.'

'It's a thought, but we don't know when they disappeared. And even if we did, how would George know who they are? After all, I don't suppose he has even seen them. They would have been far too nervous about being anywhere near a dog.'

'By picking up their scent. Dogs have a remarkable ability to find things by scent. Think of all those sniffer dogs during the war.'

'But they were trained.'

Dear Man said, 'Well, George has been trained. It is just a matter of giving him the correct command and something that is carrying their scent. Something they have been sleeping on, like a cushion. It should be easy enough.'

Having thought of this possibility during the following days, after continually searching the hillside calling their names, Dear Man and Dear Lady were becoming more and more enthusiastic to the idea of George looking for Bella and her family.

'Well, I really do think it is worth giving it a go,' said Dear Lady. 'Maybe Senora could go with him. After all, if the two of them went, the cats might not be so frightened of meeting up with a strange dog. We don't want them to take one look at him and run off. That would be terrible, and then we would never find them. I think they would trust Senora if she was with him. But I really do think it is important that we give George at least a week of rest. With plenty of food and the antibiotics doing their job, he will gain more strength. The poor dog has been through so much, and we have no idea how far he will have to travel to find Bella. In the meantime, I'll look for something the cats have used and let George smell it and get used to their scent. I know Tia slept on that deckchair over there, but I expect the soot has wiped out all of her scent.'

'What about in the garage? Are there any old rags they slept on down there?'

She thought for a moment. 'Just a minute. I did put a small cushion inside one of the boxes when the kittens were small so that they could be kept warm at night. I used to put it by the steps every evening. I am sure if they didn't use it, Tia would have. It's worth a try. I'll go and find it.'

She got up from her chair and walked across the terrace and down the steps to the garage. A few minutes later, she returned triumphant, holding the box in her arms. 'Here it is. Now all we have to do – when George is ready – is to give him the box to smell and then give him a command. Probably something like "Go find", and send both of them on their way. What do you think?'

Neither Dear Lady nor Dear Man had ever had a dog before, and they were not sure of the correct procedure for getting a dog unfamiliar with their ways to obey. The first thing they had to do was to prevent Senora from jumping into the box. As soon as she saw it, she became very excited. Obviously it was something with which she was familiar. Dear Lady prayed Senora had never used the cushion herself. If she had, the whole exercise would be pointless.

'Well, I think we have our answer, all right,' said Dear Lady. 'Look at Senora: she has definitely seen that box before. Let's hope it was used by Bella and the kittens. Now, let's give it to George to smell.'

Chapter 14

A Mission for George

They gathered on the terrace. George was more or less like his old self. His wounds were healing nicely, his leg was much less painful, and he got over his experience when the man in the white coat stuck something sharp into the back of his neck. He felt much better. He was also content that he had seen a photograph of his master. Now he knew his master's spirit would take care of him.

'Shall we give them something to eat before they go? We don't want them to get hungry and come back before they find them.' Half an hour later, when both Senora and George had eaten and had received lots of loving strokes and pats, Dear Man nudged George's shoulder firmly. 'Gentleman George!'

George immediately sat up. He hadn't heard his name since his beloved master had gone to heaven. How did Dear Man know his real name? George licked his hand, came over, and sat beside him. Could this be his new master? He knew he already loved the beautiful, elegant Senora even if she was a cat. During the days when they had been alone, they seemed to understand each other's thoughts and had become very close.

Dear Man bent over and showed George the box. 'Now, Gentleman George, I want you to do something for us. I want you to go find Bella and her family.' He gave the box to George to smell. 'Sniff inside, Gentleman George, Sniff the cushion.' George did nothing. He looked away, not understanding what was wanted of him. Dear Man picked up the cushion. 'Sniff, Gentleman George. You've sniffed it many times before, so please do it now.' Still nothing, Dear Man look helplessly at his wife. 'He doesn't understand.'

'Maybe you shouldn't use so many words. Just tell him, "Go find,"' she suggested.

Senora, who had been watching, calmly walked up to the box and put the tip of her nose inside before snuggling her head into George's neck. Three times she repeated the exercise. Then after giving George a quick pat, she ran down to the gate and back again. George watched, knowing Senora was trying to tell him something and that it was connected to the box and the gate, but he still didn't know what she meant.

Senora knew that scent, all right. Bella had often slept on the cushion inside the box after having settled the kittens in their nest in the old olive tree. As soon as she had seen it in Dear Lady's hand, she knew what it meant, and she was determined she would make George understand. Once again she rushed to the gate and back again, sniffing both the outside and the inside of the box. Although she wasn't quite sure, she was convinced Dear Lady and Dear Man wanted George to find Bella, Tia, and the kittens.

'It's hopeless,' said Dear Lady, 'but it was worth a try.' Even Senora was becoming despondent with George. Then she had an idea, which she thought would make him understand what was wanted of him.

Once more she rushed up to the terrace, and this time she dragged at George's worn collar, which was still lying on the terrace attached to the chain. She showed it to George. He gave it a sniff and cringed. Then Senora dragged the collar next to the box, pushing her nose inside as though indicating to George to do the same. Both Dear Man and Dear Lady watched, bemused.

Dear Man thought he would help Senora. 'I do believe Senora understands what we want,' he said. He pointed to the box and looked at George, who was now sitting beside it and gazing up at him. Dear Man spoke with a firm tone, lifted his head, and pointed to the hillside. 'Gentleman George, go find.' He then pushed George's head into the box and again pointed to the hillside, repeating the words. 'Go find.'

Something clicked inside George's brain. He could hear his master's voice saying 'Go find' when he wanted him to look for a lamb up in the hills. He pushed his nose into the box and breathed in deeply, and then he looked up at Dear Man and wagged his tail, 'Now I understand,' he seemed to say. 'You want me to look for this scent and bring it back to you.' He wagged his tail again and licked Dear Man's hand before walking slowly towards the gate, which was still open. Senora followed him, and together they walked side by side down the lane.

Dear Lady and her husband looked at each other, smiling. 'I really think this time it has worked. Let us pray they don't come back empty-handed.'

Chapter 15

Following the Scent

With the scent firmly in his nose, George headed for the woods, followed by Senora.

'We can't go up there,' cried Senora in agitation. 'That's where the big fire went.' She caught hold of George's tail and tried to pull him back, but he wasn't going to take any notice. He had been given a mission, and he was going to do his best to follow that scent wherever it led him. He nudged Senora to come alongside him, sensing she was afraid, but he wasn't worried. He knew he must find that scent wherever it was.

After a little while, George stopped, suddenly sniffing the air. There was something about it that was different, but he couldn't quite make up his mind what it was. Amongst the burnt trees, there were still a few that had remained untouched. The smell seemed to be coming from them. He rushed across, his tail wagging wildly. This was the same scent from the box. He had found it! He barked loudly to Senora and ran on into the woods. She followed as quickly as she could, wishing that George would not run so fast. *After all,* she thought, *this is supposed to be my resting period.* At this time of day, she could normally be found lying on her favourite cushion on the terrace, taking her customary nap. Now, here she was chasing a mad dog and looking for Bella and her family. *Life is just not the same anymore.* She sighed while running after him.

George stopped running and sat down as if he was tired, but that wasn't the reason. He had lost the scent. He would have to go back and begin again. He gave Senora a gentle lick with his wet tongue and began walking slowly back to the place where he had first picked up the scent. A few moments later, he sat down by the same tree, once more sniffing the air. His mind again went back to the hillside where his master had asked him to look in the snow for a ewe and her newborn lamb. Then he had sat in one place, sometimes for an hour or more, sniffing the air until he caught something which reminded him of the ewes. Now, he thought he would do the same.

Senora looked at him. *He's obviously too tired to go on,* she thought. *He's a lovely dog and I have grown to love him dearly. I'll just be patient and have a little doze.* With that, she cuddled up to George's hind leg and drifted into a dreamless slumber.

Moments later, George shook himself and began walking in a different direction. Yawning, Senora dutifully followed, wondering why he had changed his mind and was taking her along a different path. *Now where are we going?* she wondered. She saw him look up as a flock of starlings flew towards a small stream down in the valley. *Why on earth is he looking at all those birds? Surely he's not going to try to catch one.*

That's my job. After all, I am much lighter on my paws than a dog.

Something in George's brain suggested the scent had travelled in the same direction as the starlings. Maybe by taking the path towards the stream, he would be able to pick up the scent once more. He watched intently whilst the starlings landed in a field alongside the stream. Beside it was a narrow road, where a man with a horse and cart trundled along as if he had all the time in the world to spare.

In the distance, George could see the rooftops of buildings. *That must be a village of some sort,* he thought. His body suddenly began to shudder nervously, wondering if it was the same village he had been taken to by the horrible humans when they were drinking from the brown bottles and stealing. *What if they are still there and try to capture me again? What if they throw stones at Senora? How will we get away?*

The frightening thoughts ran through his brain as he tried to concentrate. He breathed in deeply, trying to pick up the scent. Surely that scent, whatever it came from, would try to get away from the fire and go towards the village. He made up his mind. He would follow his instincts, as he had always done in the past, and go down to the village.

Senora, having recovered from her quick nap, was now ready to keep looking for Bella, Tia, and the kittens. She had to admit that although they were sometimes very annoying – especially Wynken, Blynken, and Nod when they were chasing all over the place – she found Bella and Tia good company to talk to even though they were obviously from the country and not from a good family such as hers. Yes, she had to admit that she had grown very fond of them. Plus, of course she wanted to please Dear Lady and Dear Man by taking them back to the house so that they could all be one family again.

It was getting near nightfall when George and Senora finally reached the village. George indicated to Senora, by pressing his paw softly along her back, that he wanted her to be as quiet as she possibly could. He slowly crept into the shadows of a building and walked along the side of a wall. Senora followed silently.

Although there were only a few humans walking about, George knew he must not walk into a trap and meet up with his captors. No matter how hard he tried, he kept visualizing being tied up and having glass thrown at him. With his leg still hurting, his memories of their torture were very real. He knew he owed Senora his life. She had spent those days keeping his spirits up whilst she tried to clean his wounds. Yes, he really loved Senora and hoped they would be together always.

Senora was the first to spy the bins in the middle of a market square, but she shuddered the closer she got. She pulled at George's tail. 'Look,' she whispered, lifting her paw pointing to about a dozen cats who were jumping in an out. The lids of the bins were scattered all over the ground.

George sniffed but got no scent. Nuzzling against Senora, he gently pushed her towards the nearest wall indicating with his body movement that she should remain absolutely still. He then pulled himself up to his full height and walked towards the cats, growling quietly as he did so. That was enough, as he knew it would be. Within a few moments, all the cats had disappeared.

Sniffing the ground around him, he caught a familiar scent. He turned into an alley, indicating to Senora to follow him. At the far end was a tall building, and alongside it stood two large bins. Although there were no lights, the moon was bright enough for George to recognize that they were similar to those in the main square. He walked up to them as quietly as he could and sniffed all around. *Got it!* He was so excited that he had found what he was looking for that he barked loudly. Immediately there was loud barking and howling from every direction. It seemed that all the dogs in the neighbourhood had been alerted, and they joined in. Immediately George pushed Senora into the shadows, his tail moving sharply to give her a warning.

Finally, when the barking had died down and silence once more reigned in the village, George decided it was safe for them to move. With the scent firmly in his nostrils, he thought that at last it should be fairly easy to follow. He guided Senora out of the square and down a road. They walked for most of the night, all the time George sniffing contentedly. He knew he was heading in the right direction.

Eventually they reached another village, and George was relieved to see that the streets were quite empty. Here the scent from the inside of the box Dear Lady had shown him was very strong, but this time it was mingled with other scents that seemed to be connected.

In the middle of the market square, as in the previous village, there were waste bins, but strangely there were no cats. *Maybe they have my scent and have run away,* thought George while looking around him.

Senora, walking around the bins, noticed three large cages. She sniffed the air, catching an aroma of food. It smelt very appetising, similar to the biscuits she ate at the house. *Ooh, at last,* she thought. *We can have a meal. Of, course it won't be nearly as good as the meals I normally eat, but it will have to do.* The smell coming from each cage was very inviting, making her extremely hungry.

Keeping to the shadows, she went up to the cages, sniffing as she looked inside. She pulled at George's tail, trying to tell him to have a look in the bowl placed in the middle of one of the cages.

He pulled back, growling. 'Don't be silly Senora, I'm much too big to get in there.'

Senora then had a great idea. George needed more food than herself, so she would go into two of the cages, drag out the bowls, and give them to George, just as she had done when they were on the terrace.

Then she would go into the last cage and eat from the remaining bowl. Having eaten, she thought they would both be satisfied and able to continue their journey. She brushed herself against George's legs, purring constantly and trying to tell him what she intended. At first he was reluctant to think about food. He was anxious to follow the scents, which were exceedingly strong. But he realized Senora must be tired after having walked for so many hours, and she was probably very hungry. He sat down outside one of the cages and waited.

Slowly Senora crept to the middle of the first cage and began pulling at the bowl. Then, just as she was backing out, she heard a loud clap immediately behind her. Scared, she turned her head quickly and saw that the cage door had clamped shut. She was trapped! Immediately she jumped up and down, hissing and scratching at the sides, meowing loudly to George and pleading with him to let her out.

Seeing what was about to happen George put out his paw in an effort to stop the gate from closing, but he wasn't close enough. He inspected the cage, desperately trying to find a way to open it, but there was nowhere. The gate was firmly locked with Senora trapped inside. There was no way George could release her. He lay down beside the cage, trying to soothe Senora, who by this time was becoming hysterical in her efforts to free herself.

George thought long and hard about what he should do next, all the time aware of the hissing and scratching going on inside the cage. His mind went back to the dreadful night when his master had given him a command to stay, and in the end, because he had been so fearful for his master's safety, he had disobeyed that command and – too late – found him dead. He had no doubt he loved Senora; she had saved his life and was very precious to him. But he also knew that his new master had given him a command of 'Go find' for the scent from the cushion. He lay washing his paw, slowly convincing himself that his new master and mistress would forgive him if he looked after Senora before following their command. After all, he thought, Senora is very precious to them as well.

His mind made up, George walked away from the cages and lay down in the shadows. He didn't know how long he would have to wait, but no matter how long it took, he would wait until someone came along to free Senora.

Senora meowed quietly, her strength now gone. George whimpered back, hoping she would know he hadn't deserted her. Throughout the long night, both cat and dog waited.

Chapter 16

Unfamiliar Surroundings

Bella opened her eyes and stared at her surroundings. For a moment she thought she was by the old olive tree and looking at the hillside. Then as her eyes focused and she became fully awake, she saw her walled enclosure, and the truth dawned on her. They were prisoners. Immediately she began shaking with fright, telling herself to stay calm so that she could protect her family. She remembered the nightmare journey in the white van and being tossed around in the travelling cage, making her joints ache. The kittens and Tia were still fast asleep, so she got up slowly and silently walked around the enclosure.

She looked through the wire wall at the long line of enclosures. In some, the cats were still sleeping; in others, she could hear quiet meows. *I wonder if they are like us, and have only just arrived?* Bella thought. After standing up and stretching, she remembered the cat door. Maybe if she went out there, she would be able to find a way to escape. She pushed the small transparent door, but it wouldn't open. Then she remembered the kind, gentle lady coming into their enclosure just before dusk and locking it. Maybe, now that it was daylight, that same lady would come back and open it so that she could investigate.

'Where are we, Mama?' Nod was the first to wake. At five months, he had already become strong and muscular. His ginger and white fur was glistening in the sun peeping through the netting of the enclosure. Bella had always thought of him as a cat who would become a leader among cats and who, when the time was right, would find himself a good mate. She remembered the day when she thought he was suffocating inside the wall, and how terrified she had been. Thankfully, that experience had taught Nod a lesson, and from then on he had always obeyed Bella and had tried his best to persuade Wynken and Blynken to behave in the same way.

'This will be our new home for a short while,' Bella answered him optimistically. 'Don't worry, Nod. We will be well looked after. Those two humans who brought us into this house were very kind. Look at the lovely food we had when we arrived. I am sure they will soon be here to give us some breakfast.' She looked in the corner where last night the food bowls had been placed and saw that they were no longer there. *Oh, well. Maybe we shall have nice clean ones soon.*

'I want a drink, Mama.' The cry came from Blynken. Like Nod, he was a beautiful cat with sleek ginger fur along his back and head, revealing white fur when he rolled over. In Bella's eyes, he was the most beautiful of the three. She always excused his naughty sense of humour.

Tia was also now fully awake, and she stared at her new surroundings. 'I am really nervous about being here,' she meowed. 'I simply don't trust those humans. Remember, Mama, I have had much more experience of humans than you have.' She tried without success to add a tone of authority to her voice.

'How would you know what experience I've had?' Bella was tired and fretful, and she was ready to have an argument if Tia was going to be difficult. She had never felt it necessary to discuss her past life with her daughter, always wanting to keep to herself the cruelty she had endured. She turned to Blynken. 'The water bowl is in the corner, over there by the by the tray. Incidentally, you mustn't forget to use that tray to go pee. Please remember that, Blynken.'

'But the bowl for the water is empty,' Blynken persisted. 'We have no water.' He brushed against his mother in an effort to get her attention. 'Mama, I really am very thirsty.'

Wynken joined in with his brother. 'I'm very thirsty too, Mama, and I'm hungry. When will we have our breakfast?' It was difficult to tell Wynken and Blynken apart from a distance. Their ginger and white bodies were supple and strong.

Looking at them standing side by side, Bella thought, *It won't be long before they will be ready to go and find their mates.* She dreaded the time when all three would leave her. But thankfully they wouldn't have to endure the same experience as she had, when she'd lost Tia and Tio. The circumstances were very different. *Anyway,* she thought hopefully, *maybe they will bring their families and live at the white house with us.* For the moment whilst she was looking at them, she had forgotten that they were all prisoners and were very far away from the white house.

Chapter 17

Bella

Bella was born in the country, never knowing her father or any of her brothers and sisters. Life was very hard; in those days, the cruelty of putting kittens and puppies into waste bins was rampant. One day shortly after their birth, whilst Bella's mother was suckling her newborn kittens, a human found her hiding place. Before her mother could do anything, the human quickly grabbed four kittens, stuffed them into a plastic bag, and threw them into a waste bin. Luckily for Bella, before the human could capture her, her mother had picked her up in her mouth and climbed to the top of the nearest tree, where she stayed until nightfall.

Now, humans put out cages and make us prisoners. She looked over towards Tia. *At least putting us in cages is better than being suffocated in a bag.* Knowing a similar thing had happened to Tia's babies, Bella never wanted to talk about her own experiences.

After the terrible trauma of that day, Bella's mother had looked after her the best way she could, finding whatever scraps were available from waste bins and taking her to the woods to hunt. If she was lucky, her mother would catch a mouse, a rat, and sometimes a bird or baby rabbit. On one wonderful occasion, she had come across an injured squirrel, and they were able to feed themselves for nearly a week on the luxury.

Her mother became sick and was no longer able to hunt. Bella was only six months old, but in order to keep them both alive, she was forced to hunt. She did her best, but before long her mother was dying. There was nothing more Bella could do for her.

It was early one morning in the depth of winter when her mother lay down by the side of the road, whispering a last goodbye to her daughter and praying that she would keep herself safe. Bella was mortified and at a loss, not knowing what she should do. Weeping her heart out, she sat watching the snow cover her mother's body.

She was so saddened by the death that she didn't hear the vehicle coming down the road until it was too late. Suddenly there was a skidding sound as the driver put on his brakes before swerving into a ditch. Bella, frightened out of her life, tried to rush for cover. Large hands grabbed her by the scruff of the neck and put her into the back of the car.

She lay on the floor, shivering from the cold, her fur soaked from the falling snow. She kept wondering what would happen to her mother, praying that she would be taken to the wonderful heaven for cats. She didn't really care about herself anymore. Her mother was gone, and Bella was all alone in the world.

It was a long while before she felt the vehicle come to a standstill. She could hear the sound of dogs barking. She was very frightened; her mother had always warned her to stay away from dogs because they were very dangerous. Bella had been taught that dogs always attacked cats, so from then on whenever she had seen or smelt a dog, she ran as fast as she could in the opposite direction.

The car door opened, and the large hands once more took hold of the back of her neck. She felt as though she was being strangled. Her numbed neck with no support for her legs forced her to hang limply, not daring to scratch or to move. The hands then carried her into a barn, and before she could escape, they dropped her clumsily onto the cement floor before slamming a door. She was in darkness.

Bella stayed in the barn for many days and nights. She was given water but no food. She guessed the reason there was no food was because her job was to catch all the rats and mice running everywhere. She managed to survive, but even so, she felt herself becoming thinner. Every time the door opened, a water bowl was pushed inside and then rapidly closed; Bella was never quick enough to escape.

One night as she lay awake, she sensed and smelt a male cat. The scent was overpowering. *But how could that be?* she thought. *The only way inside is through the door.* She sat up, listening. There was a scratching noise coming from the roof. She looked up, and in the darkness she could see two yellow eyes looking down at her. 'Who are you?' she whispered, fearful of being overheard.

'Oh, just a cat, but I fancy you.'

'What do you mean, you fancy me?' Despite her shyness, Bella felt a stirring inside her.

'I have been watching you, and I think you are beautiful,' answered the cat.

'Do you have a name?' asked Bella.

'I don't know what a name is. I'm not just a cat – I am a super cat. So call me Super Cat, if you want to. But I do think your lovely white fur is wonderful, and I would like you to be my mate.' Her mother had told her a little bit about mating, but Bella was still not sure what it was.

'I will come and see you tomorrow night,' said the cat. 'We'll talk some more.' With that, he disappeared into the rafters. Bella couldn't wait for the next day to pass. Suddenly she became very excited at the thought of a male visitor.

When he arrived the following night, she brushed against him. He seemed to like that, so she did it again. Purring contentedly, he responded by washing Bella's face, and then as gently as he could, he mounted her and left.

Bella couldn't understand why the cat didn't come to see her anymore. As far as she knew, she had done nothing wrong. As the days went by, she remained alone in the barn, occasionally catching a mouse or a rat. As usual, water was left for her every day. Before long she began feeling stirrings inside her, and like her mother, she knew she would soon have some babies. In a way, she was satisfied. She was safe inside the barn.

She had only two kittens. One was a male tabby colour whom she called Tio, and the other was a female tortoiseshell. Bella decided to call her Tia. Sighing contentedly, she put both kittens to her teats, encouraging them to suckle.

As the weeks went by, Bella watched the kittens grow stronger and spent many hours playing in the straw, which was piled high in the barn. Their favourite game was to climb up to the top of the haystack and roll down again to the bottom, purring loudly as they did so. Then they would skip over to their mother and plead with her to do the same. One day when she had climbed all the way up, she spied a small hole in the rafters. Memories came back of the cat with no name, who was the father of her kittens. She wondered what had happened to him. Each day she climbed to the top of the haystack and peeped out, wondering if she dared to escape with the kittens. However, she decided to wait. Tio and Tia were still too young to be moved.

One day whilst all three were lying asleep at the bottom of the haystack, Bella woke to hear the door opening quietly. *That's funny,* she thought. *It's not the time for our water.* She saw a man coming towards her. She jumped up, hissing and spitting, but she was too late. The man bent down and quickly grabbed both kittens before running outside and slamming the door. The kittens had been taken from her. Once more Bella was alone and distressed.

That night she climbed up to the top of the haystack, determined to find out what had happened to Tio and Tia. They were her babies and were certainly not ready to have mates. She must find them. She found the hole in the rafters and climbed through. It was a very dark night. She sniffed the air, but there was no familiar scent. In the darkness, she crept around the side of the barn, all the time sniffing as she crawled. Still no scent. She saw the big black vehicle and remembered many moons ago, when she had been put into the same vehicle. The back door was slightly open, so she climbed in and sniffed deeply. There at last was the familiar scent. Bella desperately searched trying to see if her kittens had been hidden somewhere, but there was no sign of them. The vehicle was empty. Her kittens had disappeared, and she had no idea where they had gone.

The next morning, Bella hid herself in the undergrowth, all the time watching the black vehicle. Before long, she spied a human walking from a building behind the barn carrying a basket. She was quite certain she could hear meowing. *Tia and Tio must be inside.* Bella took a flying leap at the man, scratching his face, but she could do nothing more when she felt herself being pushed roughly to the ground and left slithering in the mud. After throwing the basket onto the seat of the vehicle, the man climbed in and drove away. Bella chased after him for as long as she could. When she was finally exhausted, she sat watching the empty road, broken-hearted, knowing that she would never see her babies again. Life was so cruel. First her mother, and now her babies. What more could go wrong?

Bella didn't really care what happened to her. Although she was free, she was very sad as she walked towards the village. What she didn't know was that Super Cat, the father of Tia and Tio, was now ready to mate again and was following Bella. He called out, 'Hey, there. Come here and let me comfort you. I will give you some more kittens to love.' They stayed together for some nights. Then the cat left her once more, but by this time Bella was contented, knowing that before long she would be giving birth once more.

Chapter 18

The Pin Prick

Bella and Tia could not understand why nobody had been near their enclosure since they'd arrived the previous evening. It was now daylight, and through the netting they could see other cats were eating out of bowls filled with food and water. Cat flaps had been unlocked, with several cats walking out into the fresh air. Both kept wondering why they had been ignored. They went to the side of the enclosure and climbed on to one of the shelves, whispering to each other and not wanting to worry the kittens, who were walking round and searching for a water bowl. 'It's simply not fair,' announced Nod. His meow was so loud that the cat in the next enclosure woke and scratched on the adjoining netting.

'Do you mind being quiet all of you?' He was a very large, fierce-looking black cat. 'I am trying to sleep.' With that, he lay down again and closed his eyes.

Nod took no notice of the black cat's warning. 'Mama, will you make them understand that we are all hungry?' He had spied two humans walking towards them, looking into all the enclosures stopping occasionally to go inside and take out a pee tray.

'Mama, what are they doing with the trays? Why are they taking them away?'

'Nod, you are always asking too many questions. Please be quiet.' Irritation clearly showed in Bella's voice. 'I expect they are going to fill them with clean stones.'

'Then why don't they come and take ours?' Nod was not giving up.

'I am sure they will soon. Please stop worrying about it.'

'I don't think they will ever come and take ours.' Blynken joined in the argument. 'And Mama, why won't they bring us some food? Dear Lady always gave us food, every single day.'

'And she never made us use a dirty pee tray,' argued Nod.

'For heaven's sake, both of you. Be quiet!'

The black cat stood up again. 'Oh, you won't get any food until they have done it to you,' he said.

'What do you mean, "done it" to us?' asked Bella.

'I don't know exactly what they do, but when you are new here, they starve you for ages, and then take you away and bring you back much later.' He sounded so superior that his voice reminded Tia of Senora.

'And have you no idea what happens?' she joined in nervously.

'All I can tell you is when it happened to me I felt a funny prick in my leg, and I went to sleep. When I woke up, I was in my bed with a bowl of food beside me. I've been in here ever since. I'm waiting for a forever home,' he added proudly. 'I'm sure it won't be long before I get one, because you must admit, I am a beautiful cat. Oh, I forgot. Some of the female cats have told me that afterwards, they felt very funny inside, but it only lasted a little while. Personally, I didn't feel any different – except now I can't be bothered to look for a mate anymore.'

Bella and Tia looked at each other, not really understanding everything they had been told. 'How long do you think we will have to wait for our prick?' asked Bella. 'We are all very hungry.'

'Watch out,' said the black cat. 'I think you are in luck. Two humans are coming from the other direction, and they are wearing white coats. It is always the humans wearing white coats who take you away.' He rubbed his backside against the netting close to where Bella stood on the other side and ended up with his head pointing to two humans wearing white coats walking along the corridor. Both were carrying cages.

They were two men. Bella decided she was not going to allow anyone to touch her or her family. She meowed and hissed very loudly, telling everyone to stand behind her in the corner of the enclosure.

'All claws out,' she hissed. 'Don't let them catch you.' Unfortunately, the men were wearing thick gloves, so even when Bella lashed out with her claws, she had no effect.

'Looks as though we've got some feisty one's here, Harry,' said one of the men. They were well experienced. 'You catch the white one, and I'll take care of the tortoiseshell.' With a quick movement, each man deftly picked up a cat by the scruff of their neck, thus paralyzing their movements, and put them into a cage. There was no way either cat could get out, and although both hissed and screamed at the tops of their voices, there was nothing they could do to free themselves. The needle pricking into their side was quick, and within moments they felt sleepy.

'Two done, three to go,' said the man in the white coat nearest to Wynken, Blynken, and Nod. 'Good, three males. Aren't they beautiful? The poor things are scared stiff. Let's hope the vet thinks they're old enough to castrate. Anyway, I should think they will be fairly easy to rehome.'

'Sadly, no cats are easy to rehome,' answered the second man. 'We'll just have to hope.' He pointed towards Nod. 'You grab him, and I'll get one of the others. Come on, my beauty. Let's be having you. I wish I could adopt you myself, but I've already got four.'

The three kittens screamed as loudly as they could, but all the hissing in the world didn't help their plight.

Powerful hands grabbed each one in turn and put them into a cage, locking the gate as they did so. The pin prick was very quick, and like Bella and Tia, they were soon asleep.

Chapter 19

At first light, George heard the motor arriving in the market square. A van appeared and stopped by the cages. George kept to the shadows. He knew exactly what he had to do.

A young man got down from the driver's seat, walked around to the back of the van, and opened the door, whistling cheerfully as he did so. He then went over to the cages and took a quick look inside each of them. Upon seeing two were empty, he bent over and tied a label on the cage with its one occupant, Senora. In the meantime, George stealthily crept from the shadows and walked to the front of the vehicle, where he carefully sniffed both tyres and along the front bumper. As soon as he heard the rear door close, he retreated, his ears pricked, listening to the footsteps of the man walking towards the front and climb up into the driver's seat. The driver's door slammed shut as George was creeping to the rear, taking in all the scents before disappearing back into the shadows.

The man drove away from the village square, reaching a narrow road lined with tall lime trees. George waited a few moments before following, all the time keeping to the shadows of the trees as much as he

146

could. He knew he wouldn't be able to keep up with the van for very long, especially if it increased its speed, but it didn't worry him. The scent of the van was deeply locked into his senses, as was the scent of Senora. One way or another, he would follow her wherever she was being taken. After that, George wasn't at all sure what would happen. All he knew was that he had to take care of his new friend and take her back to Dear Lady and Dear Man before fulfilling his mission of finding the scent from the cushion.

The road twisted and turned until they eventually reached another village square. The van halted alongside more cages filled with hissing cats. The man once more carefully labelled each cage and put them into the back of his van alongside Senora. While he was doing this, George made the most of his opportunity to renew the scents carried by the van so that by the time he had completed his rounds, he was quite certain that however fast the van travelled, he would be able to follow.

Running behind at a safe distance was hard. His injured leg was becoming more and more painful. He began limping as he ran in and out of the trees, knowing that he must keep out of sight. The pain was getting worse with every stride. He prayed that the van would keep to the country roads and not go through any more villages; the last thing he wanted was to lose the scent and spend wasteful hours trying to pick it up again. He kept telling himself he had to keep going for Senora's sake. Running was soon impossible, and all he could do was to hobble, trying to keep his wounded leg off the ground as much as he could.

The longer the journey progressed, the more George became despondent. With the memory of his master continually coming into his thoughts, he thought about how he had let him down on that horrible night when the fierce animals had killed the ewes. Now, he couldn't bear the thought of letting Senora down as well. She was the only friend he had left. He simply had to keep the van in sight.

At last, he breathed a sigh of relief. Up ahead and almost out of sight, the van stopped beside a filling station, and the driver got down from his seat. George hobbled as quickly as he could until he drew level, he sat down in the shadow of a tree, relieved that he could at last rest for a moment and lick his wound. The man took a long time filling his vehicle with the strong-smelling liquid, and when he had finished, George watched him walk over to a small building, open a door, and go inside. The door swung shut behind him.

George crept closer to the van, giving a quiet woof as he did so and hoping Senora would hear him. There was no answer, so he woofed again a little louder. *Surely she must hear me. I dare not call any louder.* He could hear muffled meows coming from inside the van. Beginning to despair, he crept a little closer to the van and woofed for a third time. Suddenly he was rewarded, and he could recognize Senora's answering meow. *Thank goodness,* he said to himself. *Now she knows I am following her.* He gave another reassuring woof before creeping back into the shadows to wait for the man.

'Hey, boy!' The man had returned and was standing by the door of his van, looking directly at where George was hiding. 'What's up, laddie? Come here. Come and have something to eat.'

The voice was kind, but George kept his distance. This man was a stranger, so why should he be offering him food? He watched suspiciously as the man held out a sausage. The enticing aromas drifting towards him were very inviting, especially because he was very hungry. What should he do? All the bad experiences of the past months flew in front of him. What if this man was like the youths who had been so cruel? He stood still, pondering his situation. Should he run, or should he eat the sausage?

The man knelt down, still holding the sausage in his hand. Watching his action, George relaxed a little. In the past, he had seen men do this many times when they wanted to pat a dog's head. After all, he reminded himself, his master's friend had always knelt down when he greeted George. Maybe this man really did want to be his friend – and he had to admit, he was very hungry. He limped towards the man and took the sausage from his hand.

'My goodness, your leg looks in a bad way. Let me look?' He put his hand down to touch George's leg. George immediately jumped backwards. He didn't know what the man had been saying, but as soon as

149

the hand tried to touch his leg, he became nervous, thinking the hand would hurt him. He was already regretting that he had thought the stranger was a friend.

'I'm not going to hurt you,' came the gentle but firm voice. 'I just want to help. I know you have been following me all morning, but you can hardly walk, so please let me look at your leg. Maybe I can help.'

George sat down, staring at the back of the van. Somehow he had to tell this stranger that Senora was inside. But how was he to do that when they couldn't even communicate with each other? It was nothing like talking to his master, who knew everything he was saying. He tried barking and staring at the van door, then looking back at the man, but he got no response. The man wasn't listening to George's bark; he seemed much more interested in looking at George's wound than anything else.

But George was determined not to give up. He gingerly limped across to the van and barked. Then, lifting his injured paw, he pushed it against the rear door, letting out a yelp as pain shot through his leg, which was now hurting badly.

The man looked puzzled, watching George's actions and wondering what on earth the dog was doing. Why had the dog been following him all morning? To whom did he belong? He was obviously a very intelligent animal, and although he was far too thin, he didn't give the impression of being a stray.

George woofed loudly, putting his paw to the ground and his nose to the door of the van. As he watched, the man tried to think of when he had first noticed the shaggy mountain dog. He retraced his journey back to his first pick-up of the morning in a village called San José. He remembered that just after leaving that village, he had noticed the same large dog running behind him at a fast pace. He also remembered that in San José, there had been just one cat inside a cage; he had been surprised to find the other two still empty. *He must have been following that cat all this time. Now, the poor devil can hardly walk.*

He moved very slowly towards George speaking to him as quietly as he could. 'Come on, fella. Let's have a look at you.' Still George didn't make a move. The man thought, *Maybe if I show him the cat in that first cage, he will understand that I want to help him.* Very slowly he opened the rear door of the van, only to be greeted by hissing and spitting from the cages he had collected at the last stop. He quickly closed the door, trying to think where he had put that first cage.

As soon as the van door opened, George smelt the strong scent of Senora, but he couldn't see her. He knew she must be fairly close because she had answered him when he had spoken to her whilst the man was in the building. He woofed loudly this time and limped towards the front of the van, and then he woofed again. Her response was clear; her cage was somewhere behind the man's seat.

The man followed George, hoping all the while that the dog would begin to trust him. He had grown up with dogs of all shapes and sizes, but his favourite would always be a beautiful dog very similar to the one standing before him. That dog had broken his heart when he had died at the age of nine. He had no idea why, but there was something about this mountain dog looking up at him with such sadness in his eyes that made him think this dog was lonely and needed love.

He tried again. 'Come on, fella. Let me have a look at that leg.' He took a rag from his pocket and held it out for George to sniff, indicating that he wanted to clean his wound.

George stared up into the man's face and saw the gentle eyes. His master had gentle eyes, just like this man's. He lifted his leg and allowed the man to wipe the wound. The touch was very gentle.

'Look!' His hand went into his pocket and drew out another sausage. 'This one is for being a good boy. Now, we have to find out why you are following me and where you live.' He knew the dog couldn't answer his question, but he now knew there was one cage in his van the dog was interested in. Wondering what he should do, an idea formed in his head. 'I wonder if that will work?' he mused. 'Look, fella. I know you have a friend in my van whom you want to rescue, but I am really sorry – I cannot unlock the cage here. We will have to wait until we get to the animal sanctuary. Once there, I can ask the kind people to open the cage and give you back your friend. Why don't you get in the van and come with me?'

George looked into the gentle eyes, trying his best to understand what the man was asking. He watched the man open the passenger door and tap his hand on the seat. George hesitated. He now knew what was wanted of him. His master had made the same movement many times when he had been a young puppy. Lately, all his master had to say was one word, and George would be up beside him as fast as he could.

He had to make a decision. He knew Senora was in the van. He knew it was his duty to look after her, and that in order to find the scent from the cushion, he needed Senora's help. He also knew that despite the kind man having cleaned his wound, his leg was hurting so badly he would no longer be able to keep up with the van.

The man watched the dog patiently, all the while holding the door to the passenger seat open, waiting for George to make his decision. Finally, George climbed in and sat down.

'That's a good fella. Now we'll be able to get on our way and have that wound properly looked at.' He promptly closed George's door and walked around to the other side of the van, climbing up into the driver's seat. He then switched on the engine and put the van into gear and drove slowly along the road.

The journey seemed to go on forever as they rode along country roads, passing through several villages and even two large towns where they were forced to stop because of so many cars holding up the traffic. George was happy in the knowledge that Senora was close by, and concentrated on memorizing every farmhouse and building along the route, knowing that very soon he would be able to return with Senora by his side.

It was late afternoon when George saw that they were approaching a low building enclosed behind thick wire fencing standing at the end of a narrow road. As the van slowed down, he sensed danger and heard loud barking coming from the interior. He began to whimper. He looked behind, trying to see Senora's cage, but he could only hear her loud call above all the others.

The van finally stopped in front of tall double gates. The man blew his horn and waited for them to open. George stared all around him. He had no idea where he was. In the far distance, he could see tall mountains, and with the windows of the van wide open, he noticed the air was cool. He sniffed the air, but there was nothing reminding him of anything familiar. He realized he had lost his sense of direction. Although he had carefully followed the route, he knew that it was very important to once again refresh his nostrils with the scent from the wheels of the van. How could he do that without being seen?

When the gates opened, they were greeted by cheerful voices. Two men walked around to the back of the van and began taking out the cages, placing them on a long table. George's ears shot up as soon as he heard Senora's cry. He wanted to go straight to comfort her, but the doors to the van were quickly closed before he could get out. He was trapped inside! One by one, the labels attached to the cages were checked, and the cages were removed from the table before being taken inside the building. The table was now empty. George licked his lips, trying to calm himself despite having no idea where Senora had gone. He squeezed his large body so that he was standing up on the seat and barked loudly, pleading to his new friend to open up the doors and let him out. *Doesn't he understand I must rescue Senora?*

It seemed a long time, but eventually the passenger door opened wide enough for George to jump down. A sharp pain ran through his leg, making him flinch when his foot touched the ground. Ignoring the pain, he limped towards the table where his new friend was talking to a man dressed in a white coat. He couldn't understand what was being said, but before long the stranger walked up to him.

George gave him a wary look and backed off. He didn't like the look of this at all. Men in white coats always stuck needles into him. Ever since he had been a puppy, he had hated the annual visits to the man in the white coat for what his master called his vaccinations. Then again, recently the same man had stuck a different kind of needle into him, his body had become numb, and he had gone to sleep. After that experience, George convinced himself he would never be the same dog again. The experience had been far too painful.

The man in the white coat dropped to one knee. 'Let me look at this leg,' he said gently. 'Lift.' The voice was commanding but soft. George obediently lifted his leg, allowing the man to examine his wound. When satisfied, the man drew a bottle from his pocket and soaked a white pad with liquid, gently rubbing it all over George's wound. It stung, but for only a few minutes, so George didn't feel the need to lick it off.

The two men spoke to each other at length, every few moments looking down at George. The driver kept pointing to the building where the cages had been taken and then down the road. He seemed to be telling the man in the white coat about their journey. In the meantime, someone brought George a bowl of water, which he lapped up as quickly as possible. He was very thirsty.

His new friend and the man in the white coat continued talking. They seemed friendly enough – until for some reason unknown to George, the atmosphere changed to one of apprehension when the man in the white coat suddenly bent down and took hold of George's collar, pointing to an enclosure holding dogs. George growled, afraid. He certainly wasn't going to let this man in the white coat take hold of him, even if he had cleaned his wound. He wriggled his head, trying to free himself. As he did so, his new friend spoke sharply, pulling at the man's arm and endeavouring to release George from his grip. George was having none of this. He gave a good wrench and finally managing to free himself, limping away as fast as his wounded leg would allow until he reached the safety of a wooded copse. He was breathing hard, nervous about what would happen next.

From his hiding place, George stood watching the open gates. His new friend and the man in the white coat were still arguing. He watched as a young man and a woman, both wearing white coats, carried two cages from the building and placed them on the long table. They pointed to the cages before handing his new friend a piece of paper. George could see that inside the cages were four cats; Senora was not among them.

His new friend was shaking his head, obviously still angry, and he walked to the rear of the van and opened the doors as the man in the white coat returned inside the building. His friend carefully loaded each cage into the van and closed the doors. Back in the driver's seat, he turned his vehicle around and drove out into the road. The gates automatically closed behind him.

After a few moments, the van stopped. The driver switched off the engine and opened his door. George remained hidden, sniffing the air. He wanted to make absolutely sure that he was safe from the man in the white coat before moving. When he was satisfied, he very slowly limped towards an opening amongst the trees, whining as he did so. There was something about the man that reminded him of his master, and although he was determined to find Senora and the scent from the cushion, this man was his friend, and he didn't want to lose him.

George watched as his new friend climbed down from the van and walk towards him. In one hand was a large paper bag. When he reached George, he put out his other hand. George sat down beside him and very gently licked it. It was his way of saying, 'Thank you.' Maybe together they would be able to save Senora. There must be some way he could tell his new friend what he needed to do. But how could he possibly make him understand?

'Here you are, fella,' said his friend, showing George a juicy meat sandwich. 'This will keep you going. I'll be back as soon as I can. You mustn't worry. They won't let any harm come to your pussy cat. They are really very nice people. It's just that the man in the white coat wanted to take you and put you into the dog pound with all those other dogs, until he found you a nice new home. He really only wanted to help because you are such beautiful boy.' While he talked, he gently stroked George's head.

Although George was trying his best to listen and understand what the comforting voice was telling him, he couldn't concentrate at all when such wonderful smells coming from the sandwich were right under his nose. All he wanted to do was to gulp it down. It looked and smelt so delicious. Every now and then, he twitched his ears and wagged his tail, pretending that he understood exactly what was being said to him.

'I think,' his friend chatted on, 'that you may have a good home somewhere, so I wouldn't let the vet take you into the sanctuary. Of course they would look after you very well, but it wouldn't be right, would it?' He gave George a tickle behind his left ear and laughed. 'Anyway, I also think you are a beautiful boy, so if you haven't already got a home, you and I will get along well together. Okay, you've waited long enough.' He held out the sandwich, looked at his wrist watch, and quickly gave George another stroke before returning to his van and driving away. George sat munching the delicious meat watching the vehicle disappear down the road before limping back to the safety of the trees, where he lay down, hoping he would see his friend again.

Whilst resting, although he could have eaten three times as much food, George didn't feel quite so hungry, and so he was able to think about his next move. He decided that until darkness approached, he would keep himself hidden amongst the trees in the wood. Then, when he thought it was safe, he would make his inspection. He breathed in the air. Yes, he could definitely capture the strong scent of cats. They must be fairly close. Maybe with luck, Senora would be amongst them. With her scent still very fresh in his nostrils, he was sure to pick it up and find her quickly. He decided, he would dig a hole so that she could make her escape.

As soon as he felt it was dark enough, he crept back to the entrance gates and turned to the left, carefully crawling along the wire netting. Too late, he realized the scents were changing, and he was suddenly confronted by loud barking and growling. He had made a stupid mistake and crawled to the area where the man in the white coat had wanted to put him.

The snarling and barking became louder, with some of the dogs trying to climb the fencing. Floodlights were switched on, illuminating the whole area. Men waved torches all around him. George crouched down in the undergrowth, closing his mouth and trying not to pant. He was terrified of being caught – and before he had even started. He reprimanded himself sharply, remembering the stiff scolding he would have received if his master had found out he had made such a mistake.

He lay in the same position for what seemed a very long time until eventually the dogs behind the fencing became quiet. The floodlights were still shining brightly, but he had to take a chance and get past the gates so that he could crawl in the opposite direction towards the smell of the cats. That smell was almost certainly beyond the place where he had first hidden amongst the trees and captured their scents. He kept growling to himself, furious at his own stupidity.

The floodlights made it difficult for George to remain in the shadows, but from his experience in the hills with the sheep, he knew how to crouch so low that he would not be seen. Relief spread through him when he reached the other side of the road and heard faint meows. He knew he was getting close. Now all he had to do was to pick up Senora's scent.

He slowly crept along the high wire fencing. With the floodlights shining, he could see that directly in front of him was a field littered with small bushes. He stared hard in every direction, but wherever he looked, there were no cats. His sharp ears picked up faint cries coming from the other side of the field, where he could see a low brick building with a wooden roof. *Oh, goodness,* he said to himself. *Surely Senora is not in there.* Keeping his eyes fixed on the building, he was drawn to glints of light shining on glass at the bottom of the long wall. He stared harder. He wasn't imagining things: the glinting of light came from small doors just large enough to take a cat. At the back of his mind, he remembered Senora climbing through one of these back at the white house. Maybe the field area in front of him was for cats to come out and play? If that was the case, it was a good sign. He lay down and looked around, satisfied with his conclusion.

The fencing not only looked very strong, it was far too high for George to attempt climbing over. He shuddered when he saw the great coils of barbed wire covering the top. It was impossible to climb in and impossible to climb out. How was he going to rescue Senora? Knowing how frightened she must be feeling, he badly wanted to be able to talk to her and to comfort her. He reached the end of the fencing and lay down. It seemed there was little he could do until daylight, so with that thought, he turned back until he reached the safety of the trees.

When George woke a few hours later, the sun was up. He stood, slowly stretched his legs, and yawned while looking for a place where he could find water. He remembered he had spotted a small stream a short distance from where he was standing. It didn't take him long to find it and take a good drink from the cool water.

He knew that before doing anything, he would have to creep along the length of the fencing in order to locate Senora's scent. He must keep out of sight at all costs, although there was little cover to protect him. He decided to take a chance and begin at the place where he had abandoned the task the previous night.

He had been right in thinking the wide open space with the bushes was a play area. Now in the daylight, he could see cats everywhere. Some slept, others sat in the sunshine and gave themselves a good tongue wash, and younger ones played amongst the long grasses.

He kept as close to the fence as he dared. It was whilst he was slowly creeping along taking deep sniffs from the air, trying to distinguish Senora's scent from all the others, that he noticed a scent that seemed familiar. It wasn't Senora's, so he put it to the back of his mind. However, as he crept towards the end of the fence, the scent became much stronger. He lay down, thinking. It definitely wasn't the scent of Senora, but he knew he had smelt it within the past few days. He heard loud meowing very close to him, and then a big hiss from a large white female cat with ginger and black patches on her face and ears, standing with her back arched aggressively.

'Get away!' the cat hissed. Although the fencing was between them, George instinctively backed off. The cat angrily hissed at him again and turned to some others standing behind her. 'It's a dog!' she yelled. 'Come on, everyone. Help me get rid of this monster.' As she shouted, cats ran to her aid from all directions, hissing loudly. George wasn't scared, knowing he was safe on the opposite side of the fence, so he stood his ground.

The white cat clawed at the fencing once more. 'We are not afraid of a dog as ugly as you,' she hissed. 'Go on, get away from us. We don't want you here!'

Although George heard the confrontation, he began connecting two scents. One was coming from the cat in front of him, and another was coming from the cushion in the box which Dear Man had shown him. Surely the scents were the same. Again George sniffed in deeply. Yes, he was certain. They were the same scents. He thought, *This must be the cat who had lived in the white house before the fire. Well, at least that's one job done.* He sat down, staring through the wire and thinking hard. First he had to locate Senora, and then he'd try to find a way for them to escape so that he could guide them both back to the white house. The fact that this white cat thought of him as the enemy didn't worry George. Once Senora had introduced them, he was sure they would become friends.

He moved away from the fence and lay down in the shade, pondering his next move. One by one, the cats sloped off, leaving the white cat still sitting by the fence. George wondered where the humans in the white coats had taken Senora. *She must still be somewhere in the building,* he thought. She certainly wasn't driven away during the night. If there had been a vehicle coming down the road to collect her, it would have woken him.

Satisfied that his conclusion was the correct one, his eyes searched every corner of the field behind the netting. There was no sign of Senora and no scent. Maybe she would never come out. He felt a shiver running through him. Would she disappear like his master? He didn't think he could bear it if that happened.

All day George crawled back and forth along the fence, trying to pick up Senora's scent. Every time he crawled past the cats in the field, he was aware of angry hissing from the same cat, but he tried not to take any notice. One time as he passed, he glanced through the netting and saw that the cat had been joined by three ginger kittens plus a tortoiseshell cat. Their scents were strong and were definitely intermingled with those from the cushion. Maybe these cats were also included in Dear Man's command to 'Go find'.

In their enclosure earlier that morning, the family were recovering from their ordeal. However, the only thing Wynken, Blynken, and Nod remembered was the prick in their side and waking up feeling sleepy. The three of them were very hungry and were delighted to find a bowl filled with tiny biscuits by their blankets. But later, instead of playing as was their normal habit, they settled down and went back to sleep.

Bella and Tia later woke, both feeling very odd inside their stomachs. Bella looked across at her kittens and noticed immediately that each cat had a little snip in one ear. 'What on earth have they done to us, Tia? Is my ear like the others? It feels very strange. You've had your ear chopped, Tia – did you know? Does it feel sore, like mine?'

At the time, Tia was not worried about her ear. She was worried that something was very wrong with her stomach. She stroked it, gently trying not to grimace answering her mother. 'Yes, my ear is very sore, but it's not nearly as bad as the ache in my belly. That hurts a lot, and when I tried to tongue wash it a few moments ago, I could feel some funny bits of wire sticking out. Do you feel the same?'

'Yes, I certainly do. My belly is really very painful to touch.'

'I think we have been tortured, like those nasty humans did to me in the village that time.'

'Maybe we have,' agreed Bella, sitting down and feeling very sorry for herself. 'But now, I think we have another problem. I heard a vicious dog howling just outside our fencing.'

Bella could take no more heartache, so she slowly walked to the farthest corner in the enclosure and quietly sobbed her heart out. Why had the fire come and caused their life to change so drastically? They had been carefree and happy in their forever home at the white house, and now here they were, having been tortured and locked up in a cage. To add to their misery, there was a howling dog somewhere outside.

Her sobs woke the kittens, and one by one, they cuddled up to her, trying their best to comfort the mother they loved more than anything in their world. Tia, watching the scene, decided the best thing she could do was eat something and then sleep, which was what she did.

Chapter 20

George Will Find a Way!

As soon as her cage had been unloaded from the van and placed on a table, Senora was collected by a woman dressed in a white coat. All the time her soft voice trying to quieten Senora's hisses, telling her not to be afraid. Senora was afraid. She was carried along a narrow corridor until they reached a large empty room with a square table in the centre. Her cage was placed on the floor, and the cage door was opened. Immediately she rushed around the room, trying desperately to find somewhere to escape, but there was nowhere. She heard the door of the room closing, and she was left all on her own. Terrified, she looked around. Along one wall was a long shelf, and lying on it was a large round cushion covered with a blanket. *Well,* she thought, *at least there's a comfortable bed so that I can have a sleep.* On the other side of the room, she saw a litter tray, but no food or water.

She kept wondering why the cage in the market square had suddenly closed behind her. Why hadn't George been able to get her out? There were so many questions she didn't understand. Why had she been left in this room all alone? Who were all these strangers? Her only hope was knowing that George had stayed with her in the van. Maybe he would be able to speak to someone and take her home. She thought about the man with the sausage; he had been kind to George. Maybe he could help free her.

With so many thoughts running through her head, Senora was feeling dizzy with fear, hunger, and thirst, plus the fact that she was now very angry. Why had nobody thought to give her a drink of water or bring her some food? *This is a horrible place,* she decided. All she wanted was to get back home to Dear Lady and Dear Man. She no longer cared about finding Tia, Bella, and the others. All that night, she lay on the cushion dozing fretfully, not knowing what would become of her.

Nothing about her surroundings had changed when Senora woke the following morning. Still no food or water. She couldn't understand why. She paced around the room, inspecting every tiny crack to see if, by any chance, there was a hole that might be large enough for a mouse to enter, but there was nothing. She sat down again. She couldn't escape from her prison.

She kept cleaning her coat and paws, all the time trying to convince herself that Dear Man would soon be collecting her – but in her heart she knew that would be unlikely. *Maybe George has been able to travel through the night and return to the house to collect him.* But when she thought about that idea, she remembered the wound on George's leg, and how the kind man with the sausage had tried to help him. *No,* she decided. *George will still be waiting for me nearby.*

He will surely be able to think of something and help me escape.

Suddenly she heard a bark. She stood up and ran around the room, scratching at the door and meowing loudly. 'That's George's bark! It's definitely George's bark!' She called out again as loudly as she could. 'George, George! I'm in here!' But there was no reply. 'He's going to help me. I know he will! Oh, George, I love you. Please come and find me. Please help me, George!' But there was no response to her plea.

A few minutes later, she heard the latch turn as the door opened, and she recognized the woman with the soft voice. Again the lady was wearing a white coat, but this time Senora could see that on her hands were large protective gloves. Senora winced. She hissed at the woman and quickly moved backwards, trying to hide herself in a corner. But even though she fought as hard as she could, there was no escape from the gloves lifting her up. All the time, the woman's voice spoke gently as she put Senora into a carrying cage.

She was carried along a corridor to a room smelling strongly of disinfectant. The disinfectant made her nose twitch. It was definitely similar to the smell in Dear Lady's house when she cleaned the floors, and it was always far too strong for Senora's liking. Whenever she smelt it, she would always make a rapid retreat to the terrace.

What on earth were they thinking about putting her near this horrid smell with no chance to get away from it? After a few moments, two men wearing white coats came into the room carrying overalls and rubber gloves. Senora nervously watched as one of the men took some needles out of a drawer along with a tiny bottle of clear liquid. He then pushed the needle into the bottle and began to draw out the liquid.

As Senora watched, memories flooded into her mind of the day when she was very young and had watched something similar. She remembered a prick and feeling very sleepy, but nothing else. Now she let out loud hisses and meows, desperately trying to find a way out of the cage. But nobody opened the cage door; all the voices around her were very soft and gentle. She tried to see what was happening when she felt a small prick in her leg. *Ah, well!* was her last feeling of consciousness.

She awoke in a cat enclosure with a bowl of food and water nearby. She turned over sleepily, realizing that she was no longer in the cage but lying on a soft bed.

Senora opened one eye and looked around her. She sat up and very slowly washed herself thoroughly. First she tongue washed along her outstretched legs, followed by her four paws, giving special attention in between her toes. Then she went along her neck and down her sides, finally ending her spell of cleanliness by washing her head and ears until there was no trace of the strange disinfectant smell anywhere on her body. She walked over to a bowl of food and sniffed. Her favourite was fish, but sadly she found this was just some type of biscuit. Still, because she was hungry, it didn't taste too bad, and she ate as much as she could. Then it was time to have another wash. Senora had always taken a pride in how she looked, and just because she was now a prisoner, she was not going to change her habits.

A loud meowing came from the enclosure beside her. A cat was trying to catch her attention. She took no notice and continued washing her front paw before cleaning the fur behind her ear. She didn't know anyone in this awful place, and she certainly didn't want to talk at the moment. Anyway, it was far beneath her dignity to talk to cats who were from just anywhere. The meowing continued. *Oh goodness,* she thought. *Will it never stop?*

Curiosity got the better of her, and she couldn't resist looking in the direction of the cries. Then as she looked, not only did she recognize the meows, but she could see a ginger and white kitten sitting on the other side, pressing his nose up against the netting dividing them. 'Good heavens above! Nod, is that you?'

'Yes, Senora, we're all here.' Nod, at last having made her understand, excitedly returned her call. 'Mama, Tia, Wynken, and Blynken! We're all here, and we don't know why.'

'Let me speak to your mama,' said Senora. 'Where is she?' The enclosures were in deep shade. Hanging from the outside were blinds, making it difficult to clearly see the interiors.

171

Bella and Tia came and stood by the wire netting separating them. Bella said, 'Oh, goodness, Senora. it is so good to see you. We ran away from the woods near the white house when we saw fire. We were very frightened, so we ran all the way to the village as fast as we could.' She rushed on with her explanation. 'Then we found something to eat inside some cages, and we were trapped, put into a van, and brought here. Oh, Senora, we don't know what to do. The day after we arrived, we had no food or drink, and then we were all given a pin prick and went to sleep. Thank goodness the kittens are all right, but Tia and I still feel very unwell. What's more, we all had a piece taken out of our ears.' When she finished talking, she was quite out of breath.

'Oh, dear. I am afraid those people in the white coats must have done the same to you as they once did to me. None of you will want mates now.' As she was speaking, she felt one ear. *Maybe that is why it was sore when I was washing it.* 'Bella, does my ear look like the others?'

'Yes.' Bella was certainly not paying any attention to Senora's clipped ear. She was horrified at what she had just heard. 'Do you mean to say that Wynken, Blynken, and Nod won't want to have mates? That's terrible. Now I remember – that's what the black cat told me before we were taken away. Senora, please tell me what I can do to make them better.'

'Oh, there's nothing you can do. I know, because I have always felt the same. I've never wanted a mate, so I am sure it will apply to Wynken, Blynken, and Nod, as well as to you and Tia. It's the humans' way of keeping our cat population down,' she said wisely.

'But how do you know such things?' asked Tia.

'I am pretty well educated, so I do know about most things, and I know how I have always felt. I have also spoken to several visitors who belong to friends of Dear Man and Dear Lady, and they agreed. All the male cats have said they had a prick and no longer want a mate. Sorry, but you'll just have to accept it.'

'Well, in that case. Why are you here if it has already happened to you?' asked Bella

Senora then told them her story. She didn't leave anything out and praised her new friend George for being so wonderful. She was quite sure he was outside waiting for a chance to free her. 'I heard him bark, so I know he is here somewhere. You really must not be afraid of George. He is quite a gentleman, you know, and I am sure he will find a way to save us. We will simply have to be patient.'

'That must be the dog who has been crawling around outside our play area,' said Tia. 'We kept on hissing at him because we were certain that he was very fierce, but we haven't seen him this morning, so maybe he has gone.'

'Oh, no!' replied Senora. 'He is definitely still around somewhere – probably hiding. Just before I was taken for my prick, I heard him howl and bark, so I know he will not desert us and will find a way to take us back to Dear Lady and Dear Man. He was friendly with the man who brought us here; the man gave George a sausage. He also cleaned George's wound, so maybe he will come back and take us all home. We have to trust in George – he is our only hope. Now tell me, how do we get to that play area?'

'Look over there.' Bella pointed her paw to the flap in the wall. 'If you push, it will open. I think it is just like the one you had at the white house.'

'When I have had a rest, I will go out and see if I can find George, and I'll discuss with him how we can all get out.'

'Oh, that's impossible,' Bella continued, pointing her paw through the netting of their enclosure towards the play area. 'Don't you see? The whole place is enclosed with wire netting. Even when you look up at the sky, you can see netting.'

'Well, I am sure George will find a way,' said Senora optimistically.

'Do you mean to tell me that you can talk dog language?' All the cats gathered around as Bella asked the question. Nobody could believe that a cat could talk dog language.

'Of course I can,' answered Senora, and with that she strolled back to her bed, lay down, gave herself another wash, and went to sleep.

In the other enclosure, Bella encouraged the kittens to play before they too settled down for an afternoon nap.

Chapter 21

George's Vigil

George waited patiently in the shadows of the trees, occasionally going to the stream to drink some water. The time seemed endless, but however long he waited, he saw no sign of Senora or any sign of his friend with the sausage.

While he dozed throughout the long nights, he dreamed of Senora appearing before him, gently washing his ear. All the cats with the scents from the cushion were gathered around, mewing quietly. How wonderful – he dreamed they had all escaped, and he had led them back to the white house.

He woke up with a start, looking around him. There was nothing; just the moon glinting through the trees, and leaves gently waving in a cool breeze. He whined softly. Maybe the cats were hiding from him. But there was no response. It had all been a dream. Miracles never happened!

There was nothing for it but to spend each day waiting in the shadows of the trees, hoping for a glimpse of Senora. People arrived and left through the tall gates, very often holding small baskets, but it was impossible for George to catch a glimpse inside. He could only pray that none held Senora. George was not only very hungry, but he was becoming despondent with his lack of success. He had no idea how to solve his problem.

Men and women, all wearing white coats, often came out of the building and went into the field. George kept watching anxiously in the hope that he would see someone holding Senora, but he never did. Instead, bowls lying at intervals along the back wall of the building were filled with fresh water; plants were watered; weeds were pulled; and areas of long grass were mown. Some used large brooms, clearing pathways where they had been covered with gravel blown over them by the wind; others gathered up a cat in their arms, giving them a cuddle as they did so. To George, there always seemed to be a hive of activity somewhere, but it was satisfying to see that most of the cats appeared to be content with their captors – although George did notice a few who were meowing quietly when a white coat came too close. George supposed they were frightened, and he wondered what would happen to them.

With still no sign of Senora, he was becoming bored with keeping watch. He stretched sleepily, feeling the sun warming his body. Although he knew he shouldn't, he felt he was ready to take a quiet snooze. He was confident his new friend would return before long, and together they would find Senora. Until then, he would wait.

A cat was walking along the fencing of the play area of the enclosure in the late afternoon. George recognized a meow. *Senora?* He sniffed the air. Yes, it was definitely Senora. George jumped to his feet, and without thinking, he howled loudly. A few moments later, he saw the main gate opening, and a man wearing a white coat ran out of the enclosure towards the trees where George was hiding. George could see a leather lead. At the same time, the man was taking a chew bone from a pocket.

George knew he had no time to waste. He had made a dreadful mistake by barking, and now he had to hide from the man. There was no way he wanted to be taken prisoner before he had found Senora. Because he had been resting his leg for the past two days, it felt much stronger, so he was able to run farther into the woods, where he hid in the undergrowth. He breathed a sigh of relief when he realized that the man in the white coat was returning to the main entrance, with the gates closing behind him. George stayed where he was until he felt it was quite safe to take up his watch close to the cat enclosure once more.

Chapter 22

Smithy Magoo

Being woken from her afternoon nap always made Senora bad-tempered, and this afternoon was no exception. Loud hissing and meowing coming from one of the enclosures only made matters worse. She sleepily opened an eye. 'For goodness' sake, shut up and let me get some sleep!' She turned her back on the noise, burying her head deeper into her cushion. It was no use – the cries of anguish were louder than ever.

'Mama, Mama! Help me. What's happening to us?'

'Oh, my goodness, that's Tia's voice.' Senora jumped up and was shocked when she saw what was happening in the enclosure alongside hers. Two ladies wearing white coats where picking up Bella, Tia, Wynken, Blynken, and Nod in turn and putting them into cages.

'Where are you taking them?' she leapt at the protecting netting, meowing aggressively, but she was completely ignored. One by one, the cages were carried into the corridor. 'Tell me where you are taking them!' she yelled at the top of her voice. 'They are my friends! Leave them alone! They've done you no harm.' By this time, she was getting frantic and ran back and forth in her enclosure, pushing herself against the door in an effort to escape. But it was hopeless; all she could do was to watch in dismay as they disappeared out of sight.

Exhausted, she turned around and lay down on the bed groaning. She was a prisoner and was on her own. She didn't think she could bear that. Even George had deserted her. There had been no sign of him since she'd heard him bark the previous day. She prayed nothing had happened to him; he was such a dear dog. 'It's such a mess. All our lives have been ruined. Nothing will ever be the same again!'

'Shut up, moaning all the time.' A grim-faced male tabby put his nose against the wire netting behind her, hissing loudly as he did so. 'You're being a real pain. Don't you realize we are all prisoners here until they take us back to where they picked us up?'

Senora quickly recovered at the sound of the cat's voice and jumped down from her bed, haughtily walking up to the netting. 'How do you know this?' she demanded.

'Because it's a good way to get food, silly.' If you climb into a cage in a village where there is a bowl of food in the middle, a gate will close before you can get out. The next morning, a man will collect you in his van and bring you here. After that, you have to go into a funny-smelling place, where they give you a prick. A few days later, they put you in another cage and take you back to the village. It's simple and a good way to eat without doing any work.' He stood up and arched his back, stretching his legs proudly at his intelligence. 'I've been here several times, and because they know me. I don't have to have a prick any more. I get a good brush and a comfortable bed for a few nights, with plenty of food. Life couldn't be better. So for heaven's sake, don't keep going on about your friends. They will be going back to whichever village they came from.' He sat down, thinking. 'Of course, there are beautiful cats like yourself, who are never taken back to the villages. They stay here until they are found forever homes.'

Senora's eyes widened as she listened, not knowing whether to believe the tabby cat. 'How do you know that?'

'Oh, I just know these things,' he said wisely.

To Senora, it seemed a very strange story, but she had to admit that so far, everything he said had happened to her. She did go into a cage with a bowl of food, the gate had closed, and she was brought here in a van. Oh, how she wished she could believe him – except for the bit about beautiful cats being found forever homes. Surely that wouldn't include her. She already had a forever home with Dear Lady and Dear Man. 'What's your name?' she asked.

'Don't have one', he said rudely.

'Of course you do, silly. Every cat has a name.' She sat down and washed her whiskers whilst she gave the situation some thought. 'I shall call you Smithy Magoo.'

'That's a silly name.'

'Well, it suits you. Do you have any brothers and sisters?'

'No. I take life as it comes. I did have a family once, but I don't know what happened to them. What about you?'

'Of course I have a family,' answered Senora proudly. 'I have Dear Lady and Dear Man. We live in the white house a long way from here.'

'Then how come you were brought in the van? That doesn't make any sense.'

Senora then told him about Bella and her family arriving at the white house, the fire, George, how Dear Lady and Dear Man had sent them to look for the other cats, and how she had been trapped in the cage.

'Quite a story,' said Smithy Magoo. 'And what about this dog? Where is he now?'

'I don't know, and I'm very worried. But he knows where I am, so I'm quite sure he will save me.'

Chapter 23

A Difficult Choice

George stayed in his hiding place, watching visitors drive up to the entrance gate. A few left the enclosure clutching tiny puppies. One man was leading a fluffy dog who appeared to have a problem with his rear leg. George watched as he gently lifted the dog and put it on the rear seat of his car next to a small child. A few moments later, he went back inside the enclosure, returning carrying a cat basket holding a tiny kitten. George wondered what would happen to them, but in his heart he felt the man looked kind. *Maybe he will give them a forever home like I once had,* he thought sadly, his mind full of memories of his beloved master.

It was in the middle of the afternoon when he heard the familiar sound of a van coming down the road. He recognized the noise from the engine, and he stood up, his nose alert. He made sure the driver carried the same scent as a few days ago. Yes, it was definitely the same scent. At last, his new friend had returned, and George would be able to have some of that delicious meat. He was ravenously hungry. He stood up, excitedly wagging his tail. But to his dismay, his new friend drove straight past George's hiding place without giving a glance in his direction. He drove through the open gates, came to a standstill, and switched off his engine. The men in the white coats went up to the van and opened the rear door, enabling George to see inside. It was full of cages. *Oh, dear,* he thought. *He must have been to the market square again.* Maybe he isn't my friend after all. Distraught that he would have no supper, he sat down and watched.

The cages were unloaded and taken inside the building. His friend waited by his van, smoking his white stick. A few minutes later, a man and a woman came out carrying three cages. From his hiding place, George watched them being loaded into the back of the van. By stretching his neck to get a better glimpse, he could see that one of the cages held a large white cat. Inside the other two were three ginger and white cats, plus a tortoiseshell.

George sniffed the air, staring at the cages. The smell from the cushion had returned. Could these be the same cats who had been hissing at him through the fencing? He crept as close as he dared without being seen, until he was able to pick up the strong scents from inside the van. To make quite certain, he sniffed the air once more. Yes, he was satisfied the two scents were connected. He not only smelt the scent of the hissing cat, but he also smelt the scent from the cushion. He felt proud at that moment.

But now George had an even bigger problem. George always obeyed commands, and however difficult it was, he knew it was his duty to follow the van until it stopped, and then he'd lead these same cats to the white house. He thought worriedly, *But, if I follow the van, it will mean I will have to leave Senora alone in this prison. How can I possibly do that when she saved my life?*

He returned to his hiding place, trying to decide what he should do, completely lost in thought. He became aware of the familiar sound from the van's engine coming through the gates of the enclosure and then stopping in the road.

'Hey, fella.' It was his friend who was calling to him and holding something in his hand. 'Come here. I've something nice for you.'

George was tempted, but he stayed where he was. He didn't want the man in the white coat to know he was still here.

'Come on, old fella. I promise I won't hurt you. Look, I've got some lovely sausages.' The aromas were really tempting, but George was wary. He was far too nervous to move.

'All right, then. I'll come over to you'. His friend opened the van door and stepping down into the road. He began walking towards George. In his hand were several sausages. 'There, there,' he said gently. 'That's a good chap. You eat these sausages, and then you won't feel so hungry. I'm sorry I haven't been able to get here for a few days. I don't suppose you have had anything to eat, so you must be starving by now.' He held the sausages under George's nose. Unable to resist any longer. George grabbed them quickly before his friend could change his mind.

'Now, let me look at that leg. I want to see if it is still clean. If it isn't, I have some disinfectant in the van.' He gently chatted away to George as he bent over to take a look at the wound.

'You know,' he said while stepping back. 'I think you are a lucky chap. It certainly looks a lot better than it did the other day. I don't think I need do anything to it. Now, how about a drink of water?' As he spoke, he pulled out a bottle of water and a drinking bowl from his shoulder bag. 'I always carry these for emergencies,' he said, winking at George while filling the bowl and placing it on the ground.

Finally relaxing, George sniffed his hand. It was warm and friendly and still smelled of sausages. 'All right, old chap. Let's see. I might have something else for you.' He held a small bag of biscuits under George's nose. He took three biscuits from his bag. 'These are especially for you, but first you must sit, and I will put a biscuit on the ground in front of you and tell you it's off. Then I'll say, "Take." Okay? Now, let's see how you do.'

George knew immediately what was happening. He had played this game with his master many times before, and he loved it. He sat at attention, waiting for his instructions.

'That was excellent,' said the man after the game was over, his voice softening as he spoke. He gave

George a good scratch behind the ears. In return, George stood up and wagged his tail.

Smiling, the man looked down at George. 'I think we are going to be good friends. And I'll tell you something, fella. I'm all alone in the world, so if you have no home, I would really love to be your master. What do you think of that?'

George sensed the man was asking him something very important, but he wasn't sure what it was. All he could do in response was to continue wagging his tail. He stared up at his new friend. Why was this man, with the gentle eyes and soft voice, always reminding him of his dead master? He couldn't understand. The word 'master' was familiar to him, but that had always been used in relation to his own master, and he had only ever had one master in his life.

His friend looked at his watch. 'Well, I must get going. Shall I see you tomorrow, or will you come with me in my van?'

Dear Man's command was foremost in George's mind as he watched his friend jump up into the driver's seat and close the door. He knew he had to make up his mind quickly. The scent of the cushion he had been told to find was in the back of the van and was somehow mixed up with those cats. There was no doubt it was his duty to return them safely to Dear Man at the white house. With no further hesitation, he ran towards the van as the passenger door opened, allowing him to jump up onto the front seat beside his friend. Driving away from the enclosure, George made himself a vow. As soon as he had fulfilled his mission, he would he would return to rescue Senora.

George sat looking out of the window and staring at the passing landscape, wondering where their journey would end. This was not at all like mustering the sheep. With years of experience behind him, he had always followed a series of whistles and commands: lying low on the ground and creeping up behind the sheep before rounding them up into an enclosure. That had always been so easy, but this was a very different problem. How would he be able to herd and control a group of hissing cats when they finally reached their destination? He was bewildered by the thought. Trying to talk to his friend about his problem would be of no use at all.

The narrow roads were bumpy. With the cages rattling against the sides of the van, George could hear the cats making loud meows, hissing every time it hit a bump. They stopped at a filling station, where his friend went into a nearby café, shortly returning with a mug of coffee for himself and a sandwich stuffed with lumps of meat for George.

The journey was long, but as the kilometres passed, George began recognizing landmarks. He remembered a small village where they had been forced to a stop whilst a desperate farmer tried to control his herd of goats straying all over the road. He remembered thinking at the time that if he had been in charge with his master, such a thing would never have happened.

On another occasion, he remembered the wonderful smell emanating from a café selling meat pies – a smell George could never resist. As more familiar sights appeared, George knew that they were driving back along the same route.

Alongside him, unknown to George, his friend was wishing he had left the sanctuary earlier. It was getting dusk, he was hungry, the day had seemed very long, and he was tired. All he wanted now was to deposit the caged cats in the same village where he had collected them and, after setting them free, drive home to his cottage so he could make himself soup for his supper.

After passing through yet another village, the roads became quiet. He took the opportunity of glancing down at the dog sitting quietly beside him, his ears alert while he stared through the window in front of him. He noticed the small cuts still showing on the back of George's head and neck where the fur had been cut. It seemed that his thick coat, although still shiny in places, had been neglected. *Poor animal,* he thought. *He certainly looks as though he has been badly treated recently. Maybe he really is homeless. It seems incredible that such a beautiful mountain dog like this one should have been abandoned.*

He kept wondering why the dog was on the loose, and what his life had been like before he had seen him limping behind his van. *Surely if he is lost, I would have seen notices somewhere inquiring if anybody had found a Portuguese mountain dog.*

While cruising along and pondering the situation, he once again explored the idea of the connection between this dog and the beautiful white cat he had taken to the animal sanctuary a few days previously. Why had this dog, obviously in a lot of pain with his badly injured leg, followed him for so long? *Why is he sitting beside me now, especially having been so hesitant when I beckoned him? Why on earth did he suddenly change his mind? If he was so fond of that other cat, why did he leave her back at the sanctuary?*

He tried to concentrate on the road, but every now and then, he couldn't help glancing across at George, dearly wishing he had some of the answers. He wanted to find out more about this brave, intelligent animal who was suffering his injuries without complaint. He swallowed hard. Could it be possible that he was falling in love with him?

While driving through the open countryside avoiding all the main roads, a plan developed in his mind. If he was unable to have this dog, maybe he could find a puppy and, with the money he had saved, buy a few sheep, plus a smallholding. He could begin a new life.

By the time they reached the village square, he heard the church bell chime nine o'clock. He was hungry and tired after his long day, and despite an overwhelming excitement while thinking about his plan, he wanted to get home. He stopped the van, walked around to the rear, and opened the door. He carefully took the cages out and placed them on the ground. Immediately he opened the trap doors legs pushed past him, disappearing rapidly under the covers of the market stalls.

George, still inside the van, barked loudly when he saw what was happening, frantic that the cats, along with the scent from the cushion, would disappear before he could catch up with them.

In answer to his barks, the passenger door opened, and George jumped down, wagging his tail. Although he wanted to reach his charges as quickly as possible, he wanted to make his new friend understand that it was his duty to take the scent from the cushion back to the white house. How he wished this friend could understand dog talk. After all, his master always knew what George was saying to him.

'What do you think, fella? Do you want to come with me, or do you want to go with those cats?' the man asked.

George looked at him and wagged his tail, at the same time giving the outstretched hand a warm lick before turning his attention to the covers draped over the market stalls. He sniffed the air, trying to pick up their scent, but with so many other scents mingling around the stalls, it was very difficult to single them out. He could hear soft breathing coming from underneath a stall at the end of the line. Good – he had located them. He decided to return to the empty cages and wait quietly until they made a move. The last thing he wanted to do was to panic them into running away.

He watched his friend take clean bowls from the back of the van, filling them with dried food before carefully placing them inside each cage. Then the man locked the trap, preventing the gate from closing until an animal was inside.

Calling to George, his friend climbed up into his driving seat. George remained sitting by the cages, looking at him and wagging his tail slowly. Sensing the dog wanted to stay where he was, his friend sighed. *Ah, well. Maybe I'll see you another day. I certainly hope I will.* With that, he closed his door and drove off.

The square was silent, and nothing stirred. George lay down and watched the cages, fearful that the smell from the food bowls would be too tempting to resist and the cats would become trapped again. He knew he must not allow that to happen.

Sure enough, five minutes later, he heard quiet meows behind him, and a ginger and white kitten appeared. George moved his position. He didn't want to frighten it, but he had to give a warning. Immediately the kitten backed off, and as it did so, George could hear hissing coming from behind the canvas.

George lay down, listening for some movement behind him. Would they obey his command? He knew the large white one would certainly recognize his scent. She was the one who had always been hissing at the fencing. He gave a quiet whimper, at the same time crawling a little closer to the stall. There was no reaction, so he whimpered a little louder, trying to tell them that he wouldn't hurt them. No cat appeared.

'Mama, I think that's the same dog who was crawling up and down outside our prison,' whispered Tia nervously. 'What shall we do? If we show ourselves, he may eat us.'

'Yes, I am quite sure it is the same dog – I would recognize that scent anywhere. Don't you remember? Senora telling us that he was waiting to rescue her, and that he was a gentle dog.' Bella had seen Nod creeping from their hiding place and had immediately recognized the temptation from the smell of food. 'If the dog hadn't growled, Nod would have certainly been trapped inside one of the cages. I don't think we should be afraid.' She stood up, deciding that as their mother, she would take charge. 'Stay where you are, everyone, while I have a look.' She peeked out from behind the canvas where they had taken refuge and looked around her. The square was empty. They were free and back in the same market square where they had been taken prisoners.

She gave her orders briskly. 'Wynken, Blynken, and Nod: on no account are you to go near that food in those cages. It doesn't matter how hungry you are. If you do go inside, you will be trapped again and will end up in that prison. Do I make myself clear? I will show myself to this dog. I trust Senora, and I am sure she was speaking the truth. Don't forget: she told us that the dog was hurt badly by those horrid people who'd started the fire. She also told us that both of them had been trying to find us before she was trapped in that dreadful cage and taken to the prison. He never left her side and bravely got into the machine with that man. I am going to take a chance, and we will trust him. Tia, do you agree? Please don't be silly and run away.'

'I am afraid of this dog, so please don't let him come anywhere near us, Mama. I am sure he is hungry like we are. How do you know that he won't attack and eat us?'

'For heaven's sake, Tia. Don't say such things in front of the others – you will only scare them. Anyway, if he wanted to eat us, he would have done it just now instead of warning Nod.'

Tia was still unconvinced but didn't argue with her mother anymore. She began washing her back leg, trying not to let anyone know just how frightened she really was.

Bella continued. 'Senora told us that Dear Lady and Dear Man are back at the white house, and the fire has gone, so we'll return there. I am sure we can remember the way from here, but I think if this dog wants to, he should be allowed to come with us. After all, Senora says that he needs a forever home like we do.'

Without another word, Bella stood up and gave a loud meow. With her head held high, she walked steadily out into the open. Bella was never going to admit that she was more scared than she had ever been in her whole life.

George watched the large white cat slowly walking towards him, her tail erect. He was certain these cats carried the same scent as the scent on the cushion. His only task now was to shepherd them to the white house.

Chapter 24

Why Aren't Cats Like Sheep?

Bella and George faced each other, warily keeping a good distance between them. Bella was still worried she might be attacked. George thought the white cat might spring at him and scratch out his eyes. 'Oh, dear,' he moaned. 'This is nothing like dealing with sheep. They never hissed or scratched like this one.'

The only trouble sheep ever caused was running in wide circles until he was able to direct them into their pen. From what he had seen so far, cats were impossible to control – but of course, apart from Senora, he had never really come into close contact with cats. The cats living with his master's friend had always kept their distance, ignoring him completely. The few around the various farmyards he had visited with his master were always more interested in catching rats than in George.

The white cat was free and obviously the leader. How on earth could he show her he wanted to be friends? George knew he had to act quickly; otherwise, all would be lost. He would have to take a chance. Without hesitation, he rolled over onto his back with his feet in the air and wagged his tail.

Bella watched the dog's movements, not understanding why he was being so submissive. After all, this wasn't the way dogs normally behaved. They always tried to take bites out of cats. She began to relax. She decided to copy George's movements, purring loudly as she did so. After a moment or two, she stood up and stared down at him, no longer nervous and remembering Senora's reassuring words: 'Trust George, and he will lead you safely back to the white house.'

'What's he doing, Mama?'

'Shush – I've got him under control.' She eyed his wagging tail, his body swaying slowly back and forth, and his head facing in her direction. His eyes stared directly at her. 'Why are you watching us?' Bella demanded. 'You're the same big dog who kept crawling outside our enclosure. Why are you here?'

George couldn't understand anything the cat said, so he remained lying on his back, wagging his tail and giving what he hoped would be a friendly bark in return.

Ignoring him, Bella turned to the others. 'I think he's friendly, so you can all come out, and we'll begin to find our way home. Tia, you brought us here, so you must lead the way out of the village. It is getting really dark, so it's very important to leave right away.' She turned back to George, keeping her eyes firmly on him whilst she walked over to the market stall, beckoning to the others with her paw.

George stood up, watching. One by one, the tortoiseshell cat followed by three kittens crept from their hiding place. The five cats stood, staring at George. Nobody moved. George once more began feeling uneasy, not knowing how to tackle the situation. How on earth was he going to get them to behave like his flock of sheep? While working with his master, it had always been so simple, but now there was no master and no whistle. He was on his own. He began creeping alongside them, at the same time keeping a wide berth and encouraging them to walk towards the road.

But Bella had her own ideas. Typical of her species, she was quite independent. If the dog wanted to come, it was all right by her, but as far as she was concerned, he must keep well behind them. She certainly had no intention of allowing him to interfere. To indicate how she felt, she walked straight past George with her head held high and her ears pricked, instructing her family to follow in a single line.

George was quite happy with the situation, feeling he was now in command. His flock was herded together in front of him, just as they should be.

But things didn't quite work out for either George or Bella. For the kittens, walking in a single file was boring. Playing hide and seek amongst the long grasses and climbing trees would be much more fun! Whispering amongst themselves, Wynken, Blynken, and Nod decided to disobey their mother's orders.

When George saw the kittens dispersing, he became very excited, barking at them loudly. This was not meant to happen!

Tia, immediately terrified of the bark, ran off and hid under a nearby bush.

'Now what?' Losing her patience, Bella cried out to the kittens. Wynken, Blynken, and Nod, come down from that tree at once and get back in line! Listen, everyone. We still have a long way to go. We must stay together and be very careful. We haven't even reached the bad village with all those horrible cats around the rubbish bins.'

Hearing the sharpness of her mother's voice, Tia crept from under the bush, nervously waiting for the others to obey her instructions.

In the meantime, although George finally had to admit the white cat was in charge, he praised himself. At last he had mastered the art of herding cats. Once more he took up the rear, all the while wondering how, when he had fulfilled his mission, he would be able to make the long journey back to the enclosure to rescue Senora. Although his leg was feeling much better, he knew that if he couldn't find his friend with the sausage, he would have no alternative but to walk for many, many hours. He was confident he would be able find the route from the scents on the wheels of his friend's van, but if the weather changed and the roads became wet, he would probably lose the scent completely, and that would be disastrous!

Thoughts kept racing through his mind. What if something had happened to the beautiful white cat who had saved his life? Maybe she was no longer in the enclosure. Maybe she had been taken away. He had no way of knowing. If that frightening thought was true, how would he ever find her with no trail to follow? If that had happened, he would never forgive himself for leaving her.

My first job, he reminded himself sensibly, *is to make sure these five cats, with their scent from the cushion, arrive safely back at the white house. Once there, I am certain Dear Lady and Dear Man will give me a good hunk of meat, and I'll be able to have some sleep before setting off to rescue my friend.* But however hard he tried, the bad thoughts kept returning.

Dawn was breaking. Tired, hungry, and thirsty, the bedraggled looking group walked into the market square of a large village, already crowded with people talking and laughing noisily as they unloaded small vans, filling their stalls with fresh vegetables, fruits, freshly baked bread, cooked meats, clothes, and trinkets in readiness for the day's trading.

'Quiet, everyone,' Bella hissed, urging the kittens stop. 'We must all keep well in the shadows.' Out of the corner of her eye, she spied the rubbish bins. Beside them were three large cages, two of them containing cats crouching down, trapped and terrified. She shuddered. *Poor things,* she thought. *I suppose they are going to be taken to the prison and given a prick like we were.*

Bella still couldn't understand why they had been returned to the village where they had been trapped. Why had they been captured and then set free? It was very puzzling. She had to admit that Senora seemed to know much more about such things than she. She decided if they ever met each other again, she would ask all the questions that were puzzling her at this moment.

Fortunately, the market traders were far too busy to notice five cats and one large, shaggy dog creep around the edge of the market square and out the other side. As soon as they reached the outskirts of the village, Bella broke into a run towards a road, calling to everyone to follow. When she arrived, she was delighted to see that alongside the road was the same narrow stream they had seen on their outward journey. She looked around, making sure it was safe before lying down and waiting for the others to catch up to her.

This time, George was the first to arrive, and he sat beside her. Somehow, he felt they were now friends. Bella purred and washed herself whilst George contentedly wagged his tail. Shortly after the others arrived, they went down to the stream and drank from the cool water. Bella looked up at the brilliant blue sky. It promised to be hot day, but she didn't mind. She knew that although Senora had told her that their old olive tree had been burned, they were nearly home at the white house.

After their drink, they were refreshed, and they ran up the hillside into the woods. As they progressed they could smell something strange and very strong. Only George recognized that it was the smell of burnt wood, and he remembered how he had lain on the terrace in great pain at the white house, watching the massive fire burn across the hillside whilst Senora washed his wounds. All around them, the ground was scorched, with many of the trees having lost their leaves and looking as though they were dying.

The kittens seemed to be the saddest when they saw the bleak scene. Nod cried out, 'Mama, will we ever be able to play here again?'

'Of course,' replied Tia knowingly. 'Don't you know that nothing really dies?'

'Don't talk rubbish,' answered Bella. 'If these trees are burned, it means they are dead. And according to what Senora told me, I'm afraid we will probably find that our old olive tree at the white house is dead as well.' Whilst she spoke, she gave herself a quick tongue wash, hoping that she had convinced the kittens that a few burnt trees didn't really matter. 'But don't worry, everyone. We will be in our home, and there will still be plenty of things to do and other games to play.' With that, she continued to lead the way through the woods until they came to the edge and were in sight of the house.

'There you are!' she cried excitedly, pointing a paw. 'We have finally returned to our forever home. Now, let's go down and say hello to Dear Man and Dear Lady.' She turned to George. 'Are you coming with us, big dog?'

Chapter 25

Senora's Scent

Dear Man was standing by the side of the swimming pool when he spotted movement on the hillside, just beyond the lane. He called out to his wife, 'Quickly! Come and have a look!'

Dear Lady walked along the terrace, wiping her hands on her pink apron. As she walked out into the sunlight, she could feel the beads of perspiration running down her forehead. She brushed them away with the back of her hand. 'Phew, it's going to be another hot one today. 'What are you looking at? I hope it's something urgent, because I was just in the middle of peeling the potatoes for lunch.'

Dear Man turned to her and pointed. 'I see one large white cat, three ginger kittens, and one tortoiseshell – all being followed by a large shaggy Portuguese mountain dog. Gentleman George has brought them back home. Look! Would you believe it is possible after all this time?'

Dear Lady followed his finger pointing towards the hillside. She could hardly believe her eyes. Bella was proudly leading her family down the hill towards the lane, with George walking slowly from side to side as if shepherding his flock into their pen. 'Is it really them?' she exclaimed, smiling broadly and throwing her arms in the air with delight. 'It's so difficult to believe they've really come back!' She hesitated, her eyes searching. She shaded her eyes to get a better look. 'But where is Senora, I can't see her anywhere, can you?

Dear Man shook his head. 'No, she isn't with them. Let's hope nothing has happened to her. Where on earth do you think they have all been? Oh my goodness, we've got so many questions to ask.'

'Well I'm sure they will do their best to tell you. That is, if you've learnt cat and dog language while they've been gone. But, I must say it's certainly wonderful that they've all come home.'

Impulsively, Dear Lady ran down the steps and into the lane, holding out her arms. Suddenly she stopped. Maybe after so long away, they would be cautious and run back up the hillside and hide, rather than allowing her to stroke them. As they approached, looking very bedraggled, she spoke to them softly. 'Welcome home, everyone. Tell me, where did George find you? We've been so worried.' She rushed on in her excitement. She bent down, putting her hand slowly towards them. Then as she was speaking, she felt warm fur against her legs as each cat greeted her. She turned to Dear Man, who had joined her. 'Just look at that. Bella actually brushed against me. She's never done that before! That means they must be pleased to be back home.' She looked down at Bella. 'Oh, dear Bella, it is so frustrating that we are not to be able to talk to you in your language.

204

You won't be able to tell us what you have been doing all this time.' Her voice was filled with frustration. 'Do you know what has happened to Senora? We've got to find out. She may be lying hurt somewhere.'

Dear Man put a hand on her shoulder. 'Take it easy, love. You know she would tell you if she could. I'm sure what they all need is food. I'll go get some.'

Dear Lady held out her hand to George, who until that moment had been sitting quietly watching his flock of cats, content that he had carried out Dear Man and Dear Lady's command and brought the scent of the cushion back to them. 'Do you know the answer, George?' she asked. He stood up and rubbed his back against her leg, wagging his tail proudly.

Dear Man soon returned holding two large bowls of food, which he put down in the lane. 'Here you are, everyone. One for you cats, and a very special bowl for you, George. I'm sure the only thing you will be wanting is a good meal.' He gave George a welcoming pat on his head. 'What a clever boy you are, George.'

He and his wife looked up and down the lane anxiously. There was still no sign of Senora.

Dear Man waited until George had finished his food. He was thinking that he might have a better response to the whereabouts of Senora if he used a commanding tone. 'George, where is Senora?' he asked.

George immediately understood the tone. He was being asked something important, and his instinct told him it had something to do with Senora. Now that his stomach was full, he was ready for action. He wagged his tail and barked three times before running a little way up the lane towards the woods. How was he going to make them understand that Senora was still in the enclosure, far away? Returning to the gate, he pulled Dear Man's sleeve and barked again, trying his best to indicate that he wanted Dear Man to help him rescue Senora.

Dear Man looked at him helplessly. Was George expecting him to follow? And if so, where on earth would he lead him?

In the meantime, Bella was so excited to be back home that she forgot her shyness and brushed her body back and forth against his leg. Even Tia didn't run away when she heard George barking.

'Mama, look – quick!' The cries of anguish came from Blynken, Wynken, and Nod, spying their home on the other side of the old wall. 'Look at our tree! It's all burnt and horrid. What on earth are we going to do without anywhere to sleep or play?'

Bella climbed the wall where Nod had once buried himself. That day now seemed so long ago. She saw the destruction of the old olive tree. 'It's very sad,' she agreed, 'but don't worry. It won't be long before you are fully grown, so you won't want to play, and you still have a lot of important things to learn.' She knew that they would miss the old olive tree, but she refused to allow the excitement of their being back in their forever home depress them. 'After all,' she continued, 'you have not properly learned about tracking, and of course you have never caught a bird or a large rat. So stop thinking about the old tree; we will find a nest somewhere. Come and enjoy the fact that we are home and safe at last.'

By this time, Dear Lady and Dear Man had persuaded George to move up to the terrace, and they sat in the shade. 'I'm glad to see that George's wounds have healed nicely. There's just one spot on his rear leg which could do with some antiseptic.'

Dear Lady pointed towards, Bella who was still sitting on the old wall. She said, 'Have you noticed that all the cats have a small piece cut out of one ear? I am absolutely certain their ears weren't like that before we went away.' She pondered on it.

'Maybe we just didn't notice them. Although when I think about it, don't animal sanctuaries collect street cats for sterilization and castration before returning them to the place where they picked them up? I seem to have heard something like that.'

'Yes, I believe they do. But I don't know of any sanctuaries near here, do you?'

They sat for a long time, looking at George and wondering about the stories he would be able to tell them if he could talk. 'Oh, how I wish George could tell us about their adventures,' Dear Lady exclaimed again.

Dear Man said, 'I'm sure he was trying to tell me something down by the gate, when he pulled at my sleeve. I think he knows what has happened to Senora, and I think he wanted me to follow him.' He looked over to where George was lying along the terrace. 'Come on, George. Where is Senora?'

At the sound of his name, George immediately stood up, ran down to the gate, and came back, wagging his tail until he reached the two sitting by the pool.

'Well, that proves it. He is trying to tell us something, and he wants me to follow.'

'What if we give him something belonging to Senora to smell?' volunteered Dear Lady. 'After all it worked the last time. You could give him the same command of order of "Go find". It's worth a try, don't you think?' Without hesitating, she went inside the house and brought out Senora's favourite cushion, which was on the sofa in the living room. She handed it to her husband.

'Look, George,' he said, pushing it under George's nose. 'This belongs to Senora. You sniff it and go find. 'I'll take the cushion down to the gate, let him sniff it there, and see if he understands. Of course, he could be too tired today. If he is, I'll do it again tomorrow, after he has had a good sleep.'

George followed them to the gate. He knew all about the scent. It was Senora's, and Senora was his friend. When he heard the command 'Go find', he knew immediately what he had to do. He would somehow find his way back to the enclosure and bring Senora home.

For the second time, Dear Lady and Dear Man watched George walk towards the woods.

'Good luck, old chap,' said Dear Man. 'We both wish you a safe journey, and that you will bring Senora back to us.'

Chapter 26

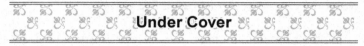

As he entered the woods, George glanced back at the white house. At this moment, although he knew where he could find Senora, he wondered how long it would take him to reach the enclosure without the help of his friend with the sausage. He remembered they had taken many hours whilst travelling along bumpy roads before they'd even reached the place where the van had stopped and his friend had given him the sausage.

So many horrible thoughts passed through his brain. What if Senora had been taken away before he arrived? How would he ever find her? One thing was certain: his command was 'Go find', and however difficult it would be, that was what he was determined to do.

He reached the road at the edge of the woods, which took him alongside the narrow stream. He remembered that he and Senora had passed the same stream before reaching the village, and it was where his flock, as he now called them, had drunk cool water. He sat down and took a drink before resting for a moment or two, gazing along the road. He could see the village in the distance. Feeling the sun sending down rays of heat on his back, he kept to the shade of the trees as

210

best he could as he walked towards the village. Whilst he was walking, he wondered if he would see cages by the rubbish bins. He hoped so. Maybe his friend would come by, and they could travel together.

The market square was still busy, causing George to dodge in and out of the crowds. He was disappointed as he looked around, because he couldn't see any cat cages anywhere. He must have missed his friend with the sausage. Maybe there would be some cages in the next village. He decided to walk on and find out.

The roads were busy with passing traffic, horses drawing carts loaded with goods, and vehicles travelling back and forth from one village to another. It took all of George's concentration not to be kicked by a horse's hoof or be run over by a van. He was lucky and eventually managed to arrive. The second village was emptying as traders packed up their unsold goods, putting them into wooden boxes, and loading them onto carts or into vans.

George skirted around the back of the stalls, keeping out of sight as much as possible. He reached the bins; again there were no cages. He sat down, disappointed, but he sensed that if he waited long enough, his friend with the sausage would return and free the cats inside his van, just as he had freed George's flock.

But then what? George asked himself. If his friend released the cats and drove off somewhere, he wouldn't be able to tell him that he wanted to be taken to find Senora. He dreaded having to wait all night in the market square with all its pending dangers, terrified he would meet up with the youths who had tied him up for so long and caused him so much suffering. He was determined he wouldn't let that happen again.

Soon he was alone in the square, the last cart having been driven away by the tired driver. Rubbish was overflowing from the bins, with even more litter spread over the ground. Well hidden behind some canvas lying under a stall, George settled down to wait. All was quiet. In the coming dusk, he spied shadows moving across the marketplace towards the bins. Three straggly cats appeared and climbed on to one of them. While watching, George couldn't help admiring the cat deftly lifting the lid, letting it slide to the ground with a heavy clatter. Immediately the other two cats poked their noses inside the bin in an effort to sniff out some supper. They then grabbed what they could and rushed away to a hiding place to enjoy their find. Very quickly four more cats arrived and took their spoils from a second bin before disappearing into the shadows.

Sometime later, George became alert at hearing the familiar sound of a van entering the square. He stood up, wagging his tail wildly as he watched the van come to a stop in front of the rubbish bins. His friend had arrived! The driver got down and walked to the rear. As George sniffed the air, he knew something was wrong. This person had a very different scent from his friend with the sausage.

He lay down again, keeping very quiet and watching carefully as the stranger put three cages by the rubbish bins and opened the gates. In a flash, two cats ran as fast as they could across the market square and out of the village. George was happy for them, knowing they were now free. The man returned to the cages, bringing with him bowls of food, which he carefully placed in the middle of each cage. After leaving the gates wide open, he climbed back into his van and drove away.

The square was quiet once more, with George still wondering what he should do. Should he leave now and walk all the way to the enclosure, or should he stay in the square and hope that when the cages were collected in the morning, his friend would be the driver? Although very hungry, he decided to stay in the market square and wait for the morning.

It wasn't long before four cats appeared, sniffed the tempting bowls of food, and slowly crept inside the cages. *Snap!* George heard the trap door to each cage lock. The cats were trapped.

For the rest of the night, there was little sleep for George, with the cats hissing, meowing, and scratching, desperately trying to escape. In desperation, George crept to a nearby alley in order to get away from the noise. How he wished he was back with his master. Would his life ever be the same?

The sound from a van's engine woke George just after dawn. Maybe today the man collecting the cages would be his friend with the sausage. He kept to the shadows, walking slowly out of the alleyway and into the market square, feeling spots of rain. Looking up at the sky, he could see black clouds forming, indicating the rain would soon be heavy.

Someone was opening the rear door to the van. George wagged his tail and then stopped. The man bending down to pick up one of the cages was the stranger from the previous evening. George was dismayed.

He watched the man lifting the cages up into the van, not knowing what he should do. The prospect of walking all the day in pouring rain until he reached the cat enclosure where Senora was imprisoned was daunting. Although his leg was healed, he knew that if he had to walk for many hours, it could bring back the pain. However, there was no question – he must rescue her somehow. Not only because he loved her, but because he had received a command from Dear Man, and he knew he always had to obey a command.

To his surprise, instead of closing the door of the van, the stranger walked to the front of the vehicle, lifted the lid of the engine, undid a cap, and looked inside. Then while leaving the lid open he walked across the square and disappeared through an open doorway. He returned a few minutes later with a bottle of water. It was then, whilst the man was busying himself with the bottle, that George made a quick decision. He ran as fast as he could over to the van and jumped in. He looked for a place to hide, and upon seeing some sacking in one of the corners, he quickly crawled past the cages, ignoring the hissing all around him. As big as he was, he managed to hide himself just as he heard the van door closing and the man jumping up into his seat. George sighed contentedly. He hadn't been discovered, and by the middle of the afternoon, he would be near Senora once more.

Chapter 27

It was late afternoon when the van finally arrived at the sanctuary. The rain had been beating down all day, soaking everything and making driving difficult as the van splashed along the muddy roads.

The front gates opened. The van drove in, and the driver switched off his engine, very relieved he had arrived without any incidents. He got down from his seat and went to the back of the vehicle, opening the door. George crouched down as far as he could, realizing even though they had arrived safely, he now had the problem of escaping without being seen.

Because of the heavy rain, he sensed the man would be in a hurry to get the cages out of the van and exchange them with others containing cats, in order to return them to the villages. Therefore, between the changeover, he had to be very quick and take his chance when the driver's back was turned away from him.

George waited until the van was empty and quietly crept from under the blanket, glad to be able to smell fresh air once more. He poked his head around the open door, where he saw a group of white-coated people huddled in the pouring rain and concentrating on sorting out the various cages and carrying them into the building.

He hesitated only a moment in order to measure his leap to the ground, and then he jumped. As he did so, he felt his back leg catching the floor of the van, making him wince with pain. Running as fast as he could towards the trees, he heard a shout behind him. He had been seen! Praying he wouldn't be followed, he thrashed his way through the bushes, glancing back quickly and seeing a man waving in his direction. Luckily, the rain saved him. When he took another glance, he saw the man was finally giving up, shaking his head in an effort to stop the rain from dripping down his wet hair onto his face. Everyone seemed to be taking cover from the downpour.

As soon as he felt safe, George lay down panting. The earth was sodden beneath him, but he didn't care. A minute later, he heard the sound of the van's engine. The van was disappearing down the road. George had escaped just in time.

Although the ground was soaking, he was able to find shelter from the thick, overhanging branches of the pine trees in the wood. Then as soon as he got his breath back, he ran towards the same narrow stream he had discovered on his previous visit and lapped up as much water as he could manage. After so long without water, he was very thirsty.

By the time he had finished drinking, the rain had eased slightly. Above the continuous buzz of insects, he heard the familiar meowing from cats inside their enclosure. There wasn't a single cat in the play area, so he decided the best thing to do would be to sleep until the weather improved. Then he would make a search of the whole area once more and try to pick up Senora's scent. After scrubbing around in the undergrowth, he eventually found a dry patch, lay down, and quickly fell into a deep sleep.

A stirring amongst the trees woke George. The rain had finally stopped, and with a break in the clouds, the moon shone through the trees, enabling him to look around. Nearby he heard the sound of an animal dragging something over fallen leaves. He quietly got to his feet and saw a fox cub battling with a rabbit just a few paces away. George growled quietly, warily looking around to see if the mother was close by; he was certain the cub wouldn't be alone. The sound of his growl alerted the cub, who looked up and fled, leaving its prey lying dead on the ground. Watching the cub disappear amongst the trees, he glimpsed the sight of its mother chasing after it. He relaxed and hurriedly picked up the rabbit, carrying it back to his hiding place, where he tore it apart with his teeth and tucked in ravenously. It tasted very good, and he couldn't help grinning to himself when he thought of how the mother fox would be scolding her cub for leaving it behind.

When George next woke, it was still dark. Millions of stars twinkled in the sky, and the omens for a dry day were good. He crept away from his hiding place and moved closer to the wire fencing of the cat enclosure, all the time sniffing the air and familiarizing himself with the scents he had picked up on his previous visit. He was reminded of the large white cat who had shown her anger by continually hissing at him from behind this same fence. Now he was content that they had finally become friends, and he was very relieved that he had been able to guide her and her family back to Dear Man.

He stared through the fencing. Nothing moved. There was silence, broken only by an owl hooting in the distance. The cats were apparently fast asleep in their enclosures.

He breathed in deeply, hoping to find Senora's scent, but there was nothing he recognized. He crawled slowly to the end of the fencing, every few moments sniffing the air, but there was still no scent reminding him of Senora. In the end, he decided that he would have to go back and search along the fence in the opposite direction.

With the floodlights still bright, George was worried, knowing that he could be seen at any time. If Senora had been moved to another part of the building, it would be very difficult to locate exactly where she was and organize her escape. He crawled along slowly, listening for the slightest sound or scent that would help him, but there was nothing.

He made his way back to the start of his search, still convinced his memory hadn't played tricks. There was something about that section that drew him back every time he crawled away. He was about to give up and take a rest when he heard hissing and smelt the strong odour of a male cat coming from the building on the other side of the play area. Could this scent be overpowering the scent of Senora? *No, that's impossible,* he told himself crossly, immediately dismissing the thought as stupid. *If Senora is there, I would know it. Anyway, she wouldn't be with a male cat – she is far too beautiful.* He lay down. Trying to be optimistic, he thought that if the morning was dry, sooner or later she would come outside. Maybe the best plan would be to wait until daylight. He closed his eyes and tried sleeping, but strange thoughts of sludgy mud and wet paws kept running through his mind. Suddenly he was wide awake. Of course – that was it!

He stood up, excitedly pawing the ground. It was very soft – ideal for digging a hole large enough for Senora to escape under the fencing. Was he dreaming, or could this really happen? The hissing from inside the building was loud and strong. The cat obviously knew there was a strange animal outside the high fence. George didn't like it.

'Smithy Magoo, for heaven's sake, stop hissing. You're waking everybody up. What on earth's the matter? Don't you realize it's still night-time?'

'I smell dog, and I don't like it.'

Senora jumped up from her bed. 'You smell dog?' she exclaimed. 'That's wonderful! It must be George. He's my dog, and he's come to rescue me.'

'Don't be silly. How can he rescue you from in here? You are a prisoner.'

Senora took no notice. She immediately went over to her cat flap and pushed. It was locked. Then she remembered that every evening, the lady in the white coat came into the enclosures and locked all the cat flaps. She would have to wait until morning. She meowed as loudly as she could. 'Please don't go away this time, George. Please don't go away.'

Outside the fencing, George heard the cries. He stood up, wagging his tail excitedly. *Yes!* He listened intently. *That's definitely Senora's cry.* Oh, thank goodness she's still here.' He stood close to the fence, hoping he would catch sight of her, but it was too dark to see very far. *Why doesn't she come outside now she knows I'm here? Something must be stopping her, but what?* He didn't dare bark; he was scared that the man in the white coat would catch him.

He looked at the high fencing. *Digging a hole is the only possible way of escape.* He dug his paw a little way into the earth. He breathed a sigh of relief. *Yes, it's definitely soft enough. I think I can do it.*

By the time daylight arrived, George was satisfied with his hole. All the time he had been digging, he did his best to spread the loose earth all around him so that it wouldn't be noticed from a distance. With his teeth and the strength of his paws, he had been able to lift a small part of the wire fencing, making the hole large enough to allow a fully grown cat to scramble through. When he had finished he went back to his hiding place by the stream and took a long drink of water. Satisfied with his night's work, he went to sleep.

The morning was cloudy, but thankfully there was no rain, so George crept towards the fencing and saw several cats who were already outside in the play area. He looked for a white cat but could see none fitting the description of Senora. He kept a short distance away, worried that some of the cats would pick up his scent and create havoc. He remembered the male cat hissing from inside the building. The last thing he wanted to do at this stage was to be noticed.

He watched the main gates, seeing cars coming and going as the morning progressed. Every now and then he glanced at the fencing, but there was no sign of Senora. By now many more cats had crept through their flaps in the wall and were enjoying themselves. Some of the younger ones were rolling onto their backs with their legs in the air, wanting to be tickled, and then they jumped up and ran as fast as they could round the small trees. Some older cats seemed content to sit chatting to each other; others, obviously restless, scratched at the fencing, trying their best to escape. George was worried not only that the hole would be discovered, but that Senora had been taken somewhere during the night. He could not understand why there was no sign of her.

Chapter 28

Instant Reaction

Senora sat in a cage on a long table in the reception area of the sanctuary, waiting to be seen by a couple who wanted to give a forever home to a white cat. They had arrived as soon as the sanctuary opened at ten o' clock and had spent a long time inspecting and talking to a number of white cats, some who had been in the sanctuary for many weeks. Others, like Senora, were new arrivals. As far as Senora could see, all the other cats were on their best behaviour, sitting and smiling eagerly. They all wanted to be chosen. But not Senora – she already had a home that she loved dearly, so she was determined not to be adopted by anyone else.

As soon as her turn came to be inspected and the cage door opened, she hissed loudly, pushing out her claws. Fortunately for Senora, the door had been opened a little too wide. Immediately realizing this was her opportunity to escape, she gave the cage door a shove with her head and leapt into the air over the shoulder of a man standing nearby. He was so shocked by her reaction that he did nothing. Everyone else in the room remained motionless, surprise evident on their faces that a cat could be so athletic.

Once free, Senora ran as fast as she could through the open doorway, looking desperately for a way to escape. She spied the front gates with their strong metal frames. Without hesitating, she took a flying leap and landed on top of the gate, wobbling precariously and trying to retain her balance before jumping to the ground, landing neatly on her front paws. Outside the perimeter, she ran as fast as she could towards a wooded area – only to be confronted by barking and howling coming from inside the dog enclosure.

Shivering with the reaction of the whole episode, but at the same time excited knowing she was free, she quickly turned away from the barking, searching the undergrowth for a place to hide. She settled for a bush of strongly scented sage. Whilst recovering, she tongue-washed herself thoroughly, anxious to wipe away all traces of the scents from inside the enclosure.

It was only moments later when she heard running footsteps. Voices called out to one another. She peeked out from her hiding place and her heart sank when she saw two people, both dressed in white coats, running up and down the road. *Oh, dear!* She shrunk back hoping she had enough camouflage to hide her white fur. She held her breath, terrified that she would be found and taken back inside. The noise from the dog enclosure was deafening. However, gradually the noises ceased, and even the dogs stopping their continuous barking. The man and the woman returned to the sanctuary building, having given up their search. With a sigh of relief Senora relaxed and nodded off to sleep.

When she woke she was aware of growling. She stood up and peeked out. Something was wrong! Why was she still hearing growls? She stared towards the tall fencing. *Horrors!* She was sure she could see large dogs moving about. *Oh, my goodness. I must be on the wrong side of the road.* She meowed loudly, and immediately barking ensued. She couldn't believe how stupid she had been. Why hadn't she paused to think for just a moment? Now, in order to reach the cat enclosure, she would have to expose herself and run the risk of being seen when she crossed over the open road to get to the other side.

Thoroughly disheartened, she lay down again. *The only thing to do now is to sleep again,* she told herself. *After all, sleeping is always the best way to solve any problem.*

As she dozed, she knew she should remain positive, convincing herself that her friend George was out there somewhere, waiting. Yes, she was certain he was there. After all, Smithy Magoo had told her he smelt dog, so it must have been George's scent and not one of the dogs from the enclosure. She was also quite certain that the dogs barking at her when she escaped were on the other side of the reception area and were too far away from the cat enclosure for Smithy Magoo to have picked up their scent. She was certain George was nearby and would take her back to Dear Lady and Dear Man. Now she had to find him.

She wondered if she should hide until nightfall, knowing that if she crossed the road in front of the entrance gates in daylight, she might be spotted. She looked up through the trees at the sky. The clouds covering the sun didn't give her any indication of the time of day, although she remembered that much earlier, she had eaten her breakfast in her enclosure and then had a good sleep on her bed. She also remembered trying to open the cat flap several times when she later woke, but it had been locked, which had surprised her because Smithy Magoo's enclosure was empty. She'd guessed his must have been opened whilst she was asleep. Of course, now she knew the reason why her flap had been kept locked. It was because the woman in the white coat wanted to show her off to those people waiting to give a cat a forever home.

As she lay in the woods, Senora thought about the couple. They had seemed nice enough. With them was a small boy who had spent most of his time running all around the reception room whilst his mother tried to catch up with him. Everyone had been laughing. Yes, Senora thought, they would probably give a cat a lovely forever home – but not for her. She loved Dear Lady and Dear Man, and now George.

Her thoughts returned to George, and she wondered what she would do if she couldn't find him. She had no idea where she was, although she did notice the air was cooler here than at her forever home in the white house. She also remembered she had seen some high mountains in the distance when the van had arrived at the sanctuary.

She thought, *Maybe if I hadn't travelled in that van, I would have been able to find my own way back home without George's help.* She had heard of cats using scents and the position of the sun and moon as a guide, walking for many days or sometimes weeks until they found themselves back at their forever homes. But she hadn't walked, so there was no doubt in her mind that unless she found George, she was lost.

Her thoughts turned to sleep. *I'll just doze here for a while and decide what to do later.* With that decision made, she stretched out lazily, thinking of the terrace back at the house and her favourite cushion lying on a deckchair.

With one eye open, she watched the couple with the young child come out of the building carrying a basket. In it, she could see a small white kitten. 'Good luck, little one,' she said as she stretched some more.

Chapter 29

A Very Proud Cat!

All day, George kept his faithful watch on the cats' play area, not understanding why Senora hadn't come out of her enclosure. He looked up, and the clouds again looked threatening enough to indicate that they would have some more rain. The depressing thought played on his mind. If that happened, he supposed all the cats would go back into their enclosures – and if the rain was really heavy, his hole would be ruined. He prayed to his doggy heaven that this wouldn't happen. He simply couldn't give up now.

His reverie was awakened by a quiet hissing and meowing coming from the other side of the fence. A cat was standing right by the hole. George crouched low on the ground just as he used to on the sheep farm when herding his flock. He watched as the cat touched the fence just above the hole and then rubbed his head against it. George made no noise, wondering what the cat would do next.

Smithy Magoo stood by the wire fence, giving it a thorough inspection. He could smell dog, all right. Most of his morning had been spent walking up and down, trying to locate the strong scent he had first smelt from inside his enclosure. But by late morning, he was bored with the activity, knowing that he was safe on his side of the wire netting. Then, just by chance, as he was about to give it up altogether, he smelt something strange close to where he was standing. It seemed to be coming from a rather ragged area of ground under the wire fencing. How could he have missed it before? He looked down, hissing and meowing and hoping that any dog on the other side would react and bark, but nothing happened. When he looked behind him, he saw that most of the cats were either playing or fast asleep, with no one taking any notice of what he was doing. He lay down on the uneven turf and meowed loudly.

Smithy Magoo was a loner. He had always found his own way, never making friends easily. As he had told Senora, he was quite content to be picked up when he was hungry, brought to the sanctuary, and then deposited back in one of the villages. But now, after hearing about Senora's life at the white house with her family, he had to admit he was jealous. Although she seemed to be very pompous, he couldn't help liking her, and he was sad when he saw her being put into a cage and carried away. It was very unlikely he would ever see her again, and his chance of visiting the white house with her family of friends had probably gone forever. The only thing staying in his mind was that she had told him about the dog who would be outside in the woods somewhere, waiting to rescue her. Now he kept wondering if the dog had seen Senora being taken away and had followed her.

Maybe it would be worth trying to see if he could find the dog and make friends with him. Senora had told him all about the fire at the white house and how the dog had been cruelly treated, all the time emphasizing to Smithy Magoo that the dog was friendly towards cats. From the early morning, as soon as his flap had been opened, he had searched along the fence trying to find the dog's scent.

He felt the earth move slightly. He stood up and began scratching with his front paws. The ground seemed to be very loose compared to a few paces away. He scratched a bit more. As he was doing so, with his nose right up against the fence, he felt the open space where George had parted the wire with his teeth. Excited, he scratched harder, pushing his paw until it reached the other side. He felt bits of wood. They felt like twigs and dried leaves, as though they had been deliberately put there to cover something up. All the time, the scent of dog became stronger. Suddenly he realized that it must have been the dog who had made the hole, and he must have made it so Senora could escape.

He poked his head through the gap. Startled, he stopped. George was staring at him from a few paces away. Hissing loudly, Smithy warned George to keep off. He was now in control. George edged backwards, not wanting to frighten the cat. He was still hopeful that Senora would appear, although he couldn't find her scent or hear her voice.

Smithy Magoo withdrew his head, satisfied that he had found something spectacular and knowing that only he held the power of telling all the cats that there was, after all, a way to escape. However, he was an intelligent cat and realized that he had to handle the situation very carefully; otherwise, there would be chaos with too many cats wanting to get through the hole at the same time.

He lay down just far enough inside the fencing so as not to cause suspicion. He slowly wiped first his whiskers, then his four very muddy paws, thinking about the situation. The clouds were getting darker, which meant it wouldn't be long before the rains came. That would be good, as long as the rain wasn't too heavy, because under normal circumstances, whenever it rained the cats would retreat into their enclosures. Whilst it remained dry, there was always a chance that someone wearing a white coat would appear in the play area. This was something Smithy Magoo had to think about.

He looked around; no white coat was to be seen. He thought, *Maybe the best solution would be to act right now. I'll summon a meeting of the cats who are out here in the play area and tell them that I know of a way to escape. I'm sure they will believe me and will be very eager to hear more. But I won't tell them anything until they promise to accept me as their leader.*

With that decision made, he nonchalantly walked over to a small hillock and sat down, calling the cats to come over and listen to what he had to tell them. A few nearby came quietly and sat in front of him. He called out again. As he did so, inquisitiveness got the better of most of them, and they gathered round eager to hear what he had to say.

He began his speech. 'I know the humans here are very kind, but none of us are free. For those who want to, I have found a way to escape.' He paused and looked around, watching amazement appear on the faces of the listeners. 'However,' he continued, 'it is extremely important that our escape is orderly; otherwise, we will be discovered, and our cat flaps will be closed so that we won't be allowed to come to the play area again. Now, for those who do not wish to escape, go back to whatever you were doing, but please act normally and say nothing to anyone. For those of you who wish to come, gather round and listen. First, I am going to be your leader. Second, it is very important that you obey my instructions. Do you all understand, and do you agree?' Every cat nodded his or her head. They were all excited at the prospect.

Smithy Magoo stepped down from the hillock, waiting patiently until he was surrounded. He looked around him, his head held high. *After all,* he thought, *I am their leader, so I must make sure they all behave.*

It was late afternoon. If they escaped now, it would give everyone a chance to disappear into the woods without being seen. But this would mean missing their supper, which was normally given to them at dusk. What an awful decision for a leader to make.

He pointed to the section of fencing where he had found the hole. 'Over there is a hole in the ground that is large enough for each of us to crawl through, but only one cat at a time.' He looked at the group before him. They were all sitting, not making a sound, and listening to everything he had to say. In that moment, Smithy Magoo was a very proud cat!

One ginger cat stood up and politely raised his paw. Smithy Magoo looked at him questioningly. 'What do we do when we go through the hole?' the cat asked.

'Well,' answered Smithy Magoo, 'I am afraid I can't answer that. Hopefully you will all be able to go back to living your lives as you did before you came here. The only difference is you will not want to search for a mate. Also, as you have all had the pin prick and the corner of one of your ears cut, you will be safe from being brought back here if you don't want to. You will be free. That is, as long as you don't get greedy and walk into one of those cages by the bins in the villages. I don't think these humans mean to be unkind to us and are cutting our ears for a purpose, which is probably to tell any female cat that we don't need a mate.' With that, he finished his speech.

Another paw went up, this time from a small black-and-white cat. 'Yes?' answered Smithy Magoo.

'Please, may we follow you instead of going on our own?'

'Of course you may.' Smithy Magoo couldn't believe that all the cats around him were so friendly and attentive. It was something that had never happened to him before. 'Now, I suggest the following,' he continued. 'I will stand by the hole and give a loud call each time it is safe for a cat to pass through. In the meantime, all you other cats must stay fairly close in a line to await your turn. But in order not to draw attention to yourselves, some of you should lie down and pretend to be asleep; others should be sitting up and washing yourselves, and the rest of you should stand and chat.' He looked behind him at the fence. One other thing I must tell you,' he continued, swallowing hard with nervousness at the prospect. 'Outside the fence, you will probably see a large, shaggy brown dog. But don't be afraid, I was told by a beautiful white cat who was taken away this morning that he came a very long way specially to rescue her and to take her back to their forever home. This beautiful white cat assured me that he is a very friendly dog, so please ignore him. I shall be travelling with the dog, so if you wish to come with me, please hide yourselves in the woods and wait for me until I have made sure everyone who wants to escape has done so. Everyone else, run straight into the woods as fast as you can. I wish you all good luck.'

With his plan now in operation, Smithy Magoo went over to the fence and stood by the hole. He looked down and was surprised to see the wooden twigs had been taken away. *That's good. He thinks Senora is coming out.*

On the other side of the fence, George was stunned when he saw one cat after another crawling through his hole. After a while he lost count, not believing what he was seeing. Very soon there were cats everywhere, some running off as soon as they were free, some lying down exhausted with emotion, and others jumping in excitement at their escape.

It was mayhem, and unfortunately for Smithy Magoo, with it came a lot of noise. As he looked at the long line of cats still waiting to crawl through the hole and hearing the meowing going on outside the wire, he became worried that he would remain trapped before every other cat had escaped. He looked towards the door of the building, expecting one of the men in a white coat to come out at any moment. 'Hurry, hurry,' he whispered anxiously.

They were down to the last six. Smithy Magoo gasped when the doors opened. A young woman walked out carrying a bucket of water and hurriedly putting it on the ground. *Please don't look up,* he pleaded, giving a quick shove on the backside of a small tabby cat struggling to crawl through the netting.

The tabby cried out in anger, his fur catching on a piece of the wire netting. 'Don't keep pushing. I can't go any quicker – it hurts.'

Just three more to go through the hole. Smithy Magoo was nervous because the woman was looking in their direction.

'For goodness' sake, hurry up,' he shrieked, shaking with fear. 'If that woman sees us, we'll be caught, and goodness knows what will happen to us.' The woman called out, and a man appeared. They both stood for a moment, looking in Smithy Magoo's direction, and then they ran towards him. Terrified, he stuck out his paws, pushing the cat in front of him as hard as he could. The cat hissed loudly, meowing as it slid through the opening, enabling Smithy Magoo to crawl through himself just as he felt a large hand grabbing his tail trying to pull him backwards. He meowed loudly, digging his paws into the ground and pushing his body forward. Suddenly he felt the hand release his tail, and he was able to crawl the rest of the way. He was free!

George kept watching until the last of the cats had crawled through the hole, beside himself with excitement when he caught a glimpse of a white cat crawling through followed by another. But despair quickly followed when neither had Senora's scent, and unlike the smooth and silky fur of Senora, their white coats were fluffy; one had a white spot on its head and nose. His Senora was nowhere to be seen.

Although most of the cats made their escape by running away in all directions, George noticed that a few were hiding themselves in the undergrowth. He wondered what caused them to stay. Why didn't they run away? Amongst them was the same tabby cat who had first discovered the hole. He seemed to be their leader, but why was he also staying here in the woods?

George decided the best thing for him to do would be to hide until the man and woman gave up their search and had gone back inside the building. But that wasn't to be. Before long, a loud siren sounded, and the front gates opened. Men and women, all wearing white coats, ran up and down the road, scattering to either side and searching for escaped cats. George crept to his hiding place by the stream whilst the few remaining cats climbed the nearest trees, seeking cover amongst the heavily clad pines. No animal stirred, and they held their breath so as not to attract detection.

The area close to the hole was thoroughly searched. Through the trees, George saw a large vehicle racing down the road in the direction of the nearest village. Then at long last, as the clouds thickened, the searchers began returning to the building, closing the gates behind them. It appeared they had given up hope of finding a single cat.

Once more peace reigned, with just the sound of insects and the occasional songbird. Smithy Magoo crawled down to the ground and stretched, telling himself all the time that he was not afraid of the large dog even though the dog wasn't safely behind the fence. He also kept telling himself that Senora had told him the dog was here to save her, and Smithy Magoo believed her – but how he wished she was with him so that she could make conversation with the dog.

He spotted George's hiding place. As bravely as he could, he walked over to him. Both looked at each other. Smithy Magoo purred quietly, showing that he meant no harm. In turn, George gave a quiet whimper. It was the sort of whimper he used to give to the baby lambs, telling them not to be afraid.

They didn't speak each other's language. and Smithy Magoo was unsure how he should proceed, and so was George. All George really wanted to know was whether this cat could tell him what had happened to Senora.

Seeing Smithy Magoo confronting the large shaggy dog, two fluffy white cats, one with a black spot on his head and nose, slowly climbed down from their hiding place. Hoping they wouldn't be noticed, they crawled under a nearby bush, where they stayed hidden to watch the proceedings. Then, as if following a signal, from beneath a mass of morning glory twined around the trunk of an old pine tree, a black-and-white cat appeared, hastily joining the other two.

Smithy Magoo turned to them, cleverly disguising his nervousness by raising his voice. 'Come on out, and remember what I told you. This dog is our friend, not our enemy. The beautiful white cat said that we must trust him, so we shall. Come and tell me your names.'

One by one, the three cats walked up to him and sat down, trying their best to ignore George. 'We don't have names,' was the answer.

'Senora says everyone should have a name, so if you want to follow me and the dog, you must have a name.' He didn't know why he was being so insistent. He had no idea why it should be important to have a name – after all he hadn't had a name since he had been born, and that was many moons ago. However, even though Senora wasn't here, he wanted to make sure the dog would take them, so he would have to make sure each of them had names.

He looked at the small black-and-white cat. 'Yes, I think Lollypop will suit you. Please remember that.'

'Fluffy white cats!' he said, pointing to the white cat with a large black spot on his head and nose. The authority in his voice was very evident. 'You shall be called Willie the Spot.' Then he turned to the second fluffy white cat. 'You haven't got any spots, so your name will be Tom Tom.' Standing back, he looked at the three cats sitting obediently in front of him. 'All of you, please remember your names. It is most important. I am called Smithy Magoo. I think Senora called this dog George, but I am not sure. However, George will do for the present.' Smithy Magoo enjoyed the superiority he had never enjoyed before.

Behind them was a rustling from a bush nearby, and out walked a young cat with smooth white fur. For a moment, George thought he was seeing things. How could he possibly have missed Senora coming through the fence? His heart sank; the scent was quite different.

The young cat shyly approached Smithy Magoo. 'Please, may I come with you?' he asked.

Smithy Magoo looked him over. 'Goodness me, I don't think so. You are surely far too young,' he said doubtfully. How old are you, do you know?'

'Well,' said the cat hesitantly, giving his paw a quick tongue wash while he thought about his reply. 'All I know is that I have been on my own in that place for ages. My mother and I were put into one of those horrid cages a long time ago, and I was given a pin prick, and my ear was cut. Then my mother died, and ever since I have been waiting for a forever home, but nobody seems to want me.'

'Well, if you don't know how old you are, do you have a name like us?'

'No, but I would love to have one.'

'I'll have to think about it.' Smithy Magoo stared down at him. 'I don't think you are old enough to take a long journey on foot. Although you had the pin prick, I think you are still a kitten.' He turned to the others. 'What do you think, everybody?'

Happy that they had been asked for their opinion by their leader, the three cats sat down and quietly discussed the problem. It didn't take them many moments to make up their minds. Willie the Spot spoke on behalf of the others. 'Well, we do agree he seems very young, but providing he behaves himself and does what you tell him, we think there is no harm in him coming with us.'

Smithy Magoo spoke to the white cat. 'Well,' he said sharply, 'you heard what Willie the Spot said. 'Providing you behave yourself, you may come and find your forever home. Now, I had better give you a name.' He thought for a moment. 'I know,' he said suddenly. 'Your name will be Young Jack.'

George, who had been standing to one side looking from one cat to another, was at a loss, wondering why these cats seemed content to stay close behind the tabby cat instead of running away like all the others. *Why aren't they afraid of me?* he thought. *Why don't they run and hide?*

Chapter 30

A Challenge

Awakened from her sleep, Senora began shaking. She could hear the sound of the siren and the continual barking of dogs. Through the open gates, men and women dressed in white coats rushed into the road in different directions. She had no idea what was happening. She crawled deeper into her hiding place, once more frightened that she would be discovered.

Why was there suddenly such a panic? Since the hunt for her had been abandoned, the wood had been relatively peaceful, with just the occasional vehicle going through the gates and driving out again a short while later. Each time a vehicle left the sanctuary, she could see the top of a basket, no doubt taking a cat to a forever home. But now everything seemed chaotic, and she had no idea why. All she could do was keep as still as she possibly could, cringing at the thought they were searching for her once again. She hardly dared breathe, hearing noises coming from every direction.

She saw a large vehicle racing away into the distance and heard more shouting and running footsteps. Maybe she would have to stay hidden forever. The thought panicked her, but she dared not move.

It seemed a very long while before the front gates were finally closed, and the searchers returned to the building. The dogs stopped barking, and it was silent once more.

Senora waited. The clouds were getting blacker. Now was her chance to cross the road before the floodlights were lit. She carefully looked around her, making sure she was quite alone. Then she ran as fast as she could and reached the woods on the other side. Crouching low, she looked behind her, making sure no one had followed. To her relief, she was alone.

Sitting up, she gave a quiet meow. 'George, are you there?' For a moment nothing happened, and then to her astonishment, there was an answering call a little distance away. But it was not a reply from George – it was a reply from a cat. For some reason, there was a cat answering her call, and the cat was in the woods close to where she was. 'Who's out there?' she called.

'Smithy Magoo,' was the answer.

Senora could not believe what she was hearing. How on earth could Smithy Magoo be out here in the woods? The last time she had seen him was early that morning, when he was inside his enclosure. She sniffed the air. 'Where are you?'

'With the dog who came to look for you. We've all escaped.'

'What do you mean, you've all escaped?'

'Come and see for yourself. We're by the narrow stream.'

As he was calling, Senora picked up Smithy Magoo's scent and moved farther into the woods. Then she saw Smithy Magoo with George alongside him; both of them walked towards her. Immediately she took a flying leap, ignoring Smithy Magoo as she did so, and landed at George's feet. She brushed against him, showing her love and relief. She couldn't stop purring, rolling over time and again while displaying her pleasure at seeing him.

George was very relieved that he had found Senora and that she was safe. He gave her head soft licks with his tongue, whining excitedly as he did so. They were together again at last and would be able to return home to the white house.

It took some moments for Senora to realize that Smithy Magoo had been speaking the truth when he had called out that they had escaped. As the three of them went back to the stream, she saw four other cats standing and waiting patiently. 'Who on earth are these cats?' she asked.

'The fluffy white one with the black spot on his head and nose is Willie the Spot. The other fluffy white one is Tom Tom, and the third small black cat with white patches is Lollypop. Oh, and that smooth-haired white cat is called Young Jack,' he added, giving a superior glance. 'He's a bit young, but I have decided to let him come along.'

'What ridiculous names,' said Senora haughtily. 'Who on earth chose those?'

'I did,' replied Smithy Magoo, somewhat downhearted that Senora should be so rude about the names he had chosen. He didn't think there was anything wrong with them. 'You told me that every cat should have a name, so I decided these names were perfect for them. Anyway, I organized their escape – and if you had been there, you could have escaped as well.' He stretched himself and slowly wagged his tail in irritation before continuing. 'If it hadn't been for me,' he emphasized, 'no one would have escaped, so I think I deserve a little more respect, thank you very much.' He then sat down in front of Senora, boldly looking straight in the eye. *That should show her,* he thought.

Senora's inquisitiveness got the better of her. 'How do you mean, you organized their escape? What did you do?'

'I found the hole that your friend George had dug for you. I told all the other cats about it, and one by one we crawled through. Of course, as the leader, I was the last cat out of the hole, and I nearly didn't make it when one of those men in a white coat grabbed my tail. I was very lucky. I think they have now closed up the hole so that no more cats will be able to escape, which is a pity. It was good fun there, and I have to admit everyone was very kind, but really it is much better to be free. At least, we all think so.'

Senora listened quietly. 'So why have these four cats stayed behind with you?'

'Because we all want to go to the white house with you and have a forever home,' he answered.

Senora looked at him in astonishment. 'I thought you said you enjoyed living in the villages and going back to the enclosure for good meals. Anyway, what makes you think there will be enough room for you at the white house? Also, how do I know that Dear Man and Dear Lady will want to take you?'

She turned to George questioningly. She doubted he understood what Smithy Magoo was asking. She wondered if he had found a way of taking Bella, Tia, and the kittens back home. If he had, it would mean Dear Man and Dear Lady would be looking after eleven cats, including herself.

There were a lot of questions that needed to be answered. The main question was, how would it affect her daily life? She certainly didn't like the idea of these strangers being allowed on to the terrace, eating alongside her and wanting to sleep on her favourite cushion. If only she could talk to George about them, but she knew she couldn't.

George slowly wagged his tail while looking at Senora. He would do anything she asked of him. Although he couldn't understand anything of the cats' conversation, he could guess what they wanted. The five cats who had stayed behind wanted to follow Senora and him back to the white house.

'How did you get out, Senora?' Smithy Magoo asked, eager to find out how she had escaped.

'I was taken to the entrance hall, where a man and a lady were waiting to take me to a forever home. But I spat and told them I already had a forever home and didn't want to go. Luckily, they let the cage door open too far, and I was able to leap out of the cage and jump over the big gates. I have been hiding in the woods on the other side of the road since early morning.'

While she was speaking, George licked Senora's head, hoping she would understand that he approved and would lead everyone safely home, protecting them along the way. After all, this was his job, and he had to admit he was very good at it.

He remembered the large gold cup his master had held between them, and how everyone had gathered around him, patting his head and telling him that he was a very clever dog. Yes, that had been a wonderful day. He reminded himself he must not be sad. He would follow the command of Dear Man and fulfil his mission by taking Senora back to the white house. If the other cats wanted to come with them, he was happy. He had no idea how Senora suddenly came to be in the woods, but that didn't matter anymore. She was safe.

Chapter 31

Shepherding His Flock

George sat down by the stream, indicating to the cats to come sit beside him. In his head, he was making a plan as to how they should proceed to the white house.

After much thought he decided the best way – although not the safest – would be to travel in the daytime. He would travel away from the mountains, but keep them in his sights. If he kept close to the roads with white lines, on which the white van had travelled, he would be able to pick up the scent from the tyres and follow them. By taking this route he would surely be able to find the villages that he and Senora had passed through when they were looking for Bella and the kittens. Then they'd find the village where Senora had been trapped in the cage.

He stopped licking Senora's head, pushed her slightly away, and lay down, stretching out. Then he waved his paw and indicated that she should lie down and sleep. Strangely enough, all the cats caught his message, and soon everyone was asleep, quite oblivious to the sounds of the soothing ripples of water from the stream close by.

George woke at sunrise. He stood up and shook himself, his long thick fur wafting a draft in Senora's direction. He gave Senora and Smithy Magoo a gentle push. They stood up immediately. The other four cats, having forgotten that there was a dog in their midst, saw him and made a mad dash into the undergrowth.

'For cat's sake,' meowed Senora loudly. 'Don't be afraid. If you want to come with us, you must come now and do exactly what George tells you. If you don't, we will leave you behind.'

One by one, three of the offenders crept sheepishly from their hiding place and stood in line behind Smithy Magoo, waiting to be given their instructions.

Frustrated there was no sign of Young Jack, Smithy Magoo meowed sharply. 'Young Jack, you had better come this instant, or we are going to leave you!' He turned to Willie the Spot. 'I knew we should never have agreed to take him. He will be nothing but trouble. Doesn't he realize that now daylight has come, we will all be in danger if we stay here for very long?'

'I can't move.' The tiny meow came from a nearby bush. 'My tail is caught on something.'

'Oh, for heaven's sake,' Senora said with a sigh, poking her head into the offending bush and coming face to face with Young Jack. She could see the bush was full of spiky thorns; it was no wonder he couldn't move. 'Hold on,' she said kindly. 'We'll help you, but it may hurt a bit. I think we will have to pull you by your paws.' Turning round, she beckoned the others to come help.

Tom Tom and Lollypop each took a paw and pulled while Senora shook the bush as hard as she could. Within moments, a tearful Young Jack was trying to shake off the prickly thorns which had stuck to his fur. He looked helplessly at Senora.

Seeing his distress, Senora began giving him a tongue wash, every now and then spitting out the offending thorns and inspecting his fur until she was satisfied there were none left. 'There you are, Young Jack. That's better.'

'Well, Young Jack,' said Smithy Magoo impatiently, 'You will have to do better than that, you know.' Turning his back on him, he called out, worried that he was losing control. 'Now for heaven's sake, everyone, please follow in a line behind Senora so that this big dog can lead us to a forever home.'

The first thing George did before starting on their journey was go to the stream and take a long drink. All except for Young Jack (who was still getting over the shock of being trapped in the bush) followed George's example, realizing they may be without food or water for many hours.

George, with Senora by his side, began the long trek. Just as Smithy Magoo had instructed, the four other cats followed in single file whilst he took up the rear. They walked slowly and carefully, listening to every sound in case of danger. Little by little, they distanced themselves from the animal sanctuary. Occasionally George would stop, sniff deeply, and change direction, keeping as close to the road as he could without exposing himself.

Suddenly George woofed and lay down, cautioning all the cats to do the same. A large van passed by, travelling towards the sanctuary. George could smell its contents through an open window; it probably contained food for all the animals. He licked his lips, realizing how hungry he was.

After what seemed like hours, Willie the Spot and Tom Tom decided it was time for a rest, and they ran into the woods and lay down. This action made Smithy Magoo furious with them. After all, he was in charge, and they should have waited for his permission before resting.

'We won't wait for you,' he shouted, 'so you had better come back now.'

'We are tired and want to rest,' called back Willie the Spot. 'Ask the big dog to let us stay here for a while.'

Senora heard his plea and turned to George, pulling on his tail and indicating to the two cats lying down just inside the line of woodland trees.

'Okay, okay. I suppose we can stop for a short while, if we have to,' he grunted. The last thing he wanted to do was to take a rest. He was the only one who knew how far they had to travel. Even Senora couldn't appreciate the distance to be covered. After all, she had been concentrating on hissing and scratching all the way to the sanctuary. However, from his previous experience of shepherding cats, he had already admitted to himself that they would do what they wanted to do anyway. Sighing, he walked over to join them.

Whilst he had been walking, George was thinking about the time when his friend with the sausage had stopped his van at the filling station and given him a large hunk of bread filled with meat. If George could find that same place, maybe he would be able to find a way of getting inside and stealing some food. He knew the cats were very hungry, and if they didn't have something to eat fairly soon, they would probably go hunting for themselves and get lost.

Their progress was slow. George looked behind him at the mountains in the distance. Heavy clouds were gathering - another sign of rain. His constant fear was rain and losing the scents from the wheels. As they tramped along the country roads, several vans passed them, but fortunately none of the drivers appeared to notice the unusual sight of a large dog shepherding six cats along the side of the road.

They came to a turning both to the left and to the right, where the roads crossed each other. George stopped, trying to get his bearings. He pushed Senora into the shadow of the trees, indicating to the other cats to follow. He ran to the middle of the crossing, hurriedly sniffing the ground and trying to pick up the scent of the van belonging to his friend with the sausage. Although aware he was in danger from the sudden appearance of a vehicle, he paced back and for forth several times until he was satisfied he had found the correct road. He ran quickly back to where the cats were hiding, pushing Senora gently, barking as he did so, telling her to follow.

Having left the woods behind, the road had very little cover. George didn't like it – they were too exposed. What if a van stopped, and the driver tried to catch them? So far luck was with them. Although no vehicle came in either direction, he kept his ears on the alert in case he had to tell the cats to hide as quickly as they could. All the while, George was on the lookout for the filling station with the shop, but there was no sign, making him think he had made a miscalculation back at the crossroad.

To make matters worse, the cats were becoming fractious. Young Jack ran away from the formation in order to catch hold of Senora's tail, pleading with her to give him something to eat. She hissed loudly. George turned in dismay, growling loudly. As soon as they heard his growl, all the cats except Senora scattered in varying directions in search of a hiding place. With little rest and no food, they were tired, hungry, and ready to give up. Even Smithy Magoo didn't have the spark and enthusiasm he had shown earlier. Luckily, Senora was still uncomplaining, quite certain George would do his best for her. The two of them lay down in the tall grasses running alongside the road, waiting.

Young Jack was the first to appear and lay down close to Senora. He had been thinking hard whilst they had been walking and had come to a decision. He would ask this beautiful lady cat if she would be his new mother. After all, she had saved him from being stuck forever on that horrible bush, and because his mother also had white fur, he was quite sure she would agree. He snuggled up to Senora. Soon he felt her rough tongue washing his head, and he knew that if he behaved himself, she would look after him.

The clouds were heavy as it began raining, at first a few spots. Then little by little, the rain fell heavily until it was pouring down. There seemed little hope that the scents from the tyres would remain on the road. George was depressed.

'Can't we go and find shelter? We'll be soaked if we keep on walking.' Smithy Magoo was fed up with getting wet. 'Look, Senora. Over there in the field on the other side of the road, isn't that a barn or something?'

Senora looked in the direction of his paw, seeing a large wooden building in the distance. She wondered if George had missed it – or had he deliberately decided to ignore it? She pulled his tail, ran across the road, and then went back to George.

George had seen the barn but had immediately dismissed it. He didn't know why, but it looked suspicious. Where there were barns, there were always guard dogs. He anxiously looked at the heavy clouds. It seemed the rain had no intention of stopping. He was aware his own sodden coat was making him feel very uncomfortable. He crossed the road, stopping to stare at the barn and hoping he wasn't making a stupid mistake. Reluctantly, he beckoned everyone to follow. One by one, at Smithy Magoo's signal, they crossed the road, crawling under the wooden fencing enclosing a field planted with watermelons. In single file, with George and Senora still leading the procession, they crept along a deep furrow around the edge.

Suddenly there was a noisy scramble. Lollypop was tearing at the earth, desperately trying to make a path around the root of a melon. He disappeared for a few moments but returned triumphantly holding a tiny mouse, which he put on the ground, watching as it tried to run away. Tom Tom, who was nearest, put his paw out sharply, but Lollypop was quicker. This was his prize, and because he was very hungry, he didn't intend to share it. Deftly he tossed it into the air, and as it fell, he allowed it to run a few paces before leaping on it and holding it between his paws. By this time the mouse was terrified, and with one snap of its neck, Lollypop killed it and enjoyed his meal whilst the other cats looked on with envy.

George was becoming anxious with the responsibility of leading these strange cats. Why couldn't they behave like his ewes? Lollypop's antics were causing an unnecessary delay, and he didn't like it. They were in the open countryside, and even though it was raining, they were at the mercy of any man holding a long rod with loud bangs, similar to the one belonging to his master. He growled angrily at the cats, indicating his displeasure as he continued to creep around the perimeter of the field, keeping his body low on the ground.

His ears pricked. He had heard barking coming from the direction of the barn, so his first instinct had been correct: there was danger in this field. But seemingly quite oblivious, the cats had overtaken him and were hurrying to find shelter. George gave a sharp pull on Smithy Magoo's tail, who in turn hissed at him. George didn't dare bark, not wanting the other dog to know where they were and that they were getting closer and closer. He knew the dog would probably be loose and be able to give chase once he picked up the scent of cat. He growled and turned.

Senora looked back, surprised he had suddenly changed direction and was purposely heading back towards the road. What on earth was he doing? She anxiously followed, at the same time whispering to Smithy to tell the others. Ignoring his loud objections, she chased after George.

When they finally reached the road and safety, Senora explained to the other cats that George was their leader and had to be obeyed. 'Only he knows the direction we must take to get to the white house and he will look after us, so you must attend at all times.'

The day was drawing to a close. They were wet, hungry, and miserable, and the hope of finding a safe barn was now remote. A short time before they had reached the melon field, George had seen a clump of tall trees on the side of a hill. He thought, *At least*

those trees will give us some protection from the rain.
He directed the reluctant cats to follow. They had had enough.

Fortunately, when they arrived, they found a lot of vegetation to give them plenty of undergrowth where they would be able to hide. He gently pushed Senora towards some bushes. Proud that she was able to understand most of George's instructions, she turned around to the others.

'Hide yourselves quickly, and get as much rest as you can. George says we shall have another long journey tomorrow, and if you don't obey him, he won't get you any food.' She smiled quietly to herself, watching all the cats obey without hesitation. *I'm getting good at this,* she thought as she hurried to the nearest bush. Young Jack immediately snuggled himself between her legs, and upon feeling the warmth of his body against her, she purred contentedly. Within moments they were fast asleep. It had been a long day.

As soon as all six cats were settled, George lay down, using his large body to protect them from any danger. Throughout the night, he knew he must remain on duty, just as he used to whilst guarding his flock. He had no idea what predators there might be in the woods a short distance away at the top of the hill, but he knew there would be some. To keep himself awake, he made an attempt at drying his sodden fur, but it was pointless. It was far too thick for his tongue to be of any use, so instead he contented himself, cleaning his muddy paws. After a while, satisfied with his efforts, he stood up and walked slowly through the trees listening. His eyes searched the darkness, and his nostrils were alert for the scent of fox, but there was nothing more sinister than the hoot of an owl, its melancholy sound echoing from far away. Finally, he went back amongst the bushes and lay down as close as he dared without waking the cats.

As soon as it was light, George stood up and shook his large head, his name tag tinkling against his collar. It was time to begin a new day of walking towards the white house. It was still raining, but from what he could see through the trees, the rain was not as heavy as previously. He gently pawed Senora. She stood up, yawned, and stretched, at the same time telling the others to do the same. Within a short while, they began following George.

They reached the road. George walked slowly from one side to the other, endeavouring to catch the scent from the tyres of the van. There was nothing; he would have to rely on his instinct and look for a road that would take them farther away from the high mountains. Already the air was becoming warmer. *That's a good sign,* he thought. Up ahead, he saw a turning. Cheerfully he quickened his pace, but as they came closer, he realized the road seemed to be heading back towards the mountains.

Once more he became unsure, wondering if they had been on the wrong road all morning. How could they be going in the wrong direction? He was certain there had been no other road. Had he made a mistake all the way back at the crossroad? He dreaded the thought. He stopped walking, looking around and sniffing the air. He knew he could not go much farther without finding the scent from the tyres of the van. He lifted his paw, touching Senora's back and telling her she must stay by the side of the road. She stopped walking, swishing her tail at the others; they halted and sat down. George slowly walked to the middle of the road, sniffing. Surely he would be able to find a scent in the middle – but the rain had washed away all the scents. Hiding his disappointment, he walked quickly to where the cats were waiting, He wagged his tail, determined not to let them know he was confused, and he indicated to everyone to keep walking.

Hunger and thirst were becoming a priority. The cats continually meowed. George was becoming more and more irritated in his frustration as their complaints grew louder and louder. He suddenly turned and growled sharply. His sheep had never behaved like this.

Senora, as always at George's side, turned and hissed at the others. 'For heaven's sake, stop complaining, all of you. Can't you see our friend George is trying his best to get us home? He can't help it if there isn't any food and our forever home is a long way away.' Having ended her admonishment, she put her tail in the air and walked steadily forward, closely followed by Young Jack, who proudly followed her actions.

George was trying to ignore his own hunger. He realized he had been so busy thinking about finding Senora that he hadn't eaten since he had left the white house. While he walked, he kept his eyes alert, looking for the filling station with the shop. He knew if they had any chance of survival, they had to find food.

They came to a junction. Then at last, he spotted it. A little way farther down the road was the filling station. Upon recognizing their surroundings there was no doubt in George's mind. They were on the right road! Very excited, he hurried forward and he barked his news. Surely now they would be able to find something to eat.

He touched Senora gently on her head, indicating that she and the other cats should lie down and hide themselves. Then he pointed his paw in the direction of the building on the other side of the road, showing her that he wanted to run across. Senora understood what he intended, although she wasn't sure why he wanted to leave them. Still, she did as he bid and hurried the other cats into a huddle, whispering to them to hide themselves.

George looked up and down the road, making sure it was empty before running across. When he reached the other side, he skirted the building, thankful that it was early in the day and still raining. Nobody was around; all the shutters and doors to the building were closed, so he knew immediately that there was no possibility of getting inside. What should he do? He remembered the bins in the villages; he had seen cats sliding in and out with food in their mouths. Maybe he could find some bins behind this building. He began to look around.

A loud meow behind him caused him to turn, and as he did so, he caught sight of a grey cat sitting on the roof of a wooden hut. The cat stood and arched its back, continually meowing at George. Within minutes, George heard more meowing behind him, and as he turned, he realized that despite his instructions to the contrary, Senora and all the other cats had decided to join him. He growled at them quietly, furious that they had disobeyed him. Now, with all the noise going on, they would surely be discovered.

He wasn't wrong. A door opened beside them, and a lady looked out in astonishment at seeing the strange cats and a dog in her back yard. 'My goodness me,' she exclaimed. As soon as she spoke, Senora and the others scattered. George stood wagging his tail. The grey cat on the roof remained with his back arched, hissing at everybody.

The lady went back inside the building, and within minutes she returned accompanied by a man. He gently put his hand out towards George, as if giving him a greeting. George, convinced that this man would be a friend because he knew he had given his own friend a big sandwich, wagged his tail and walked towards him. The man stroked George's head and spoke two words George recognized. 'Good boy!' he said as he patted George again.

The couple exchanged a few words between them, looking first at George, then towards the cats crouched in the corners, and then back to George again. They looked at each other smiling, nodding their heads. The lady went back into the building and shortly returned, holding a large piece of paper. On the front was a large picture of several cats. Of course he couldn't read the writing on the paper, but he could tell by instinct that it had something to do with the cats escaping from the sanctuary.

Once more the lady went into the building, followed by the man. Senora immediately rushed over to George and pulled his tail with her mouth before running to the road, followed by the other five. Luckily for everyone, they were quickly halted from chasing over to the other side by the appearance of a vehicle screeching around a bend in the road. Now frightened to cross without George acting as lookout, they returned to his side. All the while, George stood his ground, refusing to move. He knew these strangers were his friends.

Large bowls filled to the brim with food were put down on the ground in the yard. The strangers slowly retreated into the building. The grey cat on the roof jumped down immediately and began eating. George joined in, hungrily eating from the largest bowl, which was filled with chunks of meat and vegetables. To him it was a fantastic meal. Senora didn't hesitate. Losing her nervousness, she made a dash for the nearest bowl. The others, seeing her eating vigorously, ran over to the other bowls, ignored the grey cat, and began eating as fast as they could. To everyone's surprise, the grey cat then stood back, allowing them to take her place. She seemed to sense that these foreign cats must be very hungry and needed food; otherwise, they would never have been so rude as to push past her.

When he had finished, Smithy Magoo spoke to her. 'We have escaped from the sanctuary and have not eaten for two moons, so we are very hungry.' He tried his best to be polite. 'We are sorry if we have eaten some of your food. I hope you will forgive us.'

'What about that big dog?' the grey cat asked. 'Is he likely to attack now his belly is filled?'

'Oh, no,' replied Smithy Magoo. 'He is a very gentle dog, and he is taking us to the white house over the hills, where we will have our forever home.'

Satisfied, the grey cat jumped back onto the roof of the wooden building and watched all the cats finishing their meal.

'Everybody ready?' George asked, watching the cats washing their whiskers and cleaning their paws. He lifted his own paw, pointed towards the road, and gave Senora a nudge at the same time. She understood.

'George wants us all to hurry and go towards the hills so that we can reach them before night comes,' she said, confident that she had understood every word George had said.

One by one, after making sure the road was clear, they crossed over to the other side and continued walking in the direction of some hills. George was happy that the high mountains were now well behind them, and he tried to recall everything he had seen from the window of the white van belonging to his friend with the sausage. Of course, when he was in the stranger's van, he had been hidden underneath the blankets, so hadn't been able to see anything.

He remembered when the van had passed through a village some time before reaching the filling station, so he was certain that if they kept walking in the same direction, they would eventually reach it. All the time, he was wondering what they would do when they did arrive. It was still daytime, so there would probably be a lot of people in the market square, and he was scared they might be recognized. *After all,* George thought. *If the lady in the filling station recognized them because there were cats' faces on that bit of paper, then surely everyone else will know who they are and try to capture them and send them back to the sanctuary. I will never let that happen,* he assured himself. *We will have to be really careful, go around the village, and keep hidden at all costs.*

It took most of the day and a lot of walking before they saw the village. Many times on the way, at George's command, they had to dive into the undergrowth in order to avoid being seen by passing vehicles. On one occasion, they had to hide whilst a young boy, trying to balance on one wheel, fell over into a ditch, at the same time buckling the handlebars. It seemed to take forever before he could straighten them enough to enable him to cycle down the hillside and out of sight.

Another time they were terrified when Willie the Spot wasn't quick enough and was nearly run over by a man riding a machine making a very loud noise whilst travelling at great speed. Just in time, Lollypop managed to get hold of Willie the Spot's tail between his teeth and pull him to safety. Willie the Spot, not realizing what had happened and that Lollypop had saved his life, turned around fiercely and gave him a good swipe with his front paw, hissing wildly.

Before they reached the outskirts, George manoeuvred them away from the road and into some nearby woods. He walked steadily forward through the thick brushwood covering the ground, concentrating on the direction of the village. He had no idea of the size of the village, so could only guess at the amount of time it would take them to get through the woods and out on the other side.

Fortunately, all was quiet except for the constant noise from insects, and they made good progress, passing the village as it was getting dusk. George decided that it would probably be safer for them to sleep in the woods overnight. He would send Smithy Magoo and Lollypop back into the village as soon as it was dark to see if they could find food in any of the bins. Through Senora, who seemed to understand everything he wanted, he explained his idea. She immediately spoke to the others, telling them of George's plan.

'Smithy Magoo and Lollypop', she ordered. 'You are to go into the village, look for food, and bring it back here. Remember you must try to bring something back for everyone, including George, so don't be greedy and eat everything yourselves.'

Smithy Magoo looked at her in astonishment. 'Don't be so stupid, Senora. We have only one mouth each. How can we possibly bring enough food for everyone?'

'I don't know, but you'll just have to try. And please don't call me stupid,' Senora answered haughtily.

It was a dry but cloudy night, so fortunately for Smithy Magoo and Lollypop, there was no moon. They trekked towards the lights of the village. Once there, they crept forward, keeping close to the walls of a side street. Before long they came across a square similar to most villages. They eventually found three waste bins and then noted the cages alongside them. They looked at each other, smelling the bowls filled with appetizing food in the middle of each one.

Although very hungry, Lollypop shook his head and veered away, having learned his lesson. Smithy Magoo hesitated, wondering if he really wanted to change his lifestyle by going to the white house. When he reached the third cage, he sat down as if in a trance, trying to make up his mind what he wanted to do. Did he want to go with the others?

Lollypop gave him a loud hiss. He wanted nothing to do with those cages.

After a few moments, Smithy Magoo stood up and made up his mind. After all, they were at last getting close to the white house, and it seemed a good idea to be pampered as Senora had promised. If he didn't like his new home, he could always walk to a village and find a cage with some food so that he would be taken back to the sanctuary. Without hesitating any further, he joined Lollypop, who was busying himself smelling the waste bins.

'There's definitely food in this one,' Lollypop purred, content at the thought.

Smithy Magoo said sternly. 'You know very well if you climb up and then drop a lid, it will make a tremendous clatter and wake everyone. We must not touch the bins; we've got to find food some somewhere else.'

Disgruntled, Lollypop followed Smithy Magoo, and they both began searching under the market stalls in the middle of the square. As they poked their noses under the coverings placed over each stall, protecting them from the rain, they found nothing but empty boxes. Both cats began thinking it was a hopeless task – until suddenly Lollypop gave out a loud meow. He had smelt something.

'Quick, I think I have found food. Come and look.' When Smithy Magoo reached Lollypop, he found him lying on top of a large pack. 'What do you think is inside? I must say, it does smell good. Get down, and we'll try to open it at one end.'

Both cats chewed as hard as they could. Finally, Lollypop was able to push his paw into the opening. Out fell some crumbled biscuits. 'My goodness, this is animal food!' cried Smithy Magoo in amazement.

'Lollypop you are a magnificent cat to make such a find.' He purred loudly, brushing himself against Lollypop's back and trying to lick him on the head. As he did so, he hit his own head on a piece of wood which was holding up the stall. 'Ouch, that hurt!'

Lollypop gave him a quick tongue wash in return, very pleased with himself and knowing that when they returned to the others, they would be given lots of praise for finding enough food for everyone.

They both looked at the large pack lying in front of them. They couldn't get over their luck.

'We've got to be quick,' said Smithy Magoo, 'in case the cats in the village find us.'

'Or a dog,' echoed Lollypop, cringing at the thought.

'Let's try to lift it,' said Smithy Magoo, tugging at one of the corners. 'Mind you, Lollypop, we must be very careful not to spill any and leave a trail behind us.'

Lollypop tugged at another corner. The pack wouldn't move. After a few more tugs without success, he gave up. His mouth was already becoming sore.

'It's too heavy. We can't move it.'

'I agree,' said Smithy Magoo, releasing his corner. 'We will have to go back and tell George to come here and carry it for us, but we'll have to be really quick and not make any sound when we cross the square, in case someone finds it before we get back.'

'Shall I stay here, guard it, and fight off any cat who wants to steal it?' asked Lollypop.

'No, of course not. You wouldn't stand a chance against another cat; you are too small. And anyway, it might not be a cat – it might be a dog or a human. Come, now. Let's hurry.'

Once more keeping close to the walls, they left the village and ran as fast as they could back to the woods, where everyone was waiting expectantly.

'Quickly, Senora!' cried Smithy Magoo. 'You must tell George to come with us back to the village. We have found a big pack of food, enough for us all for several days, but it is too heavy for Lollypop and me to carry. George must carry it for us. It is in the square under one of those stall things.' He sat down for a moment, exhausted.

Senora turned to George and patted his leg, meowing loudly. He realized she was trying to convey something urgent, but as usual he couldn't understand her meows. She purred loudly, pushed her body against him, lifted her paw, and pointed it towards the village.

'Run to the village,' she called to Smithy Magoo and Lollypop. 'We will follow.' She turned to Willie the Spot, Tom Tom, and Young Jack. 'Make sure you three stay here until we come back.'

She gave George a shove against his front leg and ran towards the village, following Smithy Magoo and Lollypop. George quickly caught up with her.

As soon as Lollypop proudly showed him the pack still hidden under the stall, George crawled all around, inspecting it thoroughly before attempting to drag it into the open. He spied the open corner where the cats had chewed. He gave the pack a nudge with his head. It was too heavy for him to carry, so he thought the best idea would be to drag it behind him. He smelt each corner quickly and decided that the corner where Lollypop had made the opening would be the easiest end to hold in his mouth. By doing that, he wouldn't drop any of the biscuits and leave a trail behind him.

With the three cats acting as lookouts, he slowly dragged the pack out of the square and away from the village. By the time he reached the woods where Willie the Spot, Tom Tom, and Young Jack were anxiously waiting, George was tired. The weight inside the pack was far heavier than he had expected. However, he wasn't going to complain. They now had enough food to last them for the rest of their journey. His real problem would be when it came to dragging the large pack during the daylight hours without being seen.

He spread out some biscuits as fairly as he could. Senora pulled a face at him. 'It's food for dogs, not for cats. I can't eat this.' She turned on Smithy Magoo, hissing loudly. 'Fancy bringing us dog food. That was really stupid.'

'Well, if you think it was stupid, don't eat it, and then there will be more for us,' replied Smithy Magoo. Senora sat down, disgust showing on her face, but gradually even she had to give in and eat her share.

'Well I think it is wonderful,' concluded Tom Tom. Everyone else agreed and ate hungrily. George, also ignoring Senora's complaint, looked around happily and then began eating his meal with relish.

For the rest of the night, they slept soundly. As soon as dawn broke, they ate more biscuits and then got under way. George led the way, dragging the pack of food behind him. This time he kept in the shade of a line of lime trees that stood well away from the road. The sun was shining, with no sign of rain. Whenever they came to a turning in the road, George stopped to get his bearings, now able to memorize the route of the white van. He spied a barn in the distance. Something in his brain seemed to connect making him decide to take a route in the opposite direction, leading towards a row of tall walnut trees.

George was now much more confident that he was remembering the route. As they progressed throughout the day, the landscape became drier, with fewer trees giving shade from the hot sun. In the far distance, he could see hills, with glimpses of the sea every now and then.

By the time it was dusk, they were exhausted and hungry. George spent his time looking in every direction for some cover as far away from the road as possible. Above them was a steep ridge lined with woodland. *If we can reach the top,* he thought, *I will certainly find enough cover for all the cats under bushes amongst the trees.* He despairingly looked down at his pack of food, loathing the idea of dragging it all the way to the top. But if he wanted to feel relatively safe, there was no other way.

He turned back to warn Senora, only to find there wasn't a cat in sight. Where on earth were they? Why hadn't he heard them running away? He was completely mystified. 'Stupid cats!' he barked. He looked in all directions but could see nothing except the hillside with the road below. He barked some more, but there were no answering meows. All he could do was wait until they decided to return. *Then, they will get a good flip of my tail on their backsides.* But he was tired and knew in his heart he wouldn't dare do any such thing. He had no wish to be scratched in return. Eventually he lay down and waited.

It was Senora who gently licked his nose. Brought back from his dream world and having no idea how long he had been sleeping, he jumped up and growled angrily, but not for long. There in front of him, sitting in a straight line, were the six cats – plus two dead rabbits.

The ridge was far higher than he had anticipated, and at times he thought he would never reach the top, but he persevered. The cats, having enjoyed their meal, followed with their tails standing straight up in anticipation of a good night's sleep.

But when they reached the top, to George's dismay he found the pine trees in the woodland were so thickly spread that there were few bushes. Suitable covering was practically non-existent. *So much for my intuition,* he thought, realizing he was becoming far too despondent. He sat down, releasing his load for a moment or two. He had to pull himself together. There was no alternative but to search for an opening with bushes.

It seemed a very long while before they found an ideal spot to spend the night, and it was Senora who found it. At the time, she was leading the group, running amongst the trees, and looking anxiously from left to right. Suddenly she stopped, ran back to George, excitedly pulled his tail, and pointed with her paw. There in the dim light was an opening in the trees, giving way to a small glade with a stream twisting and turning down the hillside. The glade was thick with bushes. It was ideal.

George sat down, releasing the food pack from his aching jaws and indicating to Senora that every cat should hide themselves in the bushes and rest for the night. He had already decided it would be his duty to be on guard, keeping a watchful eye for predators, both human and animal. He then pushed his paw into the pack of biscuits and pulled out a good helping for each cat, leaving himself until last.

Soon every cat was sound asleep. George was content with the thought that by dusk the following day, if their luck held, they would be back at the white house.

Chapter 32

George woke suddenly, immediately jumping to his feet. Something was wrong. He looked around him. Was there a predator in the area? He sniffed the air but smelt nothing. He looked at the sleeping cats spread out underneath the clump of the bushes, deciding to count them to make sure they were all there. What if one of them had been stolen whilst he was dozing? If that were the case, he would never forgive himself. *Of course, that's a stupid notion,* he thought. *After all these are cats, not ewes or lambs. A cat would hiss and scratch if an animal tried to steal it, and all the others would wake to defend it. Anyway, I was on guard, so it couldn't possibly have happened.* Angry with himself for having such dismal thoughts, he counted again. Senora was there, the tabby, the black-and-white cat, plus the white kitten squeezed up against Senora. But he could only see one of fluffy cats. The fluffy white cat with the spot on his head was there, but not his brother.

George looked under all the nearby bushes, but there was no sign. *Maybe he's run off to catch another rabbit. Of course, that's the answer. He will return soon, and then we'll be able to get on our way. Just one more day, and then I will have fulfilled my mission.*

275

The thought made him relax, and he lay down again, waiting.

It was some time later, and Tom Tom still hadn't appeared when George decided to wake Senora. He gave her a gentle pat. She yawned, quickly washed her whiskers, and looked at him questioningly. She noticed the biscuit pack hadn't been opened. *That's strange. George always opens the biscuit pack before we wake up. Our breakfast is always ready. Oh, dear. I hope he doesn't expect us to start walking before we have eaten our breakfast.* She felt George nudge her again. 'All right, all right. I'm awake – no need to push me like that,' she said crossly. She stood up to see him lifting his paw and pointing towards the empty space by the side of Willie the Spot.

So, Tom Tom isn't sleeping. Nothing much wrong in that; he's probably just being private. She walked over to the food bag, sniffing at the opening. *For goodness' sake, hurry up, George. I'm hungry.* With that, she gave a loud meow in his direction, but George was adamant. He had to make Senora understand that the fluffy white cat had been missing since dawn. He gave her another nudge before walking back to the empty space where Tom Tom had lain, sniffing at it and whining.

Goodness, he must be worried about Tom Tom, for him to do that. She went over to Willie the Spot and pulled his tail. 'Willie, wake up and tell me where Tom Tom has gone,' she demanded.

Willie the Spot leapt to his feet, hissing loudly. 'Don't you dare do that to me again, Senora! How should I know where he is? He's probably being private,' he said, having the same notion as Senora.

By this time all the cats were yawning, washing themselves, and wondering what the commotion was all about.

'Have you seen Tom Tom?' Senora asked again.

'Willie the Spot, for heaven's sake, answer her. I'm hungry. What do you think has happened to him?' Smithy Magoo said as he stretched in anticipation of eating his breakfast.

'Oh, I expect he is close by; don't worry,' answered Willie the Spot. He turned to Senora. 'Will you ask the dog to give us our breakfast? When Tom Tom smells that, he will definitely come back. I am sure he hasn't gone far.'

'Well it is the first time that he has walked off without telling anyone,' said Senora, remembering the time when Nod was trapped in the old wall. 'I think we should look for him right away.' With that, she began calling Tom Tom by name. They sat listening for a reply, but there was none.

Soon all the cats were looking under bushes and calling his name at the top of their voices. Even George began howling in the hope that Tom Tom would answer. But when they stopped, there was no answering call. Tom Tom did not appear.

Willie the Spot became anxious about his brother. They had never been separated. Once they had a forever home, but that was when they were tiny kittens. Then they had been rescued by an old lady after being thrown from a car into a muddy ditch. The old lady was very loving to them, always giving them plenty to eat with lots of cuddles. In their eyes, she took the place of the mother they could no longer remember. It had been a very happy time. It ended one night when, having finished her supper, the old lady gave them each a big cuddle and a kiss and went to her room. They never saw her again.

The following day, they were put into a large basket and taken to the sanctuary. At first they had missed the old lady, but as the months went by, they learned to accept their new surroundings. They grew to trust the humans in the white coats who picked them up, giving them a cuddle whenever they brought them food or came to clean their enclosure. But the best part of each day was in the morning, when their little flap in the wall of their enclosure was opened, and they were able to go out into the sunshine and play. They loved that.

However, there were times when they became frightened at the thought of being separated. On these occasions, they were each put into a cage and taken into a room, where they were lined up alongside other cats. Strange humans whom they had never seen before talked to them, putting their noses close to their cages and nodding their heads. Whenever this happened, the kittens would move as quickly as they could manage to the back of their cage hissing loudly. They had been warned by the other cats in the enclosure that these strangers might choose them and take them away to a forever home. Much to their relief, the hissing had some effect, because it was always another kitten who was chosen and taken away by the strangers.

Then one day something different happened. Instead of going to the room to be lined up with other kittens, they were taken to room with a very strange scent. There they were given a prick, and the next thing they remembered was waking up in their enclosure feeling very sleepy.

As they grew, they heard stories from new arrivals about the joys of finding a mate. Neither could understand why those cats constantly spent their time trying to escape under the fence in the surrounding play area. When Willie the Spot and Tom Tom asked what they were doing, they were told that the most important thing for all cats was to find a mate – but neither Willie the Spot nor Tom Tom understood what finding a mate was all about.

All morning George and the cats searched, but Tom Tom was nowhere to be found. Every now and then, one or other of the cats caught his scent, but with the area covered by bushes, it soon faded away.

George quietly went off on his own, making his way back to the ridge. Along its edge, he sniffed the ground. Even with no scent to follow, he was drawn to the ridge, thinking as he searched that it was always Tom Tom who wanted to run off and play. Tom Tom wanted to chase after small vermin or climb precariously up the trunk of a tree scaring a bird. It seemed that finally his freedom had shown him the joys of becoming independent.

He looked down the hillside searching both to the left and to the right. If Tom Tom was on the hillside, he should be fairly easy to spot with his fluffy white fur standing out against the green grasses. He glanced down towards the road, already dismissing the idea that Tom Tom would have strayed so far away from the others. He looked again. There was something white lying in the middle.

George almost slid down the slope, whimpering loudly, hardly daring to believe. He reached the road and with a breaking heart walked to the middle, knowing that it would be the body of Tom Tom.

Poor, poor Tom Tom! He touched his body with his paw, seeing the deep wound in Tom Tom's head. He had crept away during the night, probably to hunt, and had been run over by a vehicle and left to die.

As gently as he could, George picked up Tom Tom's body in his mouth and walked up the slope towards the ridge. Silently he lay Tom Tom's body in front of Willie the Spot, who gave out a loud howl and lay himself over his dead brother.

'It can't be, it can't be!' he meowed loudly. 'My poor, poor Tom Tom.' He looked up at Smithy Magoo accusingly, arching his back and hissing. 'If you hadn't made up all sorts of stories and persuaded us to go through that hole, we would both still be safe in our home. It's all your fault! You killed my beloved Tom Tom!' he yelled.

The accusation shocked Smithy Magoo. Naturally he was saddened by Tom Tom's death, but he couldn't feel in any way responsible. Tom Tom should never have left their camp at night without telling anybody. Surely everyone knew that was the rule. He decided it would be of no use saying anything to Willie the Spot at the moment; the cat was far too upset. He looked across at Senora and said quietly, 'Let us bury Tom Tom before we leave here.'

The ground was still soft from the rains. George dug a hole with his paws that was large enough and deep enough to take Tom Tom's body. With Willie the Spot, who was still sobbing his heart out, he lifted him down into the hole and covered him over with the loose earth. It was a very sad occasion, and for a long while the five remaining cats, together with George, stood looking down at Tom Tom's grave.

'Willie the Spot,' Senora said as she brushed up against him, gently purring. 'It is time to move on. You know how sorry we all are to lose Tom Tom. He was a lovely boy, and we all loved him. You must try not to blame Smithy Magoo. It really wasn't his fault.'

She turned towards the waiting George, who was holding their biscuit pack in his jaws. With sadness filling their hearts, they left Tom Tom's grave and walked slowly down the hillside to the road. Willie the Spot looked back for one last time, hesitating as he did so and wondering whether he should stay with his beloved brother or travel on with the others. All he had left in the world were the wonderful memories of their lives together.

Chapter 33

The day was sunny. Throughout the morning, they made slow progress with Willie the Spot lagging behind the others, continually needing encouragement to continue. Lollypop and Young Jack, on the other hand, decided the journey was becoming a good game. They had enjoyed their biscuits, and now that their bellies were full, they were ready to play and spend their time tantalizing the others by running across their path and rolling over in front of them. With the death of Tom Tom still very much on their minds, nobody seemed to be in the mood to admonish them.

The biscuit pack seemed to be getting heavier and heavier despite the fact that it was half-empty. George's jaws were continually aching, causing him to stop and let go whilst he massaged them with his tongue, but as soon as he picked the pack up, the pain continued. Would they ever reach the white house?

Senora looked towards Lollypop, who at this moment was taking a leap in the air after seeing a butterfly. By now she was becoming more irritated by him. 'Lollypop, for goodness' sake, behave yourself. You are making us all go slower with your messing around like that. And Young Jack, you come back here and walk by me.' She knew that what they were doing was very harmless, but like George, she was becoming depressed. They seemed to be travelling forever.

'Senora, don't be angry with them; they're not doing any harm,' Smithy Magoo said. He was stronger than the other cats, and although he wouldn't dare admit to it, he was enjoying the companionship of everyone. Having friends was something he had never known in his life. Whenever he had allowed himself to be trapped in the villages and taken to the sanctuary, he was always put in an enclosure on his own, and although he had spent a lot of time in the play area, nobody had ever tried to be friendly. It seemed that most of the cats had been too scared about not knowing what was going to happen to them. But with Willie the Spot, Senora, Lollypop, and Young Jack, he was sure he had now made firm friends, and he was very much looking forward to reaching the white house and meeting Dear Lady and Dear Man, whom Senora had told him so much about.

All the cats stopped in their tracks, wondering what on earth Senora was doing when she suddenly jumped up in front of them, excitedly sniffing the air as she did so. At that moment, they were passing around the edge of a village.

Senora pulled at George's tail sharply. The action brought him out of his daze, causing him to look round to see what she was doing. He growled softly, showing his annoyance, but by now Senora was quite used to his growls and knew they didn't mean anything. Rolling on her back in front of him to show she meant no harm, she stood up again and lifted her paw, pointing it towards the village. He knew she was trying to tell him something, but as always he had no idea what. Then she sat down, put her paw behind her ear, and stared at the village. Suddenly he understood what she meant, and he too heard a bell ringing out from a tall tower. This must be the village where they had lain all night whilst Senora was in the cage. He dropped the pack, wagging his tail and at the same time giving Willie the Spot a lick on the top of his head, as if to say everything would be all right now.

He remembered the village all right, and the disaster that had befallen Senora. Now that they had returned, they knew they were nearing the end of their long journey. Just one more village to pass through before reaching the stream where Bella, Tia, and the kittens had taken a drink, then the burned-out woods, and finally the white house.

His mind was now very clear. He decided they would continue walking in the hope that they reached the second village before nightfall. Once there, they would find somewhere to hide and have some supper. Then as soon as darkness fell and he decided it was safe to travel, he would lead them in the direction of the stream. With luck they would reach it by morning when they would have another meal and sleep before their final trek through the woods.

At last his despondence left him. Wagging his tail, he picked up the pack of food in his jaws, telling Senora to walk on. Maybe it was his renewed optimism, but for some reason his jaws didn't ache quite so much. Of course, the pack was getting lighter each time he served out a meal, but he also knew that before two more nights, they would all be safe back at the white house.

They were sitting under some trees close to the second village when darkness came. George took up the lead and crept very slowly, almost on his haunches, keeping his eyes and ears wide open against any danger that could suddenly develop. He heard the sound of music and a lot of noise coming from one of the buildings, reminding him of the travellers with the brown bottles. At first he hesitated, wagging his tail from side to side as he lay down, indicating to the cats to keep still until he gave the order to proceed. Senora crawled up beside him. She too remembered the noise coming from the building and instinctively understood what George was telling them. He pushed her gently, at the same time lifting his paw a little. He wanted the cats to creep past the building before he took up the rear.

Senora understood and turning to Smithy Magoo and the others she whispered, 'We must creep past the noise and hide on the other side of the village. I will go first. Young Jack, you keep close to me, and Lollypop can follow, but wait a few moments before you do. Then, Willie the Spot, you must follow Lollypop after a few moments, and Smithy Magoo will follow Willie the Spot. George will be taking up the rear. Now, you must remember, everyone, to be as silent as you can – and on no account stop for anything. That includes you, Lollypop.' Each cat solemnly nodded.

Senora quickly looked around. She felt George's paw as he patted her back, giving her a signal to proceed. she kept to the shadows as much as she could, and she silently crawled around the market square, all the time worried not only for herself but also for both Young Jack and Willie the Spot, thinking their white fur could be noticed and they would be caught.

Eventually Senora, with Young Jack close to her tail, reached the far side of the village. Breathing a big sigh of relief, she looked around, trying to find a place to hide. She was lucky: by the side of a wooden shed, there were some old boxes. As quickly as she could, she pushed Young Jack into the largest box and crept in beside him, comforted by the warmth of his body; it was a feeling she had never before experienced. Despite her apprehension, she couldn't stop purring contentedly.

Senora anxiously waited for Lollypop to arrive. He was fairly small, so she thought he would be able to squeeze into the box beside them. She peeped out after a few moments, but there was no sign of him. Suddenly Willie the Spot ran across and squeezed in beside her. 'Where's Lollypop?' she whispered.

'I don't know. We watched him leaving, and then I saw him creeping around the square, so he should have arrived here by now. Goodness knows what he is doing.'

'He really is irresponsible,' Senora said with a sigh.

Smithy Magoo arrived shortly after Willie the Spot, closely followed by George. With his large body, George leaned heavily against the wall of the shed, trying to keep deep in the shadows.

'Did any of you see Lollypop on your way over?' asked Senora. She was getting worried. The last thing she wanted to do was to leave Lollypop behind.

'I'll go see if I can find him,' offered Smithy Magoo.

'Oh, would you?' Senora replied. 'Your fur is grey, so no one will see you.' The three of them watched Smithy Magoo creep back towards the square.

Not having any idea where Lollypop had gone, Smithy Magoo didn't know where to look first. He thought the best thing would be to retrace his steps through the village. He crept around the edge, taking the same path. Then he suddenly heard a scuffling, hissing, and spitting, followed by a loud noise of something crashing to the ground in the middle of the square. Dogs were barking from every direction. As quietly as he could, he crept around one of the stalls and immediately saw who had caused the noise. On top of the rubbish spilling out of one of the bins was Lollypop, fighting with another cat. Unfortunately for Lollypop, the other cat was getting the better of him, and Lollypop was slipping farther into the rubbish.

Smithy Magoo thought for a moment, wondering his best course of action. He had to be quick; at any time, they could be surrounded by dogs. It was certain he would have to go to Lollypop's aid, but he wasn't sure how without causing a tremendous fight – and with it a lot more noise, thus alerting the whole village.

Waiting no longer, he quietly got behind the cat and took a flying leap upwards, pulling the cat down by grabbing the back of its neck. It screeched out with shock, turned on Smithy Magoo, and scratched him sharply across the face, hissing and spitting as he did so. Fortunately for both Smithy Magoo and Lollypop, the cat took off and raced down one of the narrow streets.

In the meantime, Lollypop, shocked and shaken from his ordeal, leapt out of the bin and ran as fast as he could across the open square, only stopping when he spied George in the shadows of the wooden shed. As he sped away, Smithy Magoo heard the sounds of footsteps and loud voices coming towards him, so he too rushed out of harm's way and joined the others. A few moments later, a very sheepish Lollypop came up to him and apologized. Smithy Magoo conveyed his anger in silence by showing Lollypop his scratched face.

The atmosphere calmed a little before George decided it was safe enough to lead the way out of the village, all the time keeping a lookout for any approaching vehicle. There was a bright moon, making it easy for him to spot any vehicle approaching in the distance and thus allowing everyone time to hide amongst the bushes alongside the road.

He recognized the route quite clearly. He felt he was now in full command and was thankfully nearing the end of his mission. He began sniffing the air for the smell of the stream. There was still no sign, so they kept trudging along throughout the night. Everyone was tired and silent.

It was Senora who first heard the running water. She quickly pulled at George's tail with her mouth. He stopped and sniffed the air, listening. Yes, he too could hear the sound of running water. The stream was close, and even though it was still quite dark, by listening and using his nose, he was easily able to find it. Along its banks were tall reeds with plenty of hiding places amongst the grasses large enough to house small cats. They breathed a sigh of relief when Senora announced they could fill their bellies and then sleep until daylight. George would keep watch as usual.

George found some large, flat stones and thankfully dropped his burden. Before giving everyone a share of the biscuits, he went over to the stream. With his jaws extremely sore, he badly needed to take a long drink, allowing the cool water to soothe the inside of his mouth.

When the cats had finished eating, they went down to the edge of the stream and leaned over to take a drink. Smithy Magoo dipped his paw into the water and bathed his scratched face. Unfortunately, Lollypop, having completely forgotten his exploits in the village square, leaned over the water, attempting to catch a small fish, and he promptly fell in. He came up gasping for air and meowing loudly, trying to attract the attention of the others.

'That wretched cat!' yelled Senora. 'Quick, somebody help. Lollypop has fallen in the water. I don't want to get wet, so I'm not going in. Somebody else will have to get him out.' She knew she didn't really mean what she was shouting, but she was mad at Lollypop for continually causing so much trouble.

George looked up, glad to help. He loved swimming, and after all, this was what he had been trained to do. He would save Lollypop, just as he used to save the baby lambs if they were in trouble. He leapt into the water and quickly swam towards the middle chasing after Lollypop, who was being pulled along by the current and just managing to keep his head above water, meowing at the top of his voice.

Fortunately, with the moonlight to guide George, who was a strong swimmer, it took only moments for him to be alongside Lollypop and grab hold onto the back of his neck before carrying him to safety further along the bank. They both shook themselves, very relieved the incident was over, and they quietly walked back to the others. George received praise from the four cats who had been standing and watching anxiously. Lollypop experienced their anger at his misbehaviour. Yet again, Senora threatened that next time he was naughty, they would leave him behind. She had lost all patience with him.

'I was only trying to catch a fish for our breakfast,' pleaded Lollypop, but no one believed him or took any notice.

After their very long trek and Lollypop's misadventure, they were thoroughly exhausted. One by one, they found hiding places along the bank of the stream and slept for the remaining hours of darkness, until daylight.

By the time they woke, it was almost midday, and the sun was high. Well rested, both George and Senora were happy knowing the white house was within their reach. The road was quiet, so George picked up the biscuit pack and led the way. It didn't take them very long to reach the woods – the same woods where George had originally smelt the scent of Bella, Tia, and the kittens. It seemed so long ago. George felt as though he had been walking along tracks and roads, riding in vans, digging holes, hiding from predators, and taking his flocks of cats to the white house forever. Even the memory of his horrific time with the travellers was gradually fading.

Whilst they were walking, the anger with Lollypop, together with his exploits, faded from Senora's mind. She excitedly told the others how much they would love their new lives. At the same time, she took great pleasure in instructing them how they should behave, adding that they were definitely forbidden from walking into the white house. 'That's my prerogative,' she explained.

'What's perog … something?' asked Willie the Spot, trying his best to keep up with the elegant white cat.

'Oh, nothing for you to worry about.' It was a word Senora had heard from one of the cats who had once visited the white house whilst her owners were on holiday. To Senora, the word sounded most elegant, so she repeated it as often as she could. 'And remember always be polite to Dear Lady and Dear Man,' she concluded. She immersed herself in her own thoughts of how she longed to sleep on her favourite chair. *I wonder if the others will be there?* Sadly, she had never been able to make George understand when she asked if he knew what had happened to Bella, Tia, Wynken, Blynken, and Nod. She had often wondered if they had been able to find their way all on their own, or if they had been taken to another forever home. She knew Bella would be broken-hearted if her family was separated.

Of course, it never once occurred to Senora that Dear Lady and Dear Man might be angry when she and George finally arrived home with four more cats.

Chapter 34

Snared

The air was cool under the trees away from the sunlight, and they enjoyed themselves, knowing they were nearing the end of their travels. With familiar scents filling his nostrils and his good sense of direction, George was able to find the right pathway. He was happy his mission was nearly fulfilled.

Suddenly, agonizing pain shot through one of his back paws. The contents from his pack of biscuits scattered all over the pathway. The pain was excruciating, and there was blood all over the ground. He yelped loudly again and again.

Senora turned in shock, seeing the pain in George's eyes as he collapsed on the ground. She ran to his side, giving his body a nudge with her head. 'What on earth has happened? What's the matter?' She looked at his limp paw covered in blood. 'What's that metal thing clinging to your paw?' She gently touched it and quickly drew back. She didn't know what it was, but she was sure this object was causing George a great deal of pain. She turned to the other four.

'Come and have a look. See if you know what this is sticking through George's paw. Mind out – there is a lot of blood.'

Each cat cautiously eyed his paw. 'That metal piece seems to be caught on something in the ground,' said Smithy Magoo. They were mystified, never having seen anything like it before.

George was still whimpering with pain. He knew very well what had happened, and it was through his own carelessness. When he was still a puppy, his master had shown him all kinds of metal things, making it very clear to George that they were bad and that George must stay away from them at all costs. But in his excitement of nearing the completion of his mission, he had been careless. His paw was hurting a great deal and he was beginning to feel strange inside.

Alarmed, he immediately thought of hunters. If they stayed where they were, they would all be in danger because whoever had dug this thing in the ground would return and find them – and he had no idea when that would be. It could even be before sunset. They had to get away as quickly as possible.

He tried to get up but found he couldn't; his body wouldn't allow it. He yelped again as the sharp rod went deeper into his paw. He had to find a way to get himself and the cats away from the woods and down to the white house and safety.

The five cats sat close to George, discussing the situation. Senora said she knew the way back to the white house if George wasn't able to walk, but she didn't want to leave him here all alone in case he was in danger. However, they agreed that if George was in danger, there was very little they could do to help him. They had to think of a way to get him walking again.

Smithy Magoo came up with an idea, which they discussed at length. He told them about the time he had slipped off a rubbish bin and had badly hurt his leg. He had crawled into one of the cages with the trap door and had been taken to the sanctuary. There, the men in the white coats had looked at his leg, put two sticks on each side, and tied some kind of cord around his leg, which held the sticks in place. By doing this, he was able to limp around for a few weeks until his leg was better.

Senora spoke up first. 'That all sounds very clever, Smithy Magoo, but that's not something we can do here, even if we knew how. We shall have to think of something else.'

Ignoring her, Smithy Magoo stood up to his full height. He was determined not to be put off by Senora's interference. 'First,' he continued, we have to dig this thing out of the ground. None of us have sharp enough teeth to pull it out, so we shall have to loosen the earth all around with our paws and then pull. We will take it in turns, but we must be very careful how we dig so we don't allow any earth to touch his paw. I will go first,' he said authoritatively and immediately began by digging at the damp soil.

It took them a long time to release the ugly looking claw. The only cat trying his best but making matters worse was Young Jack so Smithy Magoo immediately relieved him of his duty.

Satisfied that George's paw was now free from the ground, Smithy Magoo thought of the next stage of the operation. He turned to the others, the present situation reminding him of his announcement about escaping through the hole in the fence back at the sanctuary. *I really do think I am a good leader!*

Senora sat down in front of George and looked across at Smithy Magoo in astonishment. 'You really can't imagine you can make your plan work. It's impossible. Even if you find these sticks, George is in far too much pain for you to try to touch him. He will bite you.'

'You said he was always gentle and would never bite.' Smithy Magoo retaliated.

'I said he would never bite me.'

'Stop arguing you two.' Willie the Spot interrupted. 'Senora is right we must think of something else. The dog might bite us if we touch him. I think we should let him rest for a while and then see if he can get up on his own.'

Apart from Smithy Magoo, everyone agreed with this plan. Having been out voted he retreated into the undergrowth and lay down.

After a while George opened his eyes and lifted his head. He winced with pain. Somehow he had to get up and complete his mission? He stared at his swollen leg, and tried to move it slowly.

Senora immediately came to his aid and gently tongue washed his head, hoping that her massage would soften the pain. All the while they had been resting she regretted being angry at Smithy Magoo. After all, she decided, he was only trying to do his best. Maybe she had been wrong. His idea might have worked if she hadn't interfered.

George took a deep breath, moving his three good legs in unison, trying to lift his body. He collapsed in pain. After a moment or two, he tried again. His weight wouldn't carry him. He cringed and cried out when the metal dug further into his paw. It was useless. He closed his eyes and rested.

Senora looked on in dismay. 'Well I hope you are now satisfied.' Smithy Magoo whispered in her ear.

Senora ignored him, thinking her only alternative was to go on ahead and try to get help. Maybe she could make Dear Man understand that George needed help.

George took in another deep breath mustering all his strength and rolled his large body over until his bad leg was clear of the ground. Then, with agony clearly showing on his face, he pushed as hard as he could with his front legs at the same time slowly manoeuvring his one good back leg until he was standing upright. The metal dragged his paw down making it feel very heavy, but he persevered.

At first he wobbled, but he managed to keep his balance until he was able to limp a little way along the pathway dragging the metal object behind him. Watching his efforts, all five cats gave loud meows of encouragement, jumping with delight at his success. They then sat down in the middle of the path, purring with delight while washing the mud from their paws.

Abandoning the pack of biscuits in the middle of the wood, they followed the path once more. George, limped slowly behind them with pain piercing his paw whenever it came in contact with the ground. All the while, there was the strong smell of burnt wood; everywhere showed signs left by the fire.

Exhausted after the events of the morning, they at last reached the edge of the wood to find the hillside bathed in sunshine. George very slowly limped to join Senora.

'Look, everyone,' Senora said as she pointed down the hill. 'There is the white house I've told you so much about. You are safe now. That will be your new forever home.'

Chapter 35

Senora Shows the Way

Senora, first to reach the garden gate, quickly jumped up and over. Then she ran as fast as she could up the steps to the terrace, where Dear Man was dozing in his deckchair. Seeing him sitting there, she immediately leapt onto his stomach, at the same time crushing the paper he had been reading.

The sudden weight on his lap and the sound of crinkling paper made him wake up with a start. He couldn't believe his eyes. 'Oh, my goodness, it's you, Senora! You're back! How wonderful! But where on earth have you been all this time?' After giving her a warm cuddle he could feel how thin she had become. In turn, Senora was so happy to be home again that she nestled into his body, purring with all her strength.

Recovering from the shock of being woken so suddenly, he called for his wife. 'Quick, hurry! Senora's back! I can't believe it.' Cuddling Senora tightly and kissing the top of her head, he whispered, 'Oh, I'm so glad you're safe. We've been so worried about you.'

Within moments, Dear Lady appeared and took Senora into her arms. She too cuddled her tightly, listening to Senora's purr of contentment. 'Oh, my goodness, I really can't believe that you have come home at last. We've missed you so much!'

They were so engrossed with welcoming Senora that neither noticed George and the four cats waiting outside in the lane. Although during the last part of their journey he had been in a great amount of pain, he was very contented that he had finally been able to carry out the command of Dear Man.

The garden gate was closed, so George knew he wouldn't be able to climb the steps up to the terrace without help. Instead, he gave a small whine and lay down exhausted. The four cats standing in the lane were hesitant, wondering if they would receive any sort of welcome from these strangers. From the beginning they had listened to Senora's stories, believing Dear Lady and Dear Man would look after them. Now that they had actually arrived, they became very fearful they would be turned away. Even Smithy Magoo was scared. He had always been full of confidence, taking his chances wherever he was, but it seemed the long journey had changed him. He had made good friends and had become a leader of cats, but upon arriving at the white house all he wanted was to be loved.

Young Jack watched his beloved Senora in the arms of the strangers, knowing it would break his heart if he lost her forever. 'Please, please don't push me away now.' Although his plea was quiet, Lollypop heard him.

'Oh, for goodness' sake, Young Jack. You've got to grow up sometime so stop moaning. Anyway, Senora crossed paws with me, so I know she won't let us down.'

'Well, it's not up to her, is it?' whispered Willie the Spot, as apprehensive as the others. Now that he no longer had Tom Tom by his side, he badly wanted to be given a forever home with Dear Lady and Dear Man.

'Oh, shush, all of you. They'll hear you, and then we'll never be allowed to stay here.' The admonishment came from Smithy Magoo, his confidence returning. He stared across at a tortoiseshell cat, a large white cat with a black patch on her head, and three ginger and white young cats, all sitting and watching them from the top of a garden wall. He thought about them for a moment or two, wondering where he had seen them before. His mind went back to the sanctuary. 'Of course!' he said suddenly, turning to the others pointing his paw towards the wall. 'See those cats? They were in the sanctuary. But how did they get here, I wonder? I distinctly remember they were put into baskets and taken out of their enclosure. Surely if Dear Man had collected them, he would have taken Senora as well.'

He looked up to the terrace, watching Dear Man still holding Senora. While thinking about the mystery, he proceeded to give his coat a quick tongue wash with the excuse that he wanted to look as manly as possible when he was introduced to Dear Man.

'Oh, dear,' whispered Willie the Spot upon seeing the two strangers walking down the steps towards them. 'Something's happening, I think we should make ourselves scarce.'

'Be quiet!' hissed Smithy. 'Don't spoil everything. We will stay where we are. Keep calm and look your best.'

Senora, having at last been cuddled and adored, suddenly remembered that she had left the others in the lane. She had made good friends with them and didn't want to let them down, so she jumped out of Dear Lady's arms and rushed down to the garden gate.

'Oh, my goodness come and look at George!' exclaimed Dear Lady when she reached the gate, catching sight of George lying in the lane. 'He's got something stuck in his paw.' She turned to Dear Man. 'Just look at that swelling on his leg and his paw is twice its normal size. He looks as though he is in agony, doesn't he?'

Dear Man bent down and inspected George's leg. 'It's a snare! The poor animal has a snare caught in his paw. I'll have to take him to the vet, his whole leg could be infected. It depends on how long the snare has been there'

Dear Lady had been so busy attending to George, she hadn't noticed Smithy Magoo, Lollypop, Willie the Spot, and Young Jack on the other side of the lane trying their best to look beautiful. She lifted her head, amazement showing all over her face as she looked across the lane. 'Who are those cats? Poor loves, they are so thin I shouldn't think they have eaten for days.'

'For heaven's sake, George,' Dear Man's voice was gentle as he stroked George's head. Where on earth did you collect them from? Surely you are not asking us to look after these strays as well as the others – plus Senora and yourself.'

Dear Lady smiled, her heart warmed looking down at the four orphans. 'Of course he is asking us, otherwise he wouldn't have brought them home. They really do look awfully sweet. That fluffy white one is simply gorgeous, and just look at the little white one; he looks as though he could still be a kitten. We couldn't possibly turn them away now. After all, where would they go?'

Dear Man sighed as he opened the garden gate. He knew he had already given in.

The four orphans, upon seeing the stranger stepping into the lane, had different ideas and nervously ran a little way up the hillside.

Senora called to them. 'Come on back here, everyone. I promise Dear Lady and Dear Man won't hurt you.'

In the meantime, Dear Lady bent down and stroked George. What has happened to you? How did you hurt your leg?' she asked, although she knew George wouldn't be able to answer her questions. George tried to lift his paw and gave a yelp, indicating that he was hurting badly. 'Oh, you poor, poor dog. You really are suffering, aren't you? But you are such a clever boy. You have brought our Senora back to us!' She bent down and kissed his head. 'Thank you, George. You are a very, very good boy.'

George recognized the words 'good boy', so he knew Dear Lady and Dear Man were pleased with him. He was satisfied that his mission had been completed. He was home.

Dear Lady and Dear Man slowly stretched out their hands towards the four cats in an attempt to show they were friendly, but despite Senora's assurance, no one moved, not quite sure what was expected of them.

Dear Man turned to Dear Lady. 'Go and get them some food. Maybe that will show them we mean no harm.'

'Good idea. I'll bring some packs of meat.' The cats watched as she turned slowly so as not to scare them. Then she walked up the garden steps before disappearing into the house.

'Who are those cats, Senora?' The meow came from Bella, who was still sitting on the old wall and watching the new arrivals.

'My goodness, how wonderful, Bella. I didn't know you had come home. Are the others with you?' Senora was so pleased to see Bella that she forgot to answer Bella's question.

'Yes, we are all here. That big dog made sure we were safe when we were returned to the village. He brought us home. I like him. I never thought I would, but he looked after us, so I really like him.' Bella got down from the wall and joined Senora. Both cats brushed against one another, sniffing the other's scents. Their tails stood straight up, showing their pleasure at being together again.

Bella repeated her question.

'Of course you don't know who they are, because you left before it all happened,' said Senora, proudly looking back at George. 'George dug a big hole in order to save me, but I wasn't there – I had already escaped. It was because of that hole that a lot of cats were able to escape. Those four cats decided they didn't want to go off on their own; they wanted to come home with me.

'It was a very long trek. We were walking for many sunrises, and then one terrible day we found that Tom Tom, who was Willie the Spot's brother, had been killed by a vehicle.' Senora looked sadly across at Willie the Spot, pointing her paw. 'He's the white fluffy one with the black spot on his head and his nose. We had to bury Tom Tom before we could continue, and it was dreadful. Poor Willie the Spot was broken-hearted. You see, they had never been parted for the whole of their lives.

'Honestly, Bella,' she rushed on, 'I have so much to tell you about our journey and how George led us back here from the sanctuary. Another terrible thing happened while we were up in those horrid-smelling woods. Some iron thing got stuck in George's paw. Now George is in a lot of pain, but Dear Man will help him like he did before.'

By this time, Dear Lady had returned to the lane carrying two large plates of food. Dear Man followed holding an even bigger plate, which he put down in front of George. Then, as soon as Dear Lady had put the plates for the cats on the ground in the middle of the lane, they retreated up the steps to the terrace with Senora in their wake, anxiously eager to be given special treatment and have her meal served on the terrace. These humans had learned a lot about cats since adopting Bella and her family, and they knew the last thing they should do was hurry or make a loud noise close to the new arrivals.

It took only a few moments before George was eating. He was extremely hungry despite his pain, and once the humans had departed, Smithy Magoo, Lollypop, Willie the Spot, and a hesitant Young Jack walked back down the hillside to the lane. First they smelt and walked all around the large plates. Then they gingerly decided to try a sample. One mouthful was sufficient, and they began eating hungrily. None of them had ever tasted food such as this.

When they finished their meal, they began to relax, purring happily to each other and giving themselves thorough tongue baths. Satisfied with his toiletry, Lollypop couldn't help giving each plate a final lick, making sure they had been licked absolutely clean.

Dear Lady and Dear Man decided the best thing to do would be to leave all the cats on their own so they could get to know each other. By this time, Senora had returned to the lane and began making the introductions. They watched with amusement as Tia, Wynken, Blynken, and Nod joined their mother and ran over to greet Senora. Before long, all the cats were eying each other shyly, occasionally giving a quiet meow and a purr, warily walking around, and sizing each other up before touching noses. The scene was charming.

Dear Man counted the total in despair. Before they had arrived at the white house, they had never owned an animal. Now it seemed they would be looking after ten cats and a dog! He turned to Dear Lady. 'Don't you realize that feeding them and having them all vaccinated will be very costly? Plus, of course we have to think about sterilization. And then to add to all that, we have to think about the cost of feeding and vaccinating George.'

His wife put a comforting arm around his shoulders. 'Oh, honestly,' she said with a smile. 'I'm sure we can manage somehow. They are all so sweet, and think of the trouble poor George has gone through in finding them and bringing them home. We couldn't possibly let them go.' Dear Lady was determined to convince her husband, although in her heart she also knew looking after them was going to be difficult

'Look,' said Dear Lady, pointing. 'Do you notice something? They all have their ears clipped – even

Senora. I wonder if that means they have been sterilized. In England, they always cut the ear after sterilization.' She turned to her husband. 'Do you think George found them at the same place he found Bella and the others? Anyway, whatever the cost I would adore looking after them all. That is, of course, if they would like to stay with us.'

Chapter 36

Dear Man telephoned the vet, explaining that George had arrived home with a snare attached to his foot.

After discussing the case for a few more moments, the vet told Dear Man that he would probably have to give George an anaesthetic, so it was important for him not to have anything further to eat or drink. 'Bring him in tomorrow morning at nine thirty, and we'll see what can be done.'

It took Dear Lady and Dear Man all their strength to carry the large dog up the steps to the terrace, where he lay all night with Senora beside him. He noticed there was no drinking bowl, and he wasn't given any food, but he didn't know the reason. He was hungry and thirsty. Why were Dear Man and Dear Lady treating him like this? *After all,* he thought, *I have obeyed all Dear Man's commands – and it was Dear Lady who called me a good boy. I just don't understand why they are being so cruel when I have obeyed all Dear Man's instructions.*

He tried to sleep, but it was impossible because the pain in his paw was bad. He wanted to die and be with his master, wherever he was. He knew Senora wanted to help. She lay beside him, occasionally washing his head and purring, but that only made him feel even sadder. He simply did not understand.

Dear Man woke him from a dream early the following morning. 'Come on, George,' he said gently. 'I'm going to take you to that nice man who made you better before.' He attached a lead to George's collar and encouraged him to stand up by pulling it gently. The pain in his paw was much worse, but he managed to hobble on his three good legs down the steps behind Dear Man. Dear Lady was standing by the car, and together they lifted George up and lay him on the back seat.

The vet closely inspected George's paw. There is no doubt that he has poison inside the paw.' He looked up at Dear Man. 'Any ideas when it happened?'

'Not really,' said Dear Man, 'maybe yesterday. I guess it was fairly near to home.' Dear Man then related the story of the fire and returning home from their vacation, only to find Bella and her family missing. He narrated how he had sent George to find them, taking Senora with him. When Senora hadn't returned with them, he had again sent George on another mission, this time to look for Senora. 'After all,' he explained, 'George is a shepherd dog – and a very intelligent one at that. I was pretty hopeful he would succeed.' He looked down at George, quivering with pain. 'And he certainly did succeed. He brought them all back home – plus four extra cats. So now, apart from Bella and her family, we have a lovely fluffy white cat, a black one

311

with a white stomach, a grey tabby who seems to be their boss, and one who is still a kitten. Of course, we still have Senora, who is always the boss of everyone, including my wife and me.' He laughed at the thought of how haughty Senora could be at times.

'Do you know where George found them?' the vet asked, wondering if his guess was going to be correct.

'No idea, but the funny thing is, they all have a piece chopped out of one of their ears.'

'In other words, they have all been sterilized. Well, you obviously haven't read the English newspapers recently. A couple of weeks ago, they printed a story about a dog digging a hole at an animal sanctuary. There is one in the direction of the mountains, about seventy kilometres away from here. Apparently thirty cats escaped through that hole, and so far, not one has been found. Hold on a minute; I think I still have the article.' He left the surgery and returned moments later, holding a newspaper.

Dear Man read the headlines: 'Thirty Cats Escape from Sanctuary.' Underneath were two photographs. The first was a photo of a number of cats in a play area at the sanctuary. The second photo was of a wire fence that showed an empty gap at the bottom, where a hole had been dug. Underneath the photographs was an article. 'Late one afternoon, a vet at the sanctuary discovered cats escaping through a hole in the fencing surrounding the sanctuary. Unfortunately, he was too late to catch any of the escapees. Later, the owners of the sanctuary said that they had noticed a Portuguese mountain dog in the area a few days before, and they suspected he might have been the culprit who had dug the hole.'

'Good heavens!' Dear Man exclaimed. 'Do you think that dog was George, and he was trying to rescue Senora? That's absolutely amazing, if it is true. When you think of the distance, it seems incredible that George was able to find her and bring her back to us. The four others must have followed. No wonder they are all so thin! The poor things couldn't have eaten properly for weeks.' Questions came tumbling out. 'What about Bella and her family? Were they in that sanctuary? It all seems very odd.' Amazement showed all over his face. 'George arrived home with Bella and her family about a month ago, and they also have a snip in one ear. Does that mean they all spent time at the same sanctuary? I don't suppose we shall ever know the answer as to how they got there or how George found them. Good old George.' Dear Man put down the newspaper, watching the vet give him an injection.

The vet looked up at Dear Man, grinning. 'I imagine they were caught in the cat traps in the villages and were taken to the sanctuary. They probably tried to get at the food bowls, but, I must admit how George found them is a bit of a mystery. Portuguese mountain dogs are certainly not very common in these parts, but we do know George is very intelligent, so I too believe he must be the culprit who dug the hole. I don't think we will say anything to anyone, do you? After all, it seems you not only have a remarkable dog, but remarkable cats as well. It will take a few moments for the anaesthetic to take effect. I will then remove the snare and give him an injection of antibiotics. I suggest you come back tomorrow morning. If all is well and I don't have to amputate, you will be able to take him home. Then bring him back for a change of dressing in a couple of days and in ten days I shall be able to remove his stitches. In the meantime, he will need antibiotic pills each day. I will write it all down for you. Oh, and please don't worry about bringing the cats to my surgery. When you want them vaccinated, I will make a visit to your home. I am quite sure if they have come from the sanctuary, they will most certainly have been vaccinated already, so you won't have to think about that problem for another year. That is just as well, because it seems from what you say, they are all street cats, so you will have to make good friends with them before persuading them to be caught and vaccinated.' The vet smiled at Dear Man as he opened the surgery door.

They shook hands, and Dear Man departed. For the moment, he was not concerned with street cats; he simply hoped that George wouldn't have to lose his leg. What a dreadful penalty it would be for following a command. He drove back to the house and relayed the news to Dear Lady, at the same time telling her about the article in the newspaper.

'Poor George.' was all she could say whilst listening to his story, tears running down her cheeks. 'Just think of all the anxiety he must have been through. He is such a super dog. It really doesn't seem fair when he was only doing his duty.' She got out of the chair she had been sitting in, walked across to her husband, and rested a soothing hand on his shoulder. 'We've got to hope for the best and pray that his leg can be saved. Oh, by the way, I have given all the cats some more food. I put the bowls by the old wall, just as we used to when Bella and the kittens first arrived. Everybody seemed to tuck in, so I think they are happy. At the moment, most of them are sleeping.' She looked over towards the pile of sleeping cats on the other side of the wall. They were all there, except for Senora, who was sleeping on one of the best deckchairs. 'It is such a dreadful shame that the fire destroyed most of the old olive tree. What do you think of the idea of buying some cat beds and putting them up here on the terrace? Do you think they will adapt?'

'Well, I suppose we could try that, but I do think they will prefer to keep to their own side of the wall. After all, they are street cats. The vet says you can't expect them to suddenly become household pets. That can only happen with time.'

As soon as they had returned home from their vacation, Dear Man and Dear Lady had set to work clearing the debris left by the fire. They hired some men who had cleared the area of burnt branches and undergrowth, and then they created a garden, incorporating crazy paving paths intermingled with a variety of wild herbs. Around the remains of the old tree, they had planted grass, over which they had hung a large straw canopy that they decided would make an ideal nest for the cats and would create plenty of shade.

'It will never be the same,' sighed Dear Lady, 'but at least it is a safe place for them to rest and play.'

Two hours after Dear Man returned back to the house, the telephone rang. It was the vet, ringing to tell them that the news was positive. George's paw would be as good as new within a few weeks. There had been very little poison in the paw, but because he had been able to limp back home, the poison hadn't spread.

The following day, Dear Man arrived at the vet's surgery to be greeted by George brushing against his legs and furiously wagging his tail. 'That's wonderful,' said Dear Man. 'He doesn't appear to be in any pain at all, and he isn't even limping.'

'Well,' said the vet cautiously, 'he mustn't be allowed to jump around too much for the time being. You should bring him back to me in a couple of days, and I will change the dressing.' He opened the door of the surgery. 'Oh, I almost forgot. There was someone here this morning asking if I knew of anyone who has a collie for sale. He brought me a puppy for its first injection and told me that he is intending to buy a ram and a few ewes. He wants to start a sheep farm and sell the wool. But in order to get him going, he needs a fully trained sheep dog who will be able to help train his new puppy.' The vet looked questioningly at Dear Man. 'He was also telling me that he has been driving his van back and forth to the sanctuary for some years. Apparently he collects the traps in the villages and returns them after they have been sterilized, and he sets them free. He mentioned that not long ago, he had made friends with a mountain dog who seemed to have an attachment with a cat inside his van.' The vet looked enquiringly at Dear Man. 'I cannot be positive, but it does seem as though the whole story fits together. Missing cats, snipped ears, and cats escaping when a mountain dog digs a hole!

'Of course,' the vet continued, 'George, isn't a collie, but he is used to living amongst sheep. He has plenty of life in him, and if you will forgive me, he may become bored and start to pine if he stays with you and is away from sheep for too long. After all, if my guess is correct, he has been working and doing his job whilst shepherding those cats across the country.'

Dear Man looked thoughtfully down at George. 'Well, it is certainly something to think about, but we couldn't accept any money for him. He isn't ours to sell. However, if the man is still interested, you could tell him where we live, and maybe he would like to come along and talk to George.'

Chapter 37

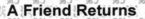

A Friend Returns

As usual, everyone was dozing. It was September, and with the sun still hot, the cats and George preferred to find somewhere in the shade for their siesta. On this particular afternoon, George and Senora were lying together on the terrace. George's paw had healed. As was normal at this time of day, Dear Man was sleeping in the shade by the swimming pool whilst Dear Lady busied herself inside the house. The remaining cats lay under the new straw canopy in the garden on the other side of the old wall. It was a very peaceful scene.

George was the first to be alerted by the sound of a vehicle coming down the lane. He stood up, sniffing the air. There was a familiar scent drifting towards him. His first thought was that his master had returned. He immediately began wagging his tail, but then he dropped it: He was never going to see his master again.

A large open truck came to a standstill outside the garden gate. George stared and listened. No, it wasn't possible; he must be mistaken. He moved his ears back, at the same time wagging his tail. He recognized the bleating of sheep, and they were coming from the truck in the lane. He ran down the steps arriving at the garden gate just in time to see a familiar face stepping down from the cart. It was his friend with the sausage, and in his arms he was carrying a small black-and-white puppy.

George couldn't stop wagging his tail, barking with pleasure. By this time, the noise had woken Dear Man, who lazily got up from his deckchair and wondered who could be arriving during siesta time. From the terrace, he saw a young man standing in the lane and holding a puppy in his arms, with George whining and wagging his tail furiously while waiting for the garden gate to be opened.

George's reaction was immediate, taking both men by surprise. They watched, laughing, as George rushed around the puppy, wagging his tail, whining happily, and licking the puppy's head in greeting.

The young man bent down and hugged George before introducing himself to Dear Man. 'You can see we are old friends,' he said, smiling.

George looked up at the two men shaking hands. At the same time, he took good care that the puppy didn't stray, and he kept a wary eye open for any cat who was likely to scare him.

'The vet told me that you might be willing to sell me your sheep dog,' the visitor said.

'First, please come in and have a cool drink. Would fresh lemonade be all right?' Without waiting for an answer, he called his request to his wife. 'The vet did warn me that you might be looking us up. Something about sheep, wasn't it? Please come this way.'

They climbed the steps up to the terrace and sat down. Very soon, Dear Lady appeared holding a tray on which were glasses and a large jug of iced lemonade. After putting the tray onto a coffee table, she served the iced drinks and opened a tin of biscuits.

Whilst they were sipping their drinks, the young man introduced himself and went on to explain his reasons for stopping by. 'When I was a child,' he began, 'my father bred a flock of sheep north from here. They were hard years; my parents were poor and relied solely on the income from selling the wool, as well as occasional livestock at the local markets. Naturally, throughout the whole of my youth, I learned a lot about sheep rearing.

'Sadly, my father passed away, and my mother had to sell the flock in order to look after herself and the rest of us. I have three younger brothers and a younger sister.

'I married a lovely girl, and for a while we were very happy, but she had a fatal pregnancy. She and our daughter died during childbirth, which was devastating.' He looked into the distance as the memories flooded back, and he took a sip of his drink. 'Anyway, since then I have been earning my living driving my van back and forth to the only animal sanctuary within seventy kilometres of here. It is owned by a British couple. I collect strays from the villages and take them to the sanctuary to be sterilized, returning them a few days later. Many of the strays are rehomed from that sanctuary. They do a tremendous job, and they are all volunteers.

'Whilst having this job, I have been saving enough money so that I can go back to sheep rearing, which is something I would love to do and which would suit my lonely lifestyle. As you see,' he continued, pointed to his cart, 'I now have a flock of white Mallorcan sheep, which I purchased last week. I have since been told Mallorcan sheep are quite valuable, so I am lucky. I have six ewes and a ram. The idea is that within a year or two, they will multiply quite nicely.'

He paused for a moment, taking another sip of his drink continuing with his story. 'One day a couple of months back, whilst on my way to the sanctuary, I saw this beautiful Portuguese mountain dog following me. He was limping badly and hardly able to walk, but he did his best to catch up with me. Poor lad was in a lot of pain. I had no idea how he hurt his leg or why he wanted to follow me, but when I arrived at a filling station, I persuaded him to let me look at his wound, and we soon became friends. When I wanted to move off, he jumped into the van, and together we drove to the sanctuary. The cats that I had picked up in the villages were in the back of my van.

'When we arrived, I asked one of the vets to look at the dog's leg, but unfortunately whilst he was putting some disinfectant on the wound, the dog became nervous, ran into the woods, and hid. I later found him and gave him a sandwich, and when I went back the next day, much to my surprise, he was still there. We became good mates after that.

'I was asked by one of the volunteers at the sanctuary to return a tortoiseshell cat plus four white cats with ginger markings to a village a short distance from here, to set them free. As I was moving away, it became clear to me that the dog wanted to climb into my van. I had no idea why. When I released the cats, I asked the dog, whom I now know as George, if he would like to come with me. He seemed to want to stay with the cats. That was the last I saw of him – until now.

'When I heard from the vet about cats escaping from the sanctuary because some dog had dug a hole under the wire fencing, it all seemed to fit, especially when he said that a Portuguese mountain dog, just like yours, had been seen in the area and was thought to be the culprit.'

'If you look over to the other side of the old wall,' said Dear Man, pointing to where Bella and her family were all sleeping, 'you will see the reason why George wanted to stay with the cats. He was doing exactly what he had been trained to do. He was on a mission to bring them home. He is an excellent shepherd dog.'

'That is an incredible story,' said the young man, looking over to George and smiling as he watched him washing the puppy. 'It looks as though he has taken to the little one, doesn't it?'

'We love George and would like to do what is best for him,' said Dear Man. 'He was left here by some travellers who started a large fire that spread all over the hillside and up to the woods. But George is not really our dog. I understand from the vet that his master was killed last year, so we wouldn't dream of accepting any money. We have given the matter a great deal of thought in case you should visit us, and we have decided to leave the decision to George. Let him decide if he would like to go with you or stay with us. By the way, where do you live?'

'I have just bought a small stone cottage up in the hills, about twenty-five kilometres from the nearest village. It is a beautiful spot for sheep, with plenty of grazing. If George would like to come with me, he would be ideal to do the job he is trained to do, and at the same time he could teach the puppy. By the way, I'm calling the puppy Boysie.'

'George, come,' Dear Man said as he stood up, touching his knee. George immediately went to his side with the puppy in tow. Dear Man stroked the puppy and looked down at George. 'How would you like to go and live with your friend?'

The three adults watched George. He seemed to have understood what Dear Man was asking. Without hesitation he went over to his friend with the sausage and licked his hand. Then he went back to Dear Man and put his paw on his knee, as if to say thanks.

In the meantime, after being woken from her sleep by the conversation between Dear Man and the stranger, Senora sat up on her cushion. She spied the black-and-white puppy sitting behind George. 'Oh, my goodness,' she meowed. 'I sincerely hope we are not going to have to put up with that thing. It really would be too much to cope with.' She had seen puppies before and had never liked them. They always chewed everything. She remembered when a visitor had brought a puppy to the house, and he had chewed Senora's best cushion. She had been furious at the time and hissed and spat at him, causing him to run and fall into the swimming pool, where he had to be rescued by Dear Lady. Senora remembered Dear Lady being very angry and refusing to speak to her for the rest of the day.

Senora wondered why the stranger, with a scent she remembered from the white van, was talking to Dear Man and Dear Lady so earnestly. Why was George licking his hand? She looked at the man closely. *Yes, she decided, he is definitely the same man who gave George the sausage. But why is he here?* A dreadful thought crossed her mind, and she meowed loudly. *Has he come to take me back to that awful place?* Horrified at the thought, she quickly jumped down, hiding herself under the chair.

But inquisitive as ever, she peeked out. She saw George lick the man's hand and then walk slowly to Dear Man, putting a paw on his knee. *What on earth is he doing that for, and why is he running down to the garden gate and making such a noise in front of that truck? Running like that could hurt his bad leg He really is being ridiculous.* Still perplexed at what was happening, she watched George walk slowly back to the terrace.

George was thinking hard. He was sure he knew what Dear Man had been asking him, and he was sure his friend with the sausage wanted to be his new master. If he didn't want to be his new master, why had he brought George the sheep and given him the puppy to wash? George was certain he understood everything, and in his heart, he knew what he wanted to do.

When he reached the terrace, he realized that in his excitement, he had completely forgotten about Senora. He walked over to her chair and poked his nose underneath. She tried not to take any notice of him, doing her best to pretend to be asleep. She felt his nose nudging her, lifted her head, and looked at him. When she saw the sadness in George's eyes, she knew something was bad, and he was trying to tell her about it. But what? Why did he nudge her, look at her despairingly, and then walk over to the man with the sausage? It was very odd. She decided to be brave. She stood up and walked boldly across the terrace, at the same time trying to ignore both the puppy and the man. *After all,* she reminded herself, *Dear Lady and Dear Man would never let anything happen to me.*

She went to George and brushed against his legs, purring loudly. She knew he would always protect her.

After all, he had brought her on the long journey home. She loved him very much.

George bent his head and licked hers. His tongue felt very wet. Something was definitely bad – his lick had never felt like this before. Then George did the strangest thing. First he went over to Dear Lady and lifted his paw. She bent over and kissed his head. He then crossed to Dear Man and again lifted his paw. He also bent over and kissed George on his head. They both looked very sad. Last of all, George then turned to Senora and gently put his paw on the top of her head, giving her a lick all along her back.

George knew no other way to say goodbye. He loved them all, especially Senora, who had saved his life on the night of the fire and again in the woods. He would never forget her. He felt very sad to be leaving, but his instinct told him there was a job of work to be done, and that his new master was to be his friend with the sausage.

With the puppy following, George and his new master walked down the steps to the garden gate. Suddenly Senora realized the truth: she was going to lose her beloved George! She rushed down after him just as he was jumping into the front of the truck. She leapt up and landed on his back, crushing her body against his, meowing and purring and trying her best to prevent him from leaving her.

Dear Man, realizing what was happening, came to George's rescue by taking hold of Senora's struggling body; at the same time, he tried his best to soothe her. He carried her to safety behind the garden gate. All the time, she was meowing loudly, pleading with George and not believing he wouldn't listen to her.

The young man got up into the driver's seat and put the puppy in between George and himself before switching on the engine. By this time, the sheep were making a lot of noise, butting their heads against the planks of wood and bleating loudly as the young man turned the truck around in the lane. He called his thanks to Dear Lady and Dear Man and waved.

As they drove away down the lane, George gave Senora one last look. In the background, he could see a line of cats watching silently from the top of the old wall. It was a very sad moment. George wondered if he would ever see any of them ever again.

'Don't worry, old chap. We'll come and visit them soon,' said George's new master, leaning over and giving him an assuring pat on the head.

The truck disappeared from sight. One by one, the cats jumped down from the wall. Wynken, Blynken, and Nod, together with Lollypop and Young Jack, resumed their game of Catch Tails. Bella, Tia, Smithy Magoo, and Willie the Spot wished George happiness in his new life, quietly thanking him for guiding them to their forever home.

In the meantime, Senora slowly climbed the stairs to the terrace, looking back longingly down empty lane, not quite believing that she had been deserted by her dearest friend. She kept asking herself, *How could George suddenly leave me and go with the man with the sausage? And what on earth was he thinking, getting into that truck with those smelly animals? Of course, he will certainly need a bath whenever he does come back.* She jumped up onto her favourite cushion and looked across at Dear Man, who was sitting in his chair and reading his paper. 'Why didn't you stop him,' she asked. Her loud meow caused Dear Man to look up.

'What's the matter, Senora? Come over here and sit by me.'

Needing no further encouragement, Senora took a flying leap and landed on Dear Man's lap, at the same time crushing his newspaper. She brushed up against his chest, purring in his ear.

Maybe things won't be so bad, she consoled herself. She was thoughtful as she looked up at his smiling face. *After all, now everyone will feel sorry for me, so I am sure to get a lot more cuddles.* With that thought, she curled herself into a ball, purred gently, and dropped off into a contended sleep on Dear Man's lap.

They arrived at the little stone cottage just before dusk. The truck came to a standstill, and George jumped down, clumsily followed by Boysie. Both stretched their legs. Boysie, who had slept most of the journey was so lively that George had to give him a tap with his paw.

He didn't have to be told that this young pup was his new student and must obey his commands. He looked around him, seeing beautiful green pastures stretching up the hillside and alongside the cottage was a large corral. *Wonderful,* thought George. *My sheep will always be protected during the night, and I will be here to guard them.*

His master attached a small slide to the back of the truck and opened the gate. Immediately the sheep slid down the short distance to the ground, picking themselves up and running off in all directions.

George was in his element. He didn't need any commands from the stick his beloved master had always put in his mouth. He knew exactly what he had to do. George was a very happy dog. He had a new master and a very important new mission. One day, Boysie would be as good a shepherd dog as Gentleman George.

About the Author

Born in Harrow, Middlesex, and educated at a boarding school on the east coast of England, Janet Goodwin went on to make a career in the production of television commercials. During this period, she and her husband, lived for four years on the island of Ibiza in the Baleares.

She is retired and living in Spain with her American husband, plus their three dogs and Lucy their cat. In 2005 they founded a charity for the protection of abandoned animals in Spain and, together with many volunteers, have been involved with the sterilization of street cats and finding 'forever homes'.

Wanted: A Forever Home is her first novel.

CPSIA information can be obtained
at www.ICGtesting.com
Printed in the USA
BVOW03s0022231017
498351BV00012B/7/P